Red Heir

Lisa Henry
&
Sarah Honey

ABOUT RED HEIR

Imprisoned pickpocket Loth isn't sure why a bunch of idiots just broke into his cell claiming they're here to rescue the lost prince of Aguillon, and he doesn't really care. They're looking for a redheaded prince, and he's more than happy to play along if it means freedom. Then his cranky cellmate Grub complicates things by claiming to be the prince as well.

Now they're fleeing across the country and Loth's stuck sharing a horse and a bedroll with Grub while imitating royalty, eating eel porridge, and dodging swamp monsters and bandits.

Along the way, Loth discovers that there's more to Grub than meets the eye. Under the dirt and bad attitude, Grub's not completely awful. He might even be *attractive.* In fact, Loth has a terrible suspicion that he's developing feelings, and he's not sure what to do about that. He'd probably have more luck figuring it out if people would just stop trying to kill them.

Still, at least they've got a dragon, right?

CONTENTS

Red Heir

Written and published by Lisa Henry and Sarah Honey

Cover by Steph Westerik at www.instagram.com/reverse_mermaid/

Edited by Penny Tsallos Editing and Proofreading

Copyright © 2020 by Lisa Henry and Sarah Honey

ISBN: 9798664322620

❀ Created with Vellum

ACKNOWLEDGMENTS

Thanks to our beta readers, Kelly, Samantha and Janni. You rock!

To the Steter peeps who perhaps know us better under our fandom names, this one is also for you!

And to Kat, who was our tireless cheerleader through this entire crazy process.

And a special thanks to Steph, who started this whole thing with her random comment about a scribe with a limp and a penchant for scarves.

CHAPTER ONE

L oth sighed and rattled the chains of his manacles, but they remained stubbornly affixed to the cold stone wall of the cell in Delacourt castle. Delacourt castle, like the rest of Delacourt, was a total shithole. Loth had only been here a few days after stumbling off the ship from Callier, but he felt more than qualified to make that judgement call. His head throbbed, either because of how much ale he'd had to drink last night or because the guards hadn't been gentle with him during his arrest. His memory of the events wasn't crystal clear, but his favourite blue doublet had a tear in it, and he was fairly certain he'd never get the stains out of the knees of his pants. Which, not for the first time, but Loth preferred to be on his knees by choice, and not because he was being dragged through the muddy streets by a bunch of thugs wearing the livery of the crown. Waking up in chains wasn't his favourite way to start the day either, that was for sure. Not unless he'd agreed to it beforehand.

"I suppose you're wondering how I got into this mess," he announced loudly in the gloom.

The pile of straw on the other side of the cell rustled, and a grubby face appeared. "I wasn't. I don't care."

"I wasn't talking to you," Loth said to his cellmate.

"Then who were you talking to?" his cellmate demanded, jutting his jaw out.

"I was soliloquising," Loth said. "Well, I was hoping to, but somebody won't shut their mouth."

"Why don't you shut *your* mouth?"

Loth snorted. "How can I soliloquise if I do that? Now, hush." He cleared his throat. "I suppose you're wondering how I got into this mess."

"I am *not* wondering!" his cellmate snarled. "I am trying to sleep! Shut up!"

"Since you're awake," Loth said, "and apropos of nothing, you wouldn't happen to know what the penalty is in these parts for pickpocketing, would you?"

"I hope it involves cutting your tongue out."

Loth hummed. "That would be a terrible loss. My tongue would be mourned throughout the land."

"I doubt that very much," his snappish cellmate replied. "You haven't said anything of import yet."

Loth grinned. "Oh, sweetheart, I didn't mean for *talking*."

Eyes widened in the shadows, and then the straw rustled again as his cellmate attempted to bury himself under it. "Shut up!"

Loth leaned his head back against the wall and chuckled. Well, at least he could entertain himself while he was here, right? His cellmate—a drab, grimy creature who appeared to be mostly composed of straw—was just the sort of prickly arsehole that was fun to torment. It was especially fun since they were chained to opposite walls, and Loth had already checked his cellmate couldn't reach him. If he attempted to attack Loth in a fit of rage, he'd be brought up short. Loth had learned very early in life that with a mouth like his, he'd needed to develop a very strong sense of self-preservation to go along with it.

Not that the straw man opposite was really any kind of

threat. Loth was reminded of an angry rodent—a quivering bundle of impotent rage, but more amusing than dangerous. He decided to poke at the little wretch some more, if only to entertain himself. "What are you in here for, anyway? Let's see if I can guess."

"No!" The grubby urchin snapped. "Go away!"

"Well I would, but..." Loth rattled his chain. "I'll tell you what, though. I get to ask you three questions, and then I get three guesses. If I can't work out your crime, I'll be quiet for the rest of the day. Deal?"

The straw parted and the boy—no, young man—sat up. He was older than Loth had first thought, long and lanky, and his features were fine enough to be called pretty under all that dirt, but he was still a dishevelled mess. "You'll really shut up?"

"I'll definitely think about it."

The boy tilted his head slightly, considering, and his hair flashed red in the sliver of sunlight coming through the tiny barred window. His shade of red was lighter than Loth's, but then, Loth's came courtesy of henna rather than genetics. His eyes were quite lovely. They shone bright green as the sunlight caught them. What a shame his scowl ruined what little he had to work with. "Fine, but yes or no questions only."

Cheeky little shit.

"I suppose I could make that work." Loth didn't really think he could guess the boy's crime, but he was going to have a lot of fun trying. Redheads were so easy to make blush—in all sorts of places.

Loth looked at the boy and made a contemplative sound, and yes, even the weight of his gaze was enough to make his victim's cheeks flush pink.

"Hmmm." Loth mused aloud. "I doubt you're a whore, although you're definitely pretty enough—I'd pay at least a gold coin."

The young man's mouth dropped open, his face went beet

red, and his eyes widened, in mortification or scandal, Loth wasn't sure which.

"Actually, I take that back. With a prissy attitude like yours, you'd need to pay me, not the other way around. You're more frigid than an ice giant's ballsack, aren't you?" Loth held one finger up when it looked like his cellmate was about to interject. "And before you ask, that wasn't a question, it was a speculation, so it doesn't count."

The boy might have been frosty, but his glare was pure fire.

"Hmm." Loth sucked on his teeth for a moment. "I wonder if it's an arrestable offence in this part of the kingdom to be a rude little twat. Because in that case, you may be looking at the death penalty. I'll bet it's something incredibly base though and suited to your low station. Like turnip theft, or horse buggery."

The young man's lips thinned and Loth could see the internal struggle going on.

It was a struggle that the youngster inevitably lost when Loth added, "Just out of interest, were you the buggerer or the buggeree? Was there some sort of harness, or do you carry a foot-stool with you? The height difference intrigues me, so do tell."

"How dare you!" he burst out. "I am a political prisoner, not a—a—"

"Lover of horses?" And oh, but wasn't that interesting? Because Loth had no doubt that this scruffy, grubby little mouse, despite his appearances was, in fact, no peasant. He might have looked like one, but his accent gave him away. And, unlike Loth, that accent probably wasn't faked. "Political, you say? Do tell. Are you the illegitimate spawn of a ranking official? Are you perhaps a spy?"

"No, and no," the boy said, outrage magically vanishing. "That's two questions," he observed, quietly smug. "One more and you have to be quiet."

Perhaps he wasn't as dim as he appeared.

Loth grinned. This was definitely entertaining, and he had no intention of being quiet regardless of what he'd said earlier, so he resolved to come up with the most ridiculous thing he could, just to see the boy stammer and sputter and blush some more. "You do look like you've been here rather a long time. And you don't have the features of a commoner. Plus, you're awfully bossy for a little slip of a thing. Could it be, I wonder? Is it possible that you, my little grub, are in fact the long-lost Prince Tarquin of Aguillon, rumoured to have been locked away by his uncle?"

He was teasing of course. Despite the rumours perpetuated by idiots and bards—same thing, really—Loth would bet the entire contents of his purse (two silver pieces and a loose button) that Prince Tarquin wasn't lost, and instead was exactly where his uncle had left him—in several pieces in an unmarked grave. That was politics for you.

The boy narrowed his eyes and jutted his chin out. "And what if I were?" he demanded mulishly.

Loth hummed thoughtfully. "No, you're definitely a horse fucker."

The boy roared in rage and leapt at Loth, despite the futility of such a gesture. His chains brought him up short, about halfway across the cell.

Really though, he should have been glad, because if he'd still been sitting where he was a moment later, he would have been crushed by the collapsing wall as an orc barrelled through it.

LOTH COUGHED and squinted through the clouds of dust. Where there had once been a wall, there was now a mountain of rubble, with an orc standing on top of it. He was big and ugly by human standards—possibly he was very attractive to other orcs—with two teeth in his bottom jaw protruding from between his lips like tusks. He was mostly bald as well, apart from a few tufts on top of his head, and the same sort of green as a rather anaemic tree frog.

"Whoops," he said, in a voice that rumbled like thunder.

A second figure climbed up beside him. This one was human. He was a young man with broad shoulders, a heroically wide stance that really must have been straining the seams of his pants, and some underwhelming facial hair that was trying a little too hard to be a rakish beard. He peered down into the cell. "Did you *squash* him? Is that why you said 'whoops'?"

"There's two of them," the orc said, which made him one of the smartest orcs Loth had ever encountered.

The human stared between Loth and his cellmate, his jaw dropping. "There's two of them."

"S'what I said! Two!" The orc seemed inordinately pleased to have his moment of mathematical genius confirmed.

"But they said he'd be alone! Rescue the redhead, they said! Nobody mentioned a second one!"

Loth had no idea what was going on, but he saw an opportunity. "And so I was," he announced. "All alone up until yesterday, when they put this unfortunate grubby fellow in here with me. You're here for me, I take it?"

His cellmate tried to say something but choked on a mouthful of dust.

A moment later, a third figure scrambled up onto the pile of rubble. "What's taking so long?"

A dwarf. It was uncommon for dwarves to travel this far south. Most of them preferred to stick to the mountains in the north, away from all that "human bullshit" as they described it. Loth couldn't really blame them. On the other hand, as one of the most bullshitty humans who'd ever bullshitted, it was also difficult not to take it personally.

The dwarf sported a thick brown beard that hung down to their knees, a shade darker than the hair on their head. The braids woven throughout the beard made Loth think the dwarf was possibly a woman, though it wasn't always easy to tell with dwarves, and it was considered rude to ask—a lesson he'd learned the hard way. The dwarf's eyes were narrowed in suspicion so it was difficult to get a decent look, but if Loth had to hazard a guess at their shade, he'd put it somewhere between 'mistrustful' and 'murderous'.

"There's two of them," the orc said proudly and gestured at Loth and his cellmate.

"Then grab the redhead and let's go!" the dwarf exclaimed.

"They're both redheads, though," the human explained. "We don't know which he is."

The dwarf sighed. "Have you *asked* them?"

"Ah!" said the human. He cleared his throat. "We are here to rescue the lost prince, Tarquin. Pray tell, which one of you is that?"

"Me, of course," Loth said because he liked the sound of the word 'rescue'.

His cellmate squawked indignantly. "It's me! I'm him!"

"There's *two* of them!" the orc whispered, eyes as wide as dinner plates.

"Ignore my grubby cellmate," Loth ordered, making what he hoped was a vaguely noble gesture. "He's a simpleton. He is also an inveterate liar, and a molester of farmyard animals."

"I am not!"

"Ah, so you admit you're not the prince? Excellent. We'll leave you behind. Now, someone said something about a rescue?"

The orc shambled down the rubble and tugged the chains securing Loth's manacles out of the wall as simply as snapping a thread.

"Marvellous," Loth said, climbing to his feet. He brushed the dust from his doublet and sketched a bow, complete with a hand flourish, in the direction of his cellmate. "Grub, it's been an experience."

"But—it's me! I'm Tarquin! He's the liar!" Grub protested, clutching at his hair. "See? Red, like my father's."

The human's brow creased in confusion.

The dwarf sighed impatiently, then said, "Bring them both.".

"Yes!" the human exclaimed. "Excellent counsel, Ada, excellent. It is my decision that we should bring them both!"

The dwarf rolled her eyes and stomped away. Loth picked his way through the rubble and followed.

The orc grunted and shrugged, picked up Grub and slung him over his shoulder, and followed.

THEIR ESCAPE from the cells at Delacourt castle went far more smoothly than it should have. They encountered no resistance at all, which Loth thought was an appalling indictment on the professionalism of the guards. They hadn't been this lax last night when they'd been arresting him. Of course, he had pickpocketed the head guard's wife, so maybe they'd taken it personally.

Still, that was all in the past now, and Loth was more concerned about his oddball little rescue party. Clearly, they thought he was the prince, which should make them amenable to at least feeding him, but at some point—hopefully some point after he'd been fed—he was going to have to part ways with them before they discovered their mistake. That was a problem for future Loth, he decided. Present Loth was well aware that although he was out of his cell, he wasn't exactly in the clear yet. He wanted to put a few hundred miles between him and the guards before he stopped looking over his shoulder.

In the meantime, he plastered a vaguely regal expression on his face and followed his rescuers toward freedom.

The dwarf led the way outside to a courtyard where an elf was waiting with some horses. He was tall and willowy with dark, lustrous locks. He was startlingly beautiful, as all elves were, and he was also wearing a scowl. Again, par for the course with elven folk.

"Was he there? You took forever," the elf grizzled, "I've been standing here so long that I smell like a horse." There was a petulance to his tone that had Loth looking closer. At a guess, he'd say the elf was a couple of hundred years old at most—a teenager in elf years, then.

Loth resisted the urge to roll his eyes—never look a gift rescuer in the mouth. Instead he said, "Apologies for the delay. There was a case of mistaken identity. My cellmate thought it would be amusing to claim he was the prince. Of course, one only has to look at him to see that he's lying."

"Cellmate?" the elf asked, grudgingly interested now. "There wasn't meant to be a cellmate."

"He only arrived last night. This," he said with a nod, "is Grub. He likes to have sex with horses, so I'd keep him away from yours. Although..." Loth made a show of looking around. "He doesn't appear to have brought his fuckery stool, so you may be safe."

"I don't... do that with horses," Grub ground out, hands clenched into fists.

"Not without your stool, you don't," Loth agreed airily, and patted him on the shoulder. "Now then, shall we put some distance between ourselves and this place, before the guards actually come and investigate the commotion?"

"Yes, my prince," the human with the beard said, stars in his eyes as he gazed at Loth.

"He's not *my* prince," the elf grumbled.

"Isn't he?" the orc asked.

"Elves don't *have* princes," the elf said and rolled his eyes. "We're collectivist anarchists."

"Is he *my* prince?" the orc asked curiously.

The elf rolled his eyes again. "No, Dave! He's a human! Orcs hate humans!"

"Oh, yeah," Dave agreed, nodding. His tooth-tusks gleamed. "I forgot."

As distracting as this was, Loth had always found it was much easier to talk people into doing what you wanted if you knew something about them, so he interrupted to say, "Who exactly *are* you people?"

The human drew himself up tall as if he'd been waiting for this moment. "We're your rescue party, m'lord! Come to save you from the clutches of tyranny!"

"And I'm exceedingly grateful. But I meant what are your names? I can't keep calling you Orc and Elf and Dwarf and Human. It makes this whole enterprise sound particularly dubious. Which I'm sure it's not," he hastened to add at the human's offended look.

"You're dubious," Grub muttered under his breath.

"Shh, my little farmyard fornicator, the adults are talking," Loth told him, despite probably being five years older than the mouthy urchin at best.

"Shall we talk while we ride, *Prince*?" the dwarf asked, hands on hips. Loth wondered if the emphasis on his fake title was because she knew he was lying through his teeth, or because she really didn't want to hang around here and get arrested. Loth couldn't blame her.

"Let's do that," he agreed. Really, it was nice to know at least one of them had a brain.

THE RESCUE PARTY, having only expected to rescue one redheaded prisoner from the nominated cell, had only brought one spare horse, which left Loth sharing with Grub. Grub rode pillion, much to his grumbling disgust. Loth wasn't sure what he was complaining about. A fellow should count himself lucky to sit rubbing up against Loth's arse like this, with his arms around his waist. Thousands would pay for the privilege! More than one had.

As they worked their way out of the streets of Delacourt, casting back occasional glances to be certain they weren't being pursued, Loth learned the names of his rescuers.

The human was called Scott. He called himself a humble former farmhand, but Loth wasn't sure he knew what 'humble' meant, since he appeared convinced he was only a peasant by accident of birth, and that he was supposed to be a nobleman instead. He spent quite a bit of time speculating about just how many bards would sing about his heroic deeds in the near future, and just how many hearts, and titles, his exploits would win him.

Still, despite Scott's enthusiasm for talking about himself, Loth did manage to learn the names of the others. Ada was the dwarf, which he'd picked up in the cells, and Dave was the orc. The teenage elf was called Calarian. Ada had joined the quest because Scott had promised to pay her. Dave didn't seem exactly sure of why he was there and what he was supposed to be doing. Calarian's mum had thrown him out of home, telling him to stop sitting around playing Houses and Humans and get out and find a job.

"What happened to the collectivist part of collectivist anarchists?" Grub muttered.

"I *heard* that!" Calarian sneered. "I have exceptional hearing!"

"Of course you do. You have ears shaped like a bat's," Loth muttered.

"I quit!" Calarian said. "I'm going home!"

"You can't leave! An elf adds class, it'll sound good in the ballads," Scott insisted. "The fearless leader and his brave band of merry men." He flinched as Ada cleared her throat loudly. "*Persons.*"

Personally, Loth thought brave was a stretch. Merry was pushing it as well. Calarian was whining about the sun ruining his complexion, Ada looked ready to murder Scott at any given moment, (although that seemed to be the effect Scott had on people generally), and Dave vacillated between confusion as to why he was here and elation that there were two of them and he'd got it right.

And Grub? He was downright sulking.

"Listen," Loth said, turning his head so that only Grub could hear his words, "I know you wanted to play the prince, but let me do it, alright? I've got the better look for it."

Grub simmered at a low boil behind him. "You seem awfully sure I'm *not* the prince!" he hissed in Loth's ear.

Loth snorted. "Of course I'm sure." He gestured to the empty street behind them. "If you were the prince, my dear Grub, then why the hell is there nobody chasing us?"

He had the reward of Grub's silence for the rest of the ride out of town.

CHAPTER TWO

The rescue party had arrived shortly after dawn, which struck Loth as odd. Odd, and inconvenient, because for all the accommodations were terrible in dungeons, the breakfasts were usually decent, and now he'd missed his. "I'm hungry," he muttered.

Grub made a noncommittal sound, probably still brooding.

Loth let him sulk, more interested in the matter at hand—that was to say, his lack of breakfast. "Tell me, Scott, where are we stopping?"

Scott startled at being addressed. "Stopping?"

They were about an hour's ride from town now, and there was no sign of pursuit, so Loth didn't think his request was particularly egregious.

"For a meal. My royal disposition is quite delicate. If I don't eat soon I may faint, and that will definitely slow us down."

"Or we could roll you into the reeds and leave you behind," Grub muttered, and my, wasn't he an annoying little tick of a thing? Speaking of ticks...

"Also, I believe my young saddle mate is infested with something," Loth announced. "He's done nothing but scratch and squirm since we started riding. Probably caught something while making time with his barnyard friends."

"I have not! I'm just itchy from the straw!"

"Hmmm. Regardless, I think we should stop somewhere with fresh water and rinse the lad off. And maybe eat?" Loth wasn't silly, and knew who was really in charge despite Scott's posturing, so he addressed this last to Ada.

She gave a curt nod. "There's food in the cart. We left it near the river."

Scott cleared his throat. "I have decided," he declared, "that the prince is in need of sustenance. We shall make our way to the riverside."

There was the tiniest breath of air on the back of Loth's neck, almost as if Grub was laughing despite himself.

"Stellar leadership," Loth murmured, and was rewarded with another puff of air, just above the drape of his scarf. His cellmate, while completely insufferable, was at least observant.

Their pace slowed as they turned off the road towards the snaking river.

The ride to the riverbank, and to the cart concealed behind a screen of bushes, was only a few more miles. Still, Loth was glad to get out of the saddle and stretch his aching muscles. It had been too long since he'd ridden. In all senses of the word, actually, but at the moment hunger was his primary concern.

He thought back to Delacourt and pondered on the wisdom of a dawn raid as he waited to be served his breakfast. It wasn't the way these things were done. And the reason it wasn't done was because it wasn't practical, or effective. Yet here they were. He looked at Scott speculatively. "Not that I, as a prince, have been rescued before, but I'm curious as to why you chose morning to stage your attack, Scott? I believe these things are normally done under cover of night?"

"Yes Scott, tell the prince why you decided that," Ada piped up from where she was rifling through the cart.

"For the ballads," Scott mumbled.

"Pardon? What was that?" Ada asked, arms folded. Loth suspected it was to stop herself from leaping down from the cart and pushing Scott into the river.

"I said, it's so it will sound dramatic in the ballads." Scott cleared his throat. *"As dawn's light broke so was our prince freed by the hero* sounds much more impressive than *by dark of night they snuck away.* And it'll stand out since there are hardly *any* ballads about dawn raids."

"That's because nobody survives them," Loth told Grub in an undertone. The boy nodded glumly, and for a moment Loth was thankful that there wasn't really a lost prince, because if this was his rescue party, things were grim.

"And what was the other reason, Scott?" Ada asked. "The reason we took twice as long to get there as we should have?"

"I was given a defective map."

Loth raised his eyebrows. "Pardon?"

"Completely inaccurate. Impossible to follow."

"It had a lot of words on it," Dave agreed. "And arrows."

Grub rolled his eyes and wandered down the riverbank. Loth glanced at Ada.

"Yes, the arrows were pointing the wrong way," Scott clarified.

"You mean you were holding it upside down," Ada muttered.

Ah, so the basic map had stymied anyone of below average intelligence. Unfortunately, it appeared that was half the rescue party. It felt a little unkind to think badly of them when they had saved him from a dungeon. Still, Loth had a feeling that their success was more down to dumb luck than anything else—dumb being the operative word.

Loth took a moment to stretch his legs and arch his back—he really was getting too old to spend the night in shackles, at least without a safe word, once his back started to twinge. Not that he was *old*. He was just a little stiffer in the mornings than he had been as a teen, that was all. Why, he was barely out of his adolescence! Those weren't crow's feet appearing at the corners of his eyes. They were character lines, and Loth would stab anyone who said otherwise.

He glanced down the riverbank where Grub was standing at the edge of the water squinting rather unattractively into the sunlight. Loth strolled over to join him.

"Daydreaming about all the pretty horses, Grub?"

"Fuck off," Grub said, scowling and scratching his nose.

"Oh, that's right," Loth remembered. "You have lice. Let me help you with that."

And he put a hand on Grub's back and pushed him into the river.

Grub yowled like a drowning cat as he broke the surface of the river, splashing and spluttering. "What the *fuck* did you do that for?"

"That's no way to talk to your prince, Grub," Loth said, as Grub waded through the reeds and hauled himself out onto the bank.

And—oh!—his wet rags clung to him like a second skin, and Loth felt a sudden jab of unease in his belly. It was an emotion he couldn't name because he wasn't sure he'd ever felt it before. Was it sympathy? Pity, even? Because the body that was revealed to Loth's gaze was thin; too thin. Grub's chest rose and fell as he glared at Loth, and Loth could see his wet shirt clinging to each individual rib. His hip bones jutted out like those of an old mule's. A droplet of water chased down his throat and over his clavicle—a sight Loth was partial to in most circumstances—and Loth thought that he could have jabbed Grub in that dip and lost his finger up to the first knuckle.

Loth wasn't usually lost for words.

More than that, he didn't understand it. Loth had spent enough time in dungeons all around the kingdom—always a misunderstanding, of course—and the worst he'd had of it was burned porridge and stale bread. He'd never been *starved*.

Grub saw him staring and glared.

"Come now," Loth said. "At least the lice will have floated away, hmm?"

"You're an arsehole," Grub snarled and stalked his way over to where the others were preparing breakfast. He dripped all the way.

Loth took the time to relieve himself in the bushes and splash cold water on his own face and hands. It *was* cold—freezing, in fact—and that tendril of unease in his gut curled a little tighter. It felt more like a knot now. It didn't help that when Loth joined the others a little way up the riverbank he saw that Grub was shivering.

Another emotion that Loth wasn't familiar with stirred in his gut. He was fairly sure this one was guilt. He wasn't a fan.

Almost against his will, he stepped closer, pulling off his cloak and thrusting it at the shaking boy. "Do wrap yourself up Grub, it's making me cold just looking at you." When Grub failed to take the cloak, instead staring at him with a furrowed brow, Loth shrugged and let it drop to the ground. "Suit yourself. But I warn you, if you get sick, we might just roll you into the reeds and leave you behind." With that he strolled off, resisting the urge to turn back and wrap the boy in the fabric—that would imply he cared, which was ridiculous.

Scott followed him, holding out a plate. "Breakfast, M'Lord Prince Majesty?" He obviously had no idea of the correct way to address royalty.

Loth wasn't quite certain either, but he didn't let that stop him saying, "Just *M'Lord* is fine," before taking the plate with a slight nod.

"Actually, it's *Your Grace*."

Loth whipped his head around at that, to find Grub giving him an exasperated look. He was wearing the cloak at least, and

Loth tried not to be pleased about it. "And what would you know about it, horse boy?"

Grub glared at him. "Kings and queens are technically still princes and princesses but should be addressed as *Your Highness* or *Your Majesty*. Otherwise, it's *Your Grace. M'Lord* implies a lower echelon and should never be used with the heir to the throne. I thought you'd know that, *Your Grace.*"

Smart little beast, Loth thought, and promptly covered his mistake with an insult. "Listen to you. Been hanging around the royal stables, have you? Eavesdropping while you wrapped your hands around a great big horse—"

"Shut up!" Grub spat out. "You don't know anything!"

"Shouldn't that be *you don't know anything, Your Grace?*" Loth asked smoothly. For a split second, watching the way the boy's fists were clenched at his sides, quivering with rage, Loth wondered if he'd gone too far, but then Grub's shoulders slumped, all the fight leaving him at once.

Grub grabbed his plate, turned his back on Loth and started to eat, attacking his meal like, well. A starving man.

It was then that Loth noticed that Grub's plate held far less than his own did. "Where's the rest of your meal?" he demanded.

It was Ada who answered. "We weren't expecting to feed two extra bodies. That's all there is. And Scott insisted that as *royalty,*" she gave Loth a narrow look, "you get the most."

Loth's gut did that squirming thing again. He looked at his own meal and privately mourned his loss. "There's far too much cheese here. It doesn't agree with my royal disposition," he said through gritted teeth, "and the cured meats seem very pedestrian. I can't possibly eat this."

He took a slab of bread and one slice of ham (the thickest one, naturally), and set the rest down next to Grub. "You may as well have it since it seems you're not picky."

Grub glared at him again, and then bent over the plate like a dog afraid someone was going to steal its bone. He was still shiv-

ering, and the squirming in Loth's gut refused to go away, quite
spoiling his appetite. He rolled his eyes and unwound his scarf
from his throat. "Here," he said, dropping it onto Grub's shoulder.
"I expect it back once you're dry. Do try not to leave any dirty
marks on it."

Grub promptly grabbed at the scarf with greasy hands and
left dirty marks on it. Loth opened his mouth to object, but
closed it again when he took in the way the boy was quick to
wrap the scarf twice, thrice around his pencil-thin neck. He
almost missed the muttered, too quiet, "Thanks."

Almost.

"You're welcome," he declared loudly. "What kind of prince
would I be if I didn't take care of my subjects? Even the lowliest
of petty criminals like poor Grub here?"

Grub actually hissed like an angry cat at that, and Loth
allowed himself a smile. At least teasing the grubby little monster
had chased away that awful, possibly sympathy emotion, which
was the point of the exercise. If Loth were to start feeling bad just
because he took advantage of someone, where would it end?
With him unemployed, that's where—pickpockets didn't build a
successful career on being decent human beings.

And he *was* successful, the odd arrest notwithstanding. But
maybe, he reflected, he could use this to his advantage, take a
break from looking over his shoulder with every dip and snatch.
His rescuers were, for the most part, thicker than treacle,
although he'd have to watch Ada. If he could successfully string
them along (and he could, he had no doubt), there was no reason
he couldn't have a nice easy ride to the capital, fed and watered
and pampered like a prince every step of the way. Once there, he
decided, he'd make the dramatic revelation that Grub was the
prince after all, and that he'd only been playing the part to
protect Grub from possible attackers. Grub would play along,
surely—his other option was to be sent back to his cell, and Loth
doubted he'd want that. The story sounded far-fetched even to

his own ears, true, but with enough dramatic flair he was sure he could pull it off, and that was one thing Loth had never been accused of lacking. Morals, yes. A conscience? Definitely didn't have one of those. But flair? That, he had in spades.

Anyway, Grub would only have to pretend long enough for Loth to make a swift escape into the crowded streets of Callier, and Loth was sure that even he could remember to stand up straight and look imperious for a few minutes.

Maybe, once he'd ditched these idiots, Loth would dye his hair again—blonde this time—and see if they really did have more fun. Perhaps he'd keep his hands out of people's pockets and slip them into their breeches instead and make his coin that way for a while. It was far less hazardous, and he did so enjoy it.

He pondered quietly as the others ate and packed up, not offering to help. He was meant to be royalty after all, and he'd never heard of a prince who'd lift a finger unless it was for his own benefit. Once the work was done, he mounted his horse and slapped the saddle. "Hurry up, Grub. I know you're not used to using a horse for its intended purpose, but we have a lot of ground to cover to get to Callier."

"No."

"Pardon?" Loth arched one eyebrow in an expression that was part incredulity, part intimidation. It was a good look. He'd practised it in the mirror, and it never failed to get him his own way.

It didn't seem to work on Grub, though. He arched an eyebrow of his own, suddenly exuding confidence and, dare Loth say it, authority. "I want to sit up front. I haven't escaped that prison after five—after a long time, only to be stuck looking at the back of your neck."

"Excuse me, it's a very nice neck!" Loth said, affronted. It was, too. Thick and muscular, he'd call it one of his best assets, except he had so many others to choose from.

"That's as may be, but I still don't want to stare at it for the next—" Grub stopped, turned to Scott. "How long will the trip to Callier take, exactly? Are we going through the mountain pass?"

Scott cleared his throat and said, "Uh," before casting a helpless glance at Ada.

"If we take the mountain pass? Six days, maybe eight if the weather's bad."

"Six days," Scott repeated, as if anyone needed to hear it again.

Loth cast an eye doubtfully at their small cart of supplies. "Forgive me for saying, but we aren't equipped for a trip that long. We'll starve." *One of us is halfway there*, he added to himself.

Scott's expression brightened. "Oh no, there are places along the way. Ser Factor sent me a list. We stop and gather our supplies, and they let him know we're still safe."

"Ser... Factor?" Loth had a working knowledge of the kingdom's noble houses—it made it easier to pick a target when he chose to do an actual burglary—but he'd never heard of Ser Factor. "And who might that be?"

"He's your glorious rescuer. Well, I'm the real rescuer," Scott clarified, just in case anyone had forgotten he was supposed to be the hero, "but he's the one holding the purse strings."

Loth's brow furrowed. Perhaps this *Factor* person was one of the new nobility that Doom had knighted in return for their support when he took the throne? He tucked the information away to ponder over later.

"Anyway. I'll be taking the front of the horse," Grub insisted.

"Make a change from you taking the back of one." Loth said airily as he dismounted. He watched as Grub struggled to pull himself into the saddle, and when it looked like he wouldn't quite make it, Loth gave a helpful shove.

Grub landed in the saddle with a solid thunk and let out an outraged yelp. "Don't you dare put your hands on me!" he hissed, and Loth was eerily reminded of every spoiled palace brat he'd ever come across.

He lifted his hands in the air, palms splayed. "Trust me, I wouldn't dream of it. I'm not sure all the lice are dead yet."

Grub's face became even more pinched, if that was possible. "Get on," he snapped finally. Loth did, making a show of swinging his leg over easily and settling right against the little monster's back, wrapping his hands around his waist just to be obnoxious. That, and Grub still had his cloak, and Loth was feeling the chill.

They set off at a brisk pace, and Loth was pleasantly surprised to find that Grub did, in fact, know how to ride. Loth wondered idly who he really was. Political prisoner he'd said, just before Loth had accused him of stallion shafting and all hell had broken loose. The son of a baron or a duke maybe, Loth mused, kept in the lockup to ensure his family's loyalty. It certainly wouldn't be the first time. He wondered if there wasn't a way to use it to his advantage—if they were wealthy, Loth was sure he could swing it so they rewarded him for the return of their lost lamb somehow. It all depended on whether the family were well situated, or one of those that boasted a name and nothing else.

Well. One way to find out. "Did you learn to ride as a child?"

"What is it to you?"

Okay, then. Still sulking.

Loth recalled that old saying about honey and flies. (He'd always wondered why you'd want to catch flies anyway, but that wasn't important right now.)

"It's just that you ride well," Loth commented. He manfully resisted the urge to make a horse joke—it wouldn't serve his purposes right now. "Almost like nobility. Didn't you say you were a political prisoner?"

"What does it matter?"

"Call me curious. Surely you have a family eager to see you again?"

Grub's shoulders stiffened. "It's none of your business," he said shortly. He twitched the reins so the horse moved into a trot, and Loth had to stop talking just to make sure he didn't lose his seat. Really, there was no point in pursuing the conversation further anyway.

He settled in behind Grub, and since it didn't seem like he'd be getting in the boy's good graces any time soon, he made himself comfortable, settling his chin on the lad's shoulder so he had a good view, and letting his hands run up and down his sides just to watch him squirm. He stopped that after a few minutes though, because the ribs jutted out disturbingly and reminded him that somewhere along the line, Grub had been treated far worse than an ordinary prisoner. Loth wasn't in the habit of entertaining disturbing ideas if he could help it, so he pushed the thoughts away. Still, a part of his mind niggled at him, asking the question.

What on earth had Grub *done*?

CHAPTER THREE

They made good time, and Loth learned over lunch that Calarian was a vegetarian. "Oh? Is that the elvish word for terrible hunter?" he asked innocently, not missing Ada's smirk.

"It's a lifestyle choice. I'm all about animal welfare," Calarian poked at his plate of greens with a distinct lack of enthusiasm.

"Yet you ride a horse," Loth observed, because hypocrisy was only okay when he was the one practising it.

"Yes, well. Questing involved a lot more walking than I expected," Calarian said with a sniff.

Loth ate his own meal, noting that a bigger portion seemed to have made its way onto Grub's plate this time. He obviously wasn't the only one who'd seen those ribs. They finished their meals in short order and struck out once more. Grub's foul mood seemed to have dissipated, and he rode with his head tilted back, obviously enjoying the weak rays of sunshine on his face. He almost smiled once. Loth, for his part, behaved on the back of the horse. It was only fun teasing someone if you lulled them into a false sense of security first, he told himself. That was the only reason. It wasn't because of that smile, no.

They stopped once or twice for Scott to pull out his map and squint at it before leading them forward. Loth had to admit he had his concerns when they rode down one path for an hour, before Ada pulled her horse up next to Scott's and hissed at him under her breath. He then consulted the map, and wordlessly led them back the way they came, but Loth wasn't too worried. As long as they had the map and Ada, they'd get where they were going, and so far it didn't seem like anyone was following them.

He was drawn from his thoughts by a low caterwauling, and at first, he glanced around to see if they'd picked up a stray cat, but no. The sound was coming from Dave. He could make out stray words as Dave... sang under his breath. If it could be called singing.

"What on earth?" he asked Ada in an undertone.

"Dave fancies himself a bard," she sighed. "He doesn't let the fact he can't carry a tune in a bucket stop him."

Loth listened closer.

"Riding through the woods with the princes, there were two of them, saving the kingdom, something something, a hero and an orc, a pretty elf and a cranky dwarf..." Dave groaned out as Ada scowled at him. He grinned cheerfully at Loth. "Startin' the ballad. Scott says there's gotta be ballads, and I'm the bard. I'll be famous, I will."

"Well, you're certainly memorable," Loth agreed because discretion was the better part of valour where seven feet of orc was concerned.

"And I'm certainly pretty," Calarian agreed, tossing his shimmering mahogany hair over his shoulder.

They passed the afternoon like that, listening to Dave attempt to remember what he'd written, Scott interjecting with instructions like, "Don't forget to mention that I'm handsome, will you?" and "Fearless. Make sure to mention fearless," while Ada and Loth rolled their eyes.

When they stopped for a break, Grub took the chance to

dismount and pull Loth's scarf up so it covered his ears. He paused mid-movement. "Why does this scarf have pockets?" His voice was muffled.

"They're very handy."

Grub regarded him flatly and pulled the scarf away from his mouth. "They're for stashing your pilfered items, aren't they?"

"They're for sentimental trifles, things I want to keep close."

"Like whatever your sticky fingers have pinched most recently, you mean." Grub pulled a silver chain with a locket out of one pocket, and a handful of foreign coins from another, holding them out in his palm like an accusation.

Loth reached out and snatched the scarf away. "Rifling through someone's pockets is just downright rude."

"Says the *pickpocket?*"

Loth decided that he'd preferred Grub when he'd been hungry and silent. "Technically, I'm a scribe," he corrected, fishing through the small pouches that ran the length of the scarf and pulling out a battered quill, waving it triumphantly. "See? Tools of my trade."

There was a beat of silence, then, "You stole that, didn't you?"

"You have such a suspicious mind!"

"And I'm sure you have very talented fingers."

Loth leered. "I've never had any complaints. Want to find out firsthand?"

Grub flushed slightly. "That's not what I meant and you know it."

"Do I? Maybe my sheer attractiveness is making you reconsider your penchant for ponies, hmm?" He waggled his eyebrows suggestively and was rewarded with Grub blushing to the very tips of his ears and scowling. "I'm very attractive, Grub. You can say it. Go on, say it."

Grub's flush deepened. "Don't try to change the subject. My point is, having a quill doesn't make you a scribe, any more than having a map makes Scott a navigator."

Loth frowned. "You're very judgemental for a wanted man. By that logic, you'd probably argue that despite freeing you this isn't a real rescue party because we don't have..." Loth cast about desperately for an example. "A dragon."

Dave stopped composing long enough to interrupt. "I have a dragon."

Loth froze, then whirled on his heel. "We have a dragon?"

"A dragon?" Scott echoed, striding over. "Excellent! All quests need a dragon!"

Dave beamed. "Yeah. Had him since I was little."

Loth was intrigued. A dragon was a rarity, and if he could get his hands on one... the possibilities were endless.

"Is he nearby?"

Dave nodded. "I'll call him." He let out a piercing whistle.

Loth shaded his face with one hand and tilted his head back, peering into the sky, while next to him Grub did the same. They both watched and waited, listening for the majestic whomping of dragon wings, all their attention focussed upward.

Which probably explained why Loth was totally unprepared for the wet tongue in his ear.

"Gah!" He leapt into the air, flailing, trying to see what it was that had attacked him. He turned his head and was greeted by a pair of wide green eyes, staring. They belonged to what was possibly the tiniest dragon Loth had ever seen, perched on his shoulder. Loth stared back. The dragon licked his cheek.

"What, exactly is that?" he asked, fascinated.

"'s my fingerdragon. Trained him from an egg, I did. Meet Pyromaneous the Third. I call him Pie."

"The Third? You have others?" Loth watched as the tiny beast, which really was no bigger than a finger, hopped down his arm and crawled into one of the pouches of his scarf.

"I forgot they could fly an' I left the window open," Dave admitted. "Mum said three strikes and no more pets, so I was careful with this one. S'why I brought him. Look, he likes you!"

And indeed, the little creature was making pleased-sounding noises accompanied by tiny puffs of smoke, kneading at the fabric of the scarf before curling around itself and settling in exactly like a kitten would. That is, if kittens had scales and breathed fire.

Well, smoke.

Loth smiled despite himself. It really was cute, in a bizarre sort of way. The scales on its body were burnished gold, but when it spread its tiny wings they were translucent, a brilliant emerald green that matched its eyes. "Look at you. Where have you been hiding, hmm?" Loth breathed, unable to resist reaching out a fingertip. "Hello, Pie."

Pie chirruped at him, sniffing the fingertip and giving it a tiny lick before going back to nesting in his scarf. "He normally lives in my sleeve," Dave explained.

Grub leaned forward. "Can I—?"

Dave nodded. "Pie likes most people."

Grub ran a fingertip down the dragon's spine, and Pie arched in obvious pleasure, so Grub did it again.

"Me next! I'm the leader!" Scott exclaimed, pushing Grub aside and attempting to remove Pie from his temporary nest.

Pie hissed and spat out a tiny flame, and Scott leapt back with a most unheroic yelp and a scowl. "You said he liked people."

"*Most* people," Dave said darkly, leaning in to make sure Pie was okay. "He's particular. Lucky he didn't bite you, messing with his nest."

"Bite me? He's not poisonous, is he?"

Dave's green brow scrunched for a moment. "No. He's not poisonous."

Loth cupped his hands under the pocket that Pie was settled in and lifted it towards Dave in offering. "Did you want to take him back?"

Dave shook his head. "Nah. Told you, he likes you."

"What good's he going to be though?" Scott asked, brow furrowed. "I mean, look at him. He's far too sm—"

"Say *small*, Scott. I dare you." Ada scowled, hands planted on her hips.

"Oh, yes do, Scott," Loth added, just as Dave's expression turned thunderous. Dave covered Pie's body completely with an enormous green hand, as if to protect his pet from any unpleasant talk.

"You got something against my dragon just cause he's little?" he demanded.

"Or little things generally?" Ada challenged, one hand moving to her axe handle. "You wanna talk about size?" For just a second Loth was afraid that the murder of their leader, for not knowing when to shut his big dumbarse heroic mouth, would stymie his rescue.

Calarian grinned broadly and picked his fingernails clean with the point of an arrow. "Can I have all Scott's stuff when he's dead?"

But even dumb animals had an instinct for danger, and Scott backed away quickly and held both hands up in a placating gesture. "Young, I was going to say he's young, that's all! I'm sure he's good for... something."

Loth was never one to miss an opportunity to make himself look good at someone else's expense, and this was no exception. "I think it's very ignorant of you to be such a sizeist, Scott. Pyromaneous the Third is magnificent," he proclaimed loudly, "and, as royalty, mine is the opinion that matters."

He ignored the choking noises Grub made.

Dave nodded, eyes wide. "You're a good boy, aren't you?" He lifted his hand away and Pie warbled at him and nodded his tiny head.

"Does he understand you?" Grub asked.

Dave nodded again, happier this time. "Watch this." He held out a massive palm, and the dragon hopped onto it. "Pie? Sit."

The dragon sat.

"Roll over."

Pie rolled over.

"Play dead."

The tiny creature fell onto its side, let out a dramatic puff of smoke and a sigh, and went completely stiff. It was very convincing.

"'S his best one," Dave said proudly. He reached down and tickled Pie's belly, which resulted in a squirming, chirruping dragon. It was bizarrely endearing, watching the massive orc grin around his tusks at his pet.

Calarian wandered over, holding out a finger, and Pie lighted onto it before flying in slow circles around his head and landing again. "A real dragon," he said, awestruck. "Wait til I tell my friends!" He chucked a finger under Pie's chin. "You're going to feature in my next campaign. I'll change it up. We'll make a new game. We'll call it... Houses and Dragons!" He frowned. "No, wait. That doesn't sound right. Anyway, I'll think of something."

"He's very, um... impressive," Scott offered, edging closer again as if unsure of his welcome. "And I wasn't being, *you know*," he said to Ada. "I have friends who are dwarves."

"Doubtful," she sniffed, but she seemed less likely to take her axe to Scott's throat, at least for now, and the palpable tension in the air eased.

"Doubtful he'd have friends at all," Grub muttered under his breath.

Loth elbowed him in the side. "Why Grub, that was positively cruel! I'm very impressed," he added quietly and was rewarded with another one of those actual smiles. (Not that a smile from Grub was a reward, he reminded himself. That would imply that he cared, and he absolutely didn't. Loth hadn't cared for anyone or anything in years, and he didn't miss it at all.)

Pie chittered and chirped at Dave, who tilted his head as

though he understood, and dumped the dragon back into the pocket of Loth's scarf. "'E wants to ride with you," he said.

Loth let Pie settle in, not inclined to argue with the orc. Besides, he thought as Pie purred from the warm confines of his scarf; they did say dragons were lucky.

DELACOURT WAS at the arse-end of the kingdom. The residents there had been perversely proud of the fact. Loth had been in worse towns, but never more remote ones. If the Kingdom of Aguillon was roughly the shape of a potato scallop, then Delacourt was on the tip of a very unnecessary appendage at the top end of it. Loth had an idea that those were called peninsulas on maps, not appendages, but he'd leave that to the cartographers.

Loth was from Callier. He'd had to leave quickly through no fault of his own. A total misunderstanding involving a game of cards, a double or nothing bet, and an extra ace that had somehow appeared in the pack—and he'd jumped on the first ship leaving the harbour. A week later, his stomach still queasy, he'd staggered off the gangplank in Delacourt. He'd always figured that when it was time to return, he'd be going by ship again, not by road. Because Loth was no fan of the sea, but he was also no fan of saddle sores, the cold, hunger pangs, and The Wilds.

They'd crossed into The Wilds that afternoon. Loth couldn't even say that he was aware of when it had happened—there were no signs proclaiming it—but turned out that entering The Wilds was like entering a cold lake. One step, and then another step, until suddenly you were in completely over your head.

The Wilds was... desolate. The trees were sparse and scrubby, and those that grew had been twisted into oddly terrifying shapes by the wind. There was a strange smell in their air: muddy, a little salty, as though even the living trees themselves were half-rotted. There was an oppressive stillness in the air, and Loth hadn't seen any wildlife in at least a few hours, not even a rabbit, although something howled in the distance. Even Ada looked concerned.

"Scott," Loth asked as they prepared camp for the night, "are you certain the map said to go through The Wilds? Because I'm pretty sure that's the Swamp of Death I can smell from here."

"Oh, yes, my Graceling," Scott said, trying to make a fire with a stack of damp wood. "Ser Factor was adamant nobody would follow us this close to the Swamp of Death. As long as we stick to the road, we'll be fine."

"Huh." Loth put his hands on his hips and squinted behind him in the gathering gloom. "And where's the road, Scott?"

Scott hurried to stand beside him and looked behind them. And then in front of them. And then behind them again.

"Huh," he echoed. He chewed his lip, and his scraggly goatee trembled like a scared little woodland creature. His brow furrowed. "It appears the road is in the wrong place, my liege."

"Must be that faulty map," Loth said, wondering how long it would be before Scott killed them all. Minutes, probably.

"Yes," Scott agreed quickly, scurrying away again. "The faulty map."

Loth swallowed a sigh and looked around at the rescue party. Calarian was sitting in the back of the cart, his long legs dangling, as he sorted through a handful of something that looked like coins, but Loth suspected were tokens from Houses and Humans.

Dave was crouching by the damp firewood, cooing encouragement at Pie as Pie puffed out wisps of smoke in the direction of the potential fire. At this rate, the poor little lizard would die of exhaustion before they ever saw a flame.

Ada was stomping up and down the edge of their sad little campsite, huffing like one of the horses.

And Grub...

Grub was standing quietly, his chin lifted, staring off into the growing darkness. There was enough distance between them that he looked almost like one of Scott's heroes, and not at all like the scrawny half-starved, bad-tempered little shit that Loth knew he was. He must have felt Loth's gaze on him—he turned, and his face settled into a familiar scowl, and then he trudged over towards Loth, his hands shoved under his armpits as though he was trying to warm them. Loth almost felt guilty for taking his scarf back.

"Scott tells me that the road is in the wrong place," he said as Grub approached.

Grub snorted.

Loth levelled a stare at him. "You don't seem too upset by the fact that we are currently lost in The Wilds."

Grub shrugged. "We'll be fine, as long as we avoid the swamp." His brows drew together thoughtfully. "And, of course, the wolves don't attack."

"The what now?"

"The wolves," Grub said. "They say they can grow as big as horses out here." He flashed Loth an evil grin. "But I'm sure that's just a nasty rumour."

"Well, you're safe," Loth said. "You'd be nothing but bone and gristle. They'd only want you as a toothpick."

Grub lifted a hand and raked his fingers through his hair. It stood up at strange angles, and Loth pushed down the urge to attempt to tame it slightly. What did he care if Grub looked like a manic haystack?

Grub's gaze found his again. "A fire should keep the wolves away if Pie can start one. Otherwise, my *Prince*, you'd do well to tell them to set a watch."

"Hmm." Loth folded his arms over his chest. "A fire might keep the wolves away, but wouldn't it attract other predators?"

Grub raised his eyebrows. "Such as?"

"Bandits," Loth suggested. "Or soldiers of the crown, given both of us are currently fugitives."

"You think that Ser Greylord would send his men into The Wilds for a pickpocket?" There was something confronting in Grub's stare.

"I have no idea who that is."

"The Shire Reeve of Delacourt."

"I still don't know who that is," Loth admitted. "And while I doubt very much the loss of one pickpocket would bother him, there's still the question of *you*, isn't there, Grub? What exactly were you doing in the dungeons of Delacourt, and who put you there?" He exhaled slowly. "Who are you, Grub? You're no peasant."

Grub's brows drew together. "What was it you said back in Delacourt? You asked me if I was the illegitimate spawn of a ranking official." He shrugged and looked away.

"A hostage, then," Loth said. "Kept in chains to ensure your father's compliance." He stretched. "Well, I'm sure he'll be glad to have you home if the wolves don't eat us. Not that you can ever show your face again, can you? Or Lord Doom will snap you right up again. Still, it'll be better than a dungeon, I suppose."

War was a messy thing, and so was politics. Loth, like most people who worked for a living, didn't give two shits about the games that rich men played. It didn't make any difference to him which royal arse was sitting on the throne. The sun still rose every morning.

Still, he snorted. "It's funny, isn't it?"

Grub was staring into the darkness again. "What is?"

"Lord Doom," Loth said.

Grub's brow furrowed.

"Lord Doom," Loth repeated. "He's called Lord *Doom*, he seized power, and nobody ever saw it coming?" He huffed out a laugh. "That's funny."

Grub blinked at him. "It's... it's actually Lord Dumesny."

"Huh." Loth wrinkled his nose. "Oh, well that's not as funny at all then."

Dave cheered suddenly, his victorious roar echoing out through the gloom. Loth saw a tiny flame flickering in the stack of firewood. Pie chirped and flew tiny victory laps around the fire. Ada clapped her hands, and even Calarian looked grudgingly impressed.

Loth slapped Grub on the back. "Ah, some good news at last! The wolves might eat us, but at least we won't freeze to death."

He hurried towards the fire.

CHAPTER FOUR

Calarian cooked surprisingly well for a vegetarian.

There'd been a brief standoff over who should do the duties, with Scott looking beseechingly at Ada, but she'd snapped, "Don't try and make it my job. That long useless streak can do something instead of moping for a change."

Calarian, the long useless streak in question, hadn't dared object. He shuffled about scowling, but he did as asked, putting together a stew of some sort. Loth would have had seconds if there'd been any left. As it was, he watched as Dave shovelled the leftovers onto Grub's plate. At least between the barely adequate servings and the exercise of riding all day, by the time they reached the capital he'd be in excellent shape for his career change. He'd probably be able to double his prices.

Of course, he'd have to ditch these idiots once he was within the walls of the city. The last thing he wanted was to get entangled in whatever political nonsense they were engaged in. If there really was some crazy rich nobleman out there who was bankrolling this entire enterprise—Scott's Ser Factor—then Loth never wanted to meet him. No, it would be much better for everyone, especially Loth, if Prince Tarquin remained dead and buried. Loth didn't have a great grasp on history, but he was fairly sure things never ended well for pretenders to the throne. Even the attractive ones.

Somewhere out in the darkness, a wolf howled. The hair on the back of Loth's neck prickled, and he was thankful Pie had managed to light the fire after all.

After dinner, everyone began to spread their bedrolls around the fire. Loth saw the issue the second that Ada approached him with a bedroll clasped in her arms and an apologetic look on her face.

"We thought we'd only be rescuing one person," she said, thrusting the bedroll at him.

Loth took it and exchanged a glance with Grub. The firelight really did bring out all the angles of his impressive scowl. His face was how Loth felt, but Loth was much better at hiding it.

"Well," he said, "as the prince, I will of course take the bedroll and—"

Grub narrowed his eyes and then stalked towards the cart, presumably to throw himself down under it and sulk.

"Kidding!" Loth called. "Grub, I was *kidding*. We can share, you cranky little goblin. Get back here. I mean unless you'd rather sleep with the horses?"

"Maybe I would," Grub shot back. "I'm sure even the geldings would put you to shame, *Your Grace*."

"Oh, Grub," Loth said. "Did you really just admit you were a horse fucker, just to make a joke about the size of my dick?"

Grub glowered. "It was worth it," he said, but he didn't sound sure.

"See?" Loth *tsk*ed and looked around the group. "He's not even ashamed of it. Those poor horses."

Grub stomped back over to him. "I fucking hate you," he muttered.

"No, you don't." Loth beamed at him. "You adore me. I'm a delight."

"I've met rats in cells that I like more than you." Grub grabbed the bedroll and shook it out. "I've had *ticks* I liked more."

"Did you catch those from the horses?"

For a moment Loth thought that Grub was going to breathe sparks like Pie, but suddenly he threw his hands up. The bedroll fell to the ground. Grub shook his head, his mouth twisting into something that Loth was surprised to discover was a smile.

Grub snorted. "I can't win with you, can I?"

"You can't," Loth agreed. "Nobody wins against royalty. I'm glad you've realised." He leaned in close. "Besides, geldings are missing their balls, and I still have mine. They're quite impressive. Would you like to see?"

Grub let out a snort.

Loth crouched down and tugged the bedroll out. A moment later Grub joined him. His hands were pale in the darkness, fluttering like pale moths against the bedroll as they worked together to lay it out flat. Loth wondered if they were still shaking from the cold.

"You can take the side closest to the fire if you want," he said airily.

Grub nodded and crawled into the bedroll. Loth crawled in after him. Around them, Loth heard the others settling. Someone was already snoring, but Loth wasn't sure who it was. Dave was the large shape nearest to them, his greenish face illuminated by the flames, and by Pie, who buzzed around him flickering like a firefly.

Lying next to Grub was like lying next to a bag of bones. He was pointy, and Loth wasn't a fan. Loth lay on his back for a moment, then rolled onto his side and pillowed his head on his arm. He watched Grub's profile for a moment, lit by the fire. Grub was staring up at the sky, eyes wide open.

"Close your eyes, Grub. You're putting me off my sleep."

Grub jolted and turned his face towards Loth briefly. "I was looking at the stars."

"Yes, yes. Stars." Loth yawned. "Very pretty."

"It's..." Grub sounded hesitant. "It's been a while."

"A while since what?"

"Since I saw the stars."

Loth felt a knot in his belly. "How long?"

"I'm not sure, exactly, but maybe... five years?"

"Five..." Loth's chest tightened. "Fuck me."

There was a moment of silence, and then Grub said, "I would, but you're not a horse."

And then the little shit rolled over and fell asleep.

LOTH WOKE to something wet dragging across his face.

"Gah!" He swatted blindly, and his hand touched scaly skin. Pie chirruped in his ear, far too cheerful for this early in the day.

Loth sat up with a scowl. His sleep had been fitful, broken up with strange dreams of sitting on a throne while a crowd chanted *imposter! imposter!* Followed by a delightful episode of being chased through the Swamp of Death by a pack of wolves. Random jabs from Grub's elbows had woken him as the boy had tossed and whined in the grip of his own dreams. Loth had ended up rolling over and wrapping himself firmly around Grub's back, hoping it meant the boy would stop flailing for five minutes. Grub had grizzled and squirmed without ever waking, but eventually he'd settled and they'd both managed a few hours' rest.

It wasn't enough.

The bedroll next to him was empty, although there was a trace of body heat lingering there. Loth rubbed his eyes with the heel of his hand, attempting to wake up properly, and peered around the camp. It appeared he was the last to wake. The smell of the Swamp of Death was tempered slightly by the smell of something cooking, possibly eggs, and Loth nodded in unconscious approval. He hauled himself out of the bedroll and wandered off to the far edge of the campsite to relieve himself and was back just in time for Scott to thrust a plate at him.

Loth was too tired for this. He peered at the contents. "What's this?" Because it certainly wasn't eggs.

"Royal porridge, your Lordiness."

Loth supposed the lumpy mess might be called porridge, if porridge was having a very bad day. He prodded at it with a finger. It jiggled in a way food shouldn't and smelled distinctly fishy. Loth hated fish. "I think I'll pass."

Scott's earnest-but-stupid face fell. "But I made it to the special recipe."

"Special recipe?"

Scott nodded. "It's the kind of porridge from the palace. Grub said it's what you'd expect. It was just lucky we had everything in the cart."

Loth smelled a rat. A stinky, fishy rat. "Remind me what's in here again? Just so I can be sure it's *proper* Royal Porridge."

"Oats, honey, cinnamon..." Scott recited, as Loth nodded along. "And of course, the dried eel," he added, and Loth's stomach dropped. "He said it's what royalty is raised on, your Princiness, and that you'd love every bite."

Loth noticed Grub watching them, smirking, and it fell into place. He should have known the little shit would try and get him back for the horse jokes.

Loth sniffed the gooey, salty mixture. Oh, he was going to make the boy pay for this. "And so I shall," he declared, and scooped up a huge bite, shoving it in his mouth before he could think better of it. He gulped convulsively in an effort to get it down his throat before his tastebuds noticed what he was doing.

He failed.

His mouth was filled with the conflicting taste of cinnamon and seawater, warm and thick and utterly gag-worthy. Normally Loth had no problem swallowing a salty treat, but the overriding flavour of eel ruined it somewhat. Still, he managed to get it down and keep it down, much to his relief.

Ada was watching him far too closely for his liking, so he was forced to make a show of humming and licking the spoon. He peered into the bowl, fighting the frown at how much of it was left. He managed another three gut-churning spoons full before he begged off. "After all my time locked away, I fear my appetite has decreased," he sighed. "Still, it's a shame for it to go to waste. Perhaps Grub can have the rest, as thanks for remembering the recipe? I'll wager you've never tasted anything like this before." He thrust the bowl into Grub's face and was rewarded with a scowl as the boy sniffed and went slightly green around the gills.

"Come on now, eat up—it's a treat!" he said, holding the spoon to Grub's thinly pressed lips, an unspoken challenge.

There was sheer murder in Grub's eyes as he reluctantly took a bite, and then another, Loth shovelling the disgusting mess down his throat as fast as he could. Loth didn't give him time to protest, pressing the spoon to his mouth like a determined mother forcing vegetables on an unhappy toddler. He wasn't a complete monster though—he relented after four or five mouthfuls and dropped the spoon into the bowl.

"Shame," he sighed. "It's gone cold, and it can't be eaten cold. Still," he said, giving Grub a particularly obnoxious smile. "I don't expect this every morning Grub, but if you do make it again, I'll be more than happy to share with you, as a thank you for this taste of home."

"It was a one-time thing. I don't think there's any more dried eel," Grub gritted out through clenched teeth.

"Oh well, in that case, I shall eat what everyone else has, like a commoner," Loth said breezily.

"Right. *Like* a commoner," Grub said, still sullen, and stalked over to the other side of the camp, arms wrapped around himself.

Loth followed and sidled up close to him because he hadn't quite had the last word. "It was a good attempt, I'll give you that," he murmured out the side of his mouth, "but don't try and play a player, my little equine eroticist."

Grub snorted at that one, and the corners of his mouth twitched up in what might have been a smile. He turned to Loth and unwrapped one arm from his body just enough to extend a hand. "Fair enough. Truce?"

Loth looked down at the thin wrist, the delicate fingers, the pale skin still marred with ingrained dirt. Clearly Grub had been through a lot. Maybe, Loth pondered, just this once, he could try not being an absolute arse. He'd heard people managed it all the time.

"Truce," he decided, giving the hand a shake, "although I'll have you know, I'll be tasting eel for weeks. Special royal porridge, my eye."

"Oh, there is a special royal porridge," Grub offered, smirking, "but it has fresh berries and cream, and it's topped with hazel-nuts, not fish."

What an odd thing for him to know.

THEY MADE SLOW PROGRESS, and Loth wasn't the only one who didn't trust Scott's sense of direction, apparently. Calarian took it upon himself to confiscate the map and appoint himself their guide.

"I know how maps work," he explained. "We use them in Houses and Humans."

It was a relief when after some twists and turns, the lost road came into view, and the party hurried towards it. Scott was still scratching his head at how it could possibly have moved so far from its appointed spot.

Grub had agreed to take turns riding pillion as part of their truce. So Loth was treated not only to the pleasant weight of Grub's body leaning against his, but also a clear view when Pie flitted up to perch on Scott's shoulder. Scott opened his mouth to say something, possibly pointing out that the dragon liked him after all. Before he had the chance, Pie lifted his tail and deposited a squirt of filth down the back of Scott's doublet. Scott squawked, and Pie chirruped and circled back to Loth.

"Good boy," Loth crooned quietly, and Grub's body shook with suppressed laughter where they were pressed close.

"He's my favourite," Grub said quietly.

"I thought I was your favourite?" Loth teased.

"No, I still hate you. But you know the saying. Keep your friends close and your enemies closer."

"That's a stupid saying. It should be, *keep your friends close and your enemies in an unmarked grave.* Or, *keep your friends close and your enemies far enough away that they're not a problem.* Or even, *keep your friends close and your enemies too busy fighting your other enemies to worry about you.*"

"The enemy of my enemy is my friend?" Grub asked.

"See, now I've said the word enemy too many times and it doesn't even sound like a real word," Loth complained. "En-em-ee. Em-en-ee. Mem-en-em-en-em-ee. I can't tell which one is right anymore."

Grub snorted. "I'm certain you'll remember. You must have enough of them."

"You really are a rude little brat, you know that?"

Loth felt rather than saw Grub shrug. "I notice you're not denying it. And you really are a terrible human being."

"Of course I am. I'm royalty, and we're all bastards, one way or another."

Grub was silent for a moment, and then he said, "Do you really believe that?"

"Of course," Loth said. "When was the last time someone with their fat arse on a throne actually gave a damn about whether or not the peasants were hungry?"

Grub was silent again. Loth discovered that he liked the

feeling of Grub's hands resting softly on his hips as they rode. He was almost regretful when, an hour or so later, they changed positions.

The day was cold, and the sun appeared faint and distant as a mist blew in over the scrubby ground. The wind-twisted trees seemed to shiver; Grub certainly did.

Loth watched the scrubby scenery for a while, then went back to watching the nape of Grub's neck, where his reddish hair curled against his pale skin. His hair needed a cut and also a wash. It appeared gritty and greasy and revolting, but for some reason Loth wasn't as willing to apply those descriptors to the man himself, despite the eel porridge incident.

A breath of cold wind brought the stench of decay with it, and Loth wrinkled his nose. "What is *that?*"

"The Swamp of Death," Grub said. "We must be very close to the edge."

"Is it called that because of the smell?"

"Yes," Grub said. "Oh, and also because it will literally kill you."

"We're still on the road, right?" Loth peered down to check, just in case, and was relieved to see they were. "At least Calarian is doing the map reading now, and not Scott."

They were in the middle of the straggling party: up ahead, Calarian led the way with Scott at his side pretending to lead. Ada rode slightly behind them. Loth and Grub followed her, and Dave brought up the rear, on his shire horse. The shire horse not only carried Dave, but it also pulled the cart. The beast was massive, but when Loth had suggested that it'd take more than a stool for Grub to deal with it—he'd need a ladder—Grub had only snorted and rolled his eyes.

They paused in a clearing to stretch and to piss. Dave kicked mud off the wheels of the cart, grumbling about the state of the road. Loth's stomach grumbled, but nobody made any move for the provisions, and so he wondered exactly how much they had left. It was probably best not to bring up for now. He'd hope for a decent meal at dinnertime.

"I suspect we have a rough afternoon ahead of us," Loth said in an undertone.

Grub nodded in agreement, and something about the movement, the light arch of his neck, made a faint tendril of want bloom in Loth's belly. He squashed it down ruthlessly, unprepared to deal with it.

When they set out again, the day growing darker as the mist rolled in further, Grub rode pillion. The bad weather brought down the mood of the party as well. Dave even stopped humming. Silence settled over them, as thick and heavy as the mist.

And then, abruptly, Calarian stopped, and leapt down from the saddle.

"What?" Scott asked. "What's happening?"

"Shut up!" Calarian hurried back down the short little column of riders. "Does anyone else hear that?"

Loth listened, but only heard the stamp and chuff of his horse as it shifted restlessly. "What can you hear?"

"Horses," Calarian said, squinting into the mist.

"We're riding them!" Scott called back.

"Shut up!" Calarian stared into the mist. "Not *our* horses!"

Ears like a bat, Loth remembered, his stomach twisting. Was he really so important that soldiers from Delacourt were searching for him? No, scratch that. Was *Grub* really that important? If he'd really been held as a hostage, then quite possibly he was, and everything Loth had talked himself into during the initial escape—that nobody cared because nobody was following them—was about to be proven false. Bad news for Grub of course, but surely the soldiers would be happy enough at getting their prisoner back that they'd overlook an insignificant pickpocket, right?

Even if he'd believed it, the thought still tasted sour in his throat when he remembered how skinny Grub was—clear evidence of how he'd been treated during his imprisonment.

"Horses," Calarian said again, his sharp features pinched. "Maybe four or five? A few miles back still, but gaining fast. We need to get off the road."

"*Off* the road?" Loth asked. "Just to clarify, you want us to get *off* the road?"

"Yes," Calarian said. "Unless you'd rather wait to be recaptured."

Grub reached around Loth and grabbed for the reins of the horse, tugging it to urge the creature to turn.

Fine. They were going off the road. The same road that was the only thing preventing them from wandering into the Swamp of Death. Which Grub had said wasn't *just* named that because of the stench.

"This is a terrible idea," Loth muttered.

"Shut up," Grub said tersely and tugged the reins harder.

They headed off the road, and into the thickening mist.

CHAPTER FIVE

D ave led the group by virtue of the size of his mount. He was able to push through the scrubby undergrowth, making it easier for those following, although the cart was an early casualty—the wheels stuck in the gluey mud and refused to move, and it took the combined strength of Dave, Ada, Calarian and Loth to drag it out of the way. Scott shouted pointless directions like "Lift it out of the mud!" and Grub paced nervously on his horse, glancing back at the road. As soon as the way was clear and Loth had climbed back on the horse, he was forging ahead.

His urgency affected the rest of the group, and it was a tense ride as they moved forward. They left the cart to the mud and Grub rode hard on Dave's heels, as though the extra two feet would make a difference if someone really was after them. Loth chanced a glance at his companion, took in the set jaw and the tense shoulders, and wisely didn't make the crack he'd been planning about Grub just wanting to get closer to Dave's horse's arse.

There was a trail—of sorts. It was more the faintest of lines through the ferns and grasses, a hint that they weren't the first ones to make their way through here, that someone or something else was walking in the swamps besides them. Loth wasn't sure if that was a comfort or not. Regardless, they were here now. The stench was growing steadily worse, and the thick stands of trees obscured the light almost completely, leaving them guessing as to where they should be going. They were no longer able to ride and had to dismount and lead the horses. After they'd forged ahead for half an hour driven by guesswork and panic, Scott called a halt. "I can't see," he complained. "I need the map."

"It's too dark to read the map," Calarian countered, clutching the document tightly.

"As your leader, I demand the map," Scott snapped, and lunged forward and snatched it out of Calarian's hand.

"Fine, but it's still too dark to read it," the elf said with a sniff.

Dave spoke up unexpectedly. "We got Pie."

"We don't need fire, Dave," Scott sighed. "we need light."

Dave's brow furrowed. "Fire... light?" he ventured.

At that, Scott's expression brightened. "I have Had A Thought," he proclaimed, and Loth could hear the capital letters. "We shall use the dragon as light to read the map, and I shall lead us to safety."

Well, he'd certainly lead them somewhere, of that Loth had no doubt. He just wasn't sure that he wanted to follow. Still, he nudged at Pie where he was sleeping in the pocket of his scarf.

"Come on, little one," he murmured, "go keep our great and glorious leader happy."

Up until then, Loth never knew that a dragon could roll its eyes, but Pie managed it just fine. Then he stretched his wings and flapped them once or twice, yawning, and glided over to land on Scott's shoulder. Loth was pleased to see that once again, the dragon crapped down Scott's back. It was almost like it was deliberate.

Scott was blissfully unaware as he held up the parchment. "I NEED YOU TO BREATHE FIRE ON THIS," he said loudly, pointing at the map.

So Pie did.

The scroll caught alight almost instantly, and Scott flailed wildly and dropped it into the mud, where the flame burned inexplicably brighter for a second, consuming the entire thing. Pie made a pleased sound, and flapped over to Dave, chittering excitedly. Loth couldn't be sure, but it sounded like the dragon was congratulating himself on a job well done. Really, Loth couldn't entirely blame him—normally when he produced a flame, he was fussed and fawned over.

The rest of the party stared at the smouldering remains before Ada summed it up for them: "Well, fuck."

"It—I didn't—that dragon is defective!" Scott exclaimed, pointing wildly at Pie, and Loth was overcome with an over-whelming desire to shove Scott face first into the stinking mud.

But it was Grub who spoke up. "The dragon did what he was told, and although we don't have time to stand here arguing about whose fault it was, it was definitely yours. Now pick up the reins of your horse before it wanders off." He pointed at Scott.

Loth was struck by the air of authority that Grub suddenly wore, like an invisible cloak.

"We need to get moving," Grub repeated. "Come on."

Dave nodded in agreement and led them forward, and the rest of the party followed, not quite silently. Loth caught mutterings of "useless" and "... sure we can't drown him?" and he had to admit, it was quite nice not to have those sentiments directed at him, for once.

Without the map, and with the darkness closing in, their progress slowed to a crawl, and Loth could feel the nervous energy radiating off Grub. He wasn't feeling the best himself, he realised. His mind was foggy, his vision not quite right. It was as if he'd indulged in some of the so-called 'medicinal herbs' that you could buy if you knew the right person, the ones that gave off an intoxicating vapour.

Glancing around the party, he saw that he wasn't the only one and that the darkness wasn't the reason they'd slowed. Every one of the party was wearing a dazed expression. He shook himself and tried to unglue his tongue from the roof of his mouth. It took him a minute to form words. "Grub, how does the swamp kill people?"

The reply was slow, dazed. "Kills 'em. Poison air, then they fall in." He paused, and then he said, more urgently, "Shit. *Poison air.*"

This was bad.

Loth scraped together his remaining motor skills and wasted no time pulling his scarf off, unrolling it to its impressive full length, then wrapping it half around his face and half around Grub's so they were at least somewhat protected from the fumes. It meant that they were shoulder to shoulder like some sort of conjoined twin, but Loth didn't care—his focus right now was on not dying. In no time at all, his mind started to clear, and he waved his arms at the rest of the party, shouting "ovr yr mfhth!"

"What?" Calarian grinned at him lopsidedly and cupped his bat-like ears.

Loth huffed and dragged the scarf down. "Cover your face. We're breathing poison gas."

Calarian's eyes widened. He dug in his saddlebag for a length of cloth and tied it around his face, and it was obvious when it started working, because he blinked and shook his head, and his posture straightened. A moment later he pulled out another length of cloth and tied it around the muzzle of his horse.

Loth took a moment to curse that he hadn't thought to do the same, and after looking about, he dragged his doublet over his head. It was torn anyway, he silently consoled himself as he handed it to Grub who froze for a second, eyes wide, before taking it and tying it around the horse's muzzle.

The rest of the party followed suit, and it was apparent as they walked that the effects of the swamp gas were quick to wear off. Dave led the way with one hand extended, Pie perched on a fingertip, letting out breaths of flame and light that allowed them to pick their way carefully forward. Grub's arm was slung around Loth's shoulder to allow them to share the scarf, fingers cool against his bare skin. It wasn't unpleasant, and Loth only felt slightly guilty that he'd made no move to find something else for Grub to wear as a mask. After all, he reasoned, neither had Grub.

At first Loth thought it was his imagination, but as they advanced it became clear that the undergrowth was gradually thinning. They were able to make faster progress, and Loth guessed that whoever was pursuing them, they were well out of their grasp by now. He glanced over at Grub to see if he shared his opinion, and found him paler than usual, sweat beading his forehead, obviously exhausted. He stopped abruptly. "We need to take a break."

"Why?" Scott whined. "I'm leading you to safety!"

Loth wasn't exactly sure how Scott was leading from the rear, but he let that fact go in favour of one far more pertinent. "Because if we don't, Grub's going to pass out, and I'm not carrying him."

Scott blinked at him. "We could just..."

"Just what?"

Scott shrugged. "Roll his body into the swamp?" He doubled over abruptly as Ada kicked him in the nuts. "What? He's only a peasant!" he protested once he could breathe again.

"So are you, dickhead!" Ada snarled.

"Well, yes," Scott said, massaging his groin, "but not for much longer! I'm a hero, and I'm going to have ballads written about me, and other rewards too. Like land, and coin, and a title!"

"I don't think Grub's a pissant," Dave said staunchly.

"Peasant," Calarian corrected. "Some stupid human thing. Elves don't believe in a class structure."

"Do orcs?" Dave asked worriedly.

"No," Calarian said. "It's too complicated for you."

"Oh, good. Cause I can't spell it either." Dave brightened

slightly. "I can spell Dave, though!" Which for an orc was quite an achievement. He waved at Grub. "I like you, Grub."

Grub's mouth twitched under his makeshift mask. "Thanks, Dave. I like you too."

"You shouldn't have sex with horses though," Dave said. "They're probably not into that."

"I..." Grub's brow furrowed. "I'll keep that in mind?"

Dave gave him a thumbs up, while Loth tried not to chortle.

Grub wrapped his hand in the reins of the horse and urged it forward. "We should keep moving. The longer we stay here, the more likely we are to succumb to the fumes."

"You need to rest," Loth argued, even as he wondered why he cared. It was because he needed Grub to be his patsy and play prince once they reached the capital, he told himself. This was survival, not sentiment.

Grub raised his eyebrows. "If we stop now, we die."

Well, Loth supposed he had a point when he put it like that. Survival, he reminded himself, and not sentiment.

They continued on into the swamp, following the boggy paths, and picking their way around the strange, bubbling patches of mud that stank of sulphur and death. The trees here were twisted and ominous, their branches stripped bare of leaves. Most of them were rotting. Loth wondered how they'd even managed to grow in the first place.

The day darkened, and Loth had no idea if it was because night was approaching, or if the mist was growing thicker.

"Could we turn back?" he asked. "Try to find the road again?"

"That would have been much easier if we still had a fucking map," Calarian pointed out.

They continued on, Loth subtly tugging Grub closer and taking his weight as they walked. "I know what you're doing," Grub groused.

"What am I doing?"

"You think I can't walk by myself when I'm perfectly capable." Grub stumbled as he spoke, giving lie to his words.

"Nonsense," Loth replied. "I'm just allowing you the pleasure of touching my near-naked body, that's all. It seems like that charitable thing to do after you've been locked away for so long."

"I..." Grub swayed alarmingly. "What?"

Loth put an arm around Grub's waist, and Grub didn't even try to fight him.

"We can't stop," Grub mumbled, blinking rapidly. "Can't stop in the swamp."

"Yes, the gas," Loth said. "We won't stop. We'll keep going. Reach some higher ground, perhaps."

"No," Grub said, squinting sidelong at Loth. "Not the gas. The *monsters.*"

And then he pitched forward spectacularly into the mud, and Loth was so surprised that he let it happen.

FIVE MINUTES later they were picking their way through the Swamp of Death still. Grub was slung over the back of the horse like a saddlebag. He had a strip of cloth torn from Loth's doublet wrapped around his face, since they could no longer share the scarf and Loth wasn't about to part with it—there were limits to his generosity—and the doublet was ruined anyway. Loth was relieved that nobody had taken Scott's advice to just roll Grub's body into the swamp and leave him there. Pie flitted about Grub like a drunk will-o'-the-wisp, eventually settling on his arse and folding up his tiny wings to rest.

"He said monsters, didn't he?" Loth queried. "Definitely *monsters?*"

"I like monsters," Dave said, and then thought for a moment. "No, wait. I like mustard."

Loth's throat was beginning to hurt, and he was fairly certain the swamp gasses were starting to addle his brain again. "Does anyone here have any actual knowledge about the Swamp of Death?"

He stared at four very blank faces.

"I'm not from around here," Ada said at last.

"Me neither," said Calarian.

"Mustard," said Dave.

They looked to Scott.

"Well," Scott said, scratching his nose and making his makeshift mask dance, "I *have* heard things. But we're fine. We're the heroes."

"What have you heard, Scott?" Loth asked.

"Oh." Scott waved his hand dismissively. "Nothing to worry about, your Worshipfulness. Just this story about some monster who lives in the Swamp of Death who catches lost and unwary travellers and then kills them and eats their flesh and wears their skin as clothes."

"Huh," said Loth. "You see, the issue is that *we're* currently lost and unwary."

"Actually, I'm pretty fucking wary after hearing that," Ada muttered.

"Point," Loth said. A thought struck him. "Who exactly told the story, Scott?"

Scott shrugged. "Just a stranger in town. He was probably making it up for the glory and the free drinks."

Loth glanced at Grub's prone figure and resisted the urge to pet his arse. "Except Grub also knew about monsters in the swamp. And he wasn't out drinking with any strangers in taverns, was he?"

For someone who'd claimed to have been a hostage in Delacourt's dungeons, Grub knew an awful lot of things, actually. Loth didn't trust it—Loth didn't trust anything, but that was beside the point. Grub was definitely not being honest with him. And maybe they'd gotten off on the wrong foot what with Loth telling everyone he fucked horses, but was that anything to hold a grudge over? Besides, if Grub hadn't been so delightfully prickly when they'd met, Loth wouldn't have felt the need to continually poke at him. He only had himself to blame.

"Anyway," Scott continued blithely, "I'm sure that the monster doesn't *really* have claws the size of ploughshares and red eyes that burn like flames."

"Or vicious fangs dripping with the blood of his enemies," Dave agreed. Everyone swivelled to look at him. "Monsters, you said. Not mustard. Monsters in the swamp, yeah, I've heard of *those*. They're terrifying."

And then he *shuddered*. And Loth didn't want to even imagine what kind of monsters made an orc shudder. Except he had to imagine it, didn't he? Because here they fucking were, in the Swamp of Death, which, it now turned out, had monsters. He really, really should have stayed in a dungeon cell in Delacourt, even if he had been given the world's most annoying cellmate.

"Well, that's just *great!*" Ada threw up her hands. "We're about to be consumed by a bloodthirsty something, and I haven't even been paid yet!"

"What? That's your main concern here?" Loth stared, openmouthed.

"It's a matter of principle, for a dwarf. Never die with unresolved debt. It brings dishonour to the family." She fixed Scott with a glare. "So before we get munched, crunched, and spat out, I want my gold, or else it won't be the monster you have to worry about."

"We won't get munched and crunched," Scott maintained stoutly. "It's a fairy story. And we're the heroes! Whoever heard a ballad where the hero got eaten?"

"Um," Calarian ventured, "maybe those don't get written, because the hero isn't around to tell about how they got eaten?"

Scott went deathly pale as reality finally penetrated. "We're—

we might be in actual danger here," he whispered, horrified. "We might be the heroes who don't make it home."

"I don't think they're called heroes, Scott," Loth said gently. "I think they're called victims."

"Or lunch," added Ada.

Scott paled further, his pallor almost matching Grub's. "I—" A strange gurgling noise came from his lower midsection. "I —excuse me!"

And he dashed off behind the nearest tree.

"Did he—" Ada threw up her hands again. "Did we not just talk about how there are monsters in the swamp, and he goes off alone to shit his pants?"

"I am not shitting my pants!" Scott called from behind the trees. "I'm shitting *without* my pants! Besides, what do you think is going to happen? That some monster is going to grab me while my breeches are around my ankles and drag me away? I don't think that's very—"

But whatever else Scott was going to say was cut off by a roar, a thwack, and a thud as a monster—Loth presumed—dragged him away

"Well," Ada said moments later as they peered down at the steaming pile of shit left behind, "they probably won't put that in the ballads."

CHAPTER SIX

The trail left by the monster dragging Scott through the swamp—Calarian insisted on calling them skid marks —was easy enough to follow, even in the rapidly gathering darkness.

"This is probably a trap, you know," Ada said.

"Probably," Calarian agreed, with a gleam in his eye as he crept ahead. He held his bow in front of him, an arrow notched and ready to loose, and he looked every part the dangerous elven warrior. Unfortunately, Loth heard him murmur "Roll for initiative!" as he moved ahead. The fact that he was treating this moment like it was something out of Houses and Humans didn't inspire much confidence.

"Are we sure we want him back?" Dave asked.

"Yes," Ada said firmly. "He's our only contact for Ser Factor. If we don't get Scott back, we don't get paid."

"I'm gonna buy dragon eggs with my share of the reward money," Dave said conversationally to Loth as they plodded along with the horses after Calarian and Ada. "Calarian is going to throw his into a bog and then spit on it because collectivist anarchists oppose the retention of money."

"Do you know what any of that actually means?" Loth asked gently.

"*Bog*," Dave said, a frown creasing his green forehead. "And *spit*."

Fair enough.

Loth absently patted Grub's arse and received a half-hearted groan in return. He was still alive then. That was a good thing, and probably more than they could say for Scott at this point. He reflected briefly on the irony of having to rescue his rescuer, before patting Grub's arse again. Grub grunted and raised his head, one eye open and peering at Loth. "Whu?"

"You fainted. And now Scott's managed to get himself captured by the swamp monster, and we're currently following a trail of his shit to try and rescue him."

"Skid marks," Calarian chimed in from ahead of him, and Loth snorted.

Loth paused in his walking so Grub could struggle upright in the saddle. "So he got captured...?"

"While he was shitting himself in fear, yes," Loth confirmed.

Grub's face screwed up. "Why are we rescuing him again?"

"Cause he's the one who knows how we can get paid," Dave supplied. He paused, thinking, and added, "If we're not dead by then."

Grub groaned and made a move to climb off the horse, but Loth put a hand on his thigh, stopping him. "No. Stay there."

Grub raised his eyebrows.

"I don't have the energy to pick your pitiful bones up out of the mud again," Loth said.

Grub rolled his eyes, but he stayed on the horse.

Calarian slowed and held up a hand. "Up ahead," he whispered, pointing.

The trail of shit stains veered sharply to the left, through a gap in the stunted, twisted trees. The group slowed as they approached and went deathly silent—Loth wasn't sure if it was from competence or caution. His money was on the second one.

"I'll go ahead," Calarian said, looking over his shoulder as if he expected someone to try and stop him. Absolutely nobody did. Loth didn't blame them—he couldn't speak for the others, but he wasn't about to go rushing headlong to meet his demise. Loth had a well-developed sense of self-preservation, and right now it was screaming at him to *run*. The only reason he was ignoring it was because in this instance, it really was a case of safety in numbers. Just look what had happened to Scott.

Calarian's shoulders drooped at the lack of response, but after a few seconds he breathed deeply, straightened up, and strode down the path, bow and arrow extended in front of him. Loth waited for the inevitable sounds of battle and the devious, self-serving part of him that had kept him alive all these years wondered if they'd be able to grab Scott and run while the monster was busy eating the elf. He liked Calarian, and personally wouldn't have chosen him to be devoured first, but Scott was the money guy. Or at least the guy who knew the money guy. And Loth had always liked money.

There was a roar that seemed to go on forever, and then Calarian's voice rang out in the gloom as he addressed the monster. Loth had to give him credit—he sounded confident, for someone who was about to be eaten. "Show yourself, foul beast, and release the prison—"

The roaring cut off suddenly, and they heard, "Cal? Is that you?"

A moment's silence, then Calarian hesitantly asked, *"Benji? Cousin Benji?"*

The mist in front of them seemed to part as a figure stepped through it. It wasn't a monster at all. It was an elf—Cousin Benji, presumably—except instead of wearing the brown and green earth tones that Loth associated with his people, this one was wearing all black, except for the gleaming metal stud through his lip. And his ear. And his eyebrow. His hair was black and straight, and he was wearing thick chunky boots that seemed way too big for his slender frame. A studded belt hung loosely around his narrow hips, and he was holding some sort of bullhorn—the source, Loth assumed, of the roaring.

"Benji! It is you! It's been years!" Calarian exclaimed. He lowered his bow. "Did you kidnap a human just now?"

Benji showed him a look of utter disgust which could only come from meeting Scott up close and personal.

"Wow, you're still doing that to people?" Calarian turned to face the others. "This is my cousin, Benji."

"Ebenjilarian," the elf clarified.

"Gesundheit," Loth muttered.

"That's racist," Benji snapped back. "Also, death to the establishment!"

Loth raised an eyebrow.

Calarian shrugged. "Most elves are collectivist anarchists, but Benji's just an antisocial arsehole."

"I believe in taking direct action against the state through civil disobedience," Benji said.

"Antisocial arsehole," Calarian repeated with a grin.

"Which one of you is the prince?" Benji asked, looking at them curiously. He shrugged. "The human started trying to bargain his own life for some prince's the second I grabbed him."

Loth sighed. Of course he had.

"Did you kill him?" Calarian asked, and there may have been a touch of hopefulness in his tone.

"No." Benji shrugged again. "I figured if he really had a prince, it'd be more of a political statement to capture him instead."

Loth took a step back.

"You can't," Calarian said. "He's part of my quest." He clapped Benji on the shoulder. "I can't believe you're living in the Swamp of Death. That's so hardcore."

"It's pretty great," Benji said. "I don't have to talk to people. I can just work on my manifesto in peace."

Grub swayed alarmingly in the saddle.

"Excuse me," Loth said. "Calarian? I think Grub's about to pass out again."

"Right!" Calarian widened his eyes. "We really need to get out of this swamp gas, Benji. How do you, you know, not die?"

"My house is built on a pit full of charcoal," Benji said. "It's also built out of charcoal. And all my furniture is charcoal. Oh, plus I paid a witch to perform a spell of purification around the house, but I think she was talking a lot of bullshit, so I mostly rely on the charcoal."

Well, that explained why he dressed entirely in black.

Benji eyed the group again. "Whichever one of you is the prince, don't think you're getting any special treatment. I despise your system of government, and when the revolution comes, you'll be first against the wall." Calarian elbowed him in the ribs. "But since you're part of Cal's quest, I suppose for now you can come with me."

Loth took a cautious step forward. "I have no intention of standing in the way of your revolution, I promise. But if we don't get out of this gas, my young companion won't be alive to see it."

Grub made a noise of protest, but it was overshadowed by him sliding right out of the saddle, forcing Loth to catch him before he hit the ground.

Again.

BENJI'S HOUSE was indeed made entirely out of charcoal. It was a squat little cottage that had been built on a small piece of raised land within the Swamp of Death. Half-dead trees surrounded it, with wreaths of grey moss hanging from their branches. The cottage was only two rooms. One was filled with charcoal-smudged books, and one was Benji's bedroom. He had, for very practical reasons, an outdoor kitchen.

The cottage wasn't as cold as the swamp outside, but it wasn't a lot better either since there were no open flames allowed. Jars full of fireflies, which gave the light a flickering, ethereal quality, illuminated the interior. Benji huffed and grumbled as he dug through his things, eventually dragging a few grubby blankets out of a trunk and thrusting them in the party's direction. His angry expression softened slightly as it fell on a very woozy Grub.

"I'll get him some water," he said. "And a charcoal tablet."

"He could probably just nibble on your bookshelf or something," Calarian suggested. He narrowed his eyes at Benji. "Oh, where's Scott, by the way? The human you abducted?"

"Tied up around the back," Benji said. "He was covered in shit. I wasn't going to let him inside my *house*."

Dave and Pie went to see to Scott, Pie trilling as he perched on Dave's shoulder.

"Please don't let your dragon burn down my house!" Benji yelled after them.

For all that Benji was an antisocial arsehole, he put on a decent spread for dinner. Even Grub, once he'd had his water and his charcoal tablet, rallied enough to enjoy the food that Benji cooked on the outside grill.

"So *you're* the monster," Loth mused as he chewed on a piece of fried turnip which was a lot better than it sounded. Benji knew his way around spices.

"There *was* a monster, I think," Benji said. He flicked a shank of black hair over his shoulder. "But he was either dead or retired by the time I moved here. He had claws the length of ploughshares, apparently. Anyway, I like it here. The human soldiers are too scared to come here, and so are the other elves, mostly. I'm 'too radical' for them." Air quotes.

"You burned down a school classroom," Calarian said.

"That was one time."

"It was three times!"

"It was one classroom!" Benji countered. "If they didn't want me to keep burning it down, they should have stopped rebuilding it."

"The collective kicked him out after that," Calarian told the others.

Benji smiled proudly.

Loth hummed consideringly. "If you're the vicious swamp killer, why were you so nice to Grub, getting his water and charcoal? Those don't seem like very homicidal actions."

Benji rolled his eyes "Well he's obviously oppressed right? I'm not gonna kill the oppressed, am I?"

"I don't buy it," Loth declared. "You don't seem like a killer." Benji looked distinctly shifty, so Loth prodded a bit more. "What really happens to your victims?"

"I mean I never claimed I *was* a killer. I just let the rumours do the talking. Mainly, if anyone's stupid enough to come this way, I seduce my victims and then take all their money while they're rolling in the afterglow." Benji smirked and winked. "I have an afterglow that leaves them dazzled for *days*."

Loth didn't doubt it.

Calarian nodded. "You always did have a reputation as a ladies' man."

"And a man's man," Benji said. "An anyone's man, really." At Loth's raised eyebrows, he shrugged. "It's a great way to pass the time."

"But not Scott?" Calarian asked.

"Have you *seen* him?" Benji shuddered. "Even I have limits. Anyway, the point is, there *was* a deadly swamp monster here once, but it left, or died, or retired, or something. The only monster here now is the one in my pants."

Grub's jaw dropped as the elves high-fived.

Moments later, Scott bustled through the door. He stank of

swamp water. His clothes were soaked, and his hair was dripping. "Dave threw me in the swamp!"

Dave lumbered in after him. "You smelled like shit."

"My Prince!" Scott exclaimed, his gaze falling on Loth. "You're alive!"

"No thanks to you, I hear," Loth said, and Grub snorted beside him.

Scott affected a look of wide-eyed innocence. "I don't know what you mean, your Highnessness?"

"The little matter of offering to sell me out to your captor? Ring any bells?" Loth arched an intimidating eyebrow.

Scott paled. "What? Oh—no, I was—that was—a misunderstanding, my liege! I was warning the monster to leave you alone, that's all. Alerting him to your presence so you could pass through the swamp safely. Yes, safely," he repeated, his gaze darting around the room.

"Really?" Benji asked, scowling. "You're going with that, Mr *I'll give you the prince if you let me go?*"

Scott licked his lips nervously and sidled closer to Dave. "Um…"

Loth decided abruptly that Scott wasn't worth his time right now. He was more concerned about how they were going to get out of the swamp. "Tell me Benji, I don't suppose you have a map out of here?"

Benji frowned. "You don't have a map? What kind of idiot doesn't have a map on their quest?"

"We had one, but Scott set it on fire."

All eyes turned to Scott, who was still standing there dripping. "It was the dragon," he whined. "Anyway, you should respect me as your leader and stop blaming me when things go wrong!"

"That's how leadership works, Scott. If you want the glory of success, you have to take the blame for the failures," Loth pointed out.

Scott's eyes widened as if that had never occurred to him. "You mean, if this all goes wrong, the ballads will…"

"Mock you, yes. You'll be famous as Scott the Swamp Shitter, probably."

"Ooh, I like that!" Dave perked up. "I'm gonna start working on a song! What rhymes with shit?"

"Git, tit, full of it," Grub listed, grinning. Loth was relieved to see that he was well enough to take part in the conversation, so he encouraged it.

"Brainless twit, biscuit, misfit…" he recited happily, taking great pleasure in Scott's scowl.

"Yeah," Dave nodded. "Th' ballad of Scott and his… his squat!"

Dave looked inordinately pleased with himself, and Loth couldn't blame him. It had a certain ring to it, and he suspected that even if they did make it back to Callier safely, Scott would be immortalised in song for all the wrong reasons. The thought of it made his petty heart sing with glee. Really, it served the little turd right for trying to sell him out.

They did still need a map to make it out safely though, so he turned his attention back to Benji. "Is there a safe passage out of here? We're heading for the capital."

"I don't have any maps," Benji said, "but I know the swamp. I can take you back to the Delacourt road, or I can lead you through to the other side, which puts you on the Torlere road."

"Torlere?" Grub asked, his eyes widening. "I can find the way to Callier from there, at least I think I can. And there are plenty of villages along that road."

"Well, aren't you just a handy little homing pigeon?" Loth asked. "For me, at least. And where is your home, Grub?"

"Near Callier," Grub said, without even hesitating.

"How very vague of you," Loth murmured.

Grub just quirked his mouth in a grin and shrugged his skinny shoulders.

"You people are stupid," Benji announced. "Why would you want to go to Callier anyway? It's full of *people*. I hate people."

"It's part of the quest," Calarian said, and chewed on some kind of anaemic-looking carrot.

"A—a *noble* quest!" Scott piped up. "The most noble quest! We are going to restore the lost Prince Tarquin to the throne, as the rightful ruler of Aguillon!"

"All kings are tyrants," Benji said, and Calarian fist-bumped him.

"Yes, but Lord Doom is *more* of a tyrant!" Scott exclaimed.

"Well, that's true," Benji said thoughtfully.

Scott's face lit up. "You should join us! With the Monster of the Swamp of Death at our side, we would be invincible!"

"No," said Benji. "That's actually very offensive. Also, fuck off."

"But—but I can pay you!" Scott scurried closer, bringing a whiff of swamp mud with him. "Well, *I* can't pay you, but Ser Factor can!"

Loth couldn't help but be curious about Scott's mysterious patron. "Scott, I think it's about time you told me exactly who's behind this rescue mission."

Grub, surprisingly, nodded in agreement. "Who wants the prince freed and why?"

Scott gave a helpless shrug. "All I know is, I was at the tavern one night, telling my friends how I was sure I could be a hero if I could just find a quest. A man came up to me and told me to meet him in the woods the next night. When I got there, he gave me a letter from Ser Factor." Scott fished down the front of his doublet and drew out a grubby slip of parchment.

Loth took it without asking and scanned it quickly. It was, indeed, a proposition for Scott to assemble a band of rescuers and extract the prince from the prison at Delacourt. There was a promise of payment and a list of towns along the Delacourt road where he could replenish supplies and report his progress. Loth squinted at the elaborate signature, and Scott poked at it over his shoulder. "See? Ser Factor. Beany Factor, right there. Maybe he's one of the new nobles that Lord Doom knighted?"

Loth blinked, reading the elaborate, looping signature again, and struggled to keep his voice even, stifling his laughter. "That's not a name Scott. It appears you have a benefactor."

Scott stiffened. "How did you know about that?" he demanded.

"It's written on the paper, right here. *Bene-fac-tor.*" Loth sounded it out as one might for a child. "A benefactor is someone who gives money to help a cause, Scott. What did you think it was?"

Scott blushed. "I always thought that was the thing where you have one undescended testicle. And anyway, my mother took me to the healer, and she said it's normal, and the other one should catch up eventually."

Grub let out a snort. Loth caught his eye and was surprised to find a smile, brighter than any he'd seen before. It was a far better look than Grub's usual constant scowl.

"Ignoring your genital abnormalities for just the moment, Scott, this person funding the operation, have you ever met him?" Loth asked, suddenly uneasy. Maybe the prince was in more danger than he first thought.

At that thought, he shook himself mentally. There *was* no prince. Lord Doom *claimed* that his nephew was somewhere in safekeeping until he reached his majority, but nobody really believed it. The hidden prince was a fairy story, a fantasy, and definitely dead and buried if Lord Doom had any sense.

Scott was biting his lip. "Not met-met, but everything in the letter has been true," he said. "The cell, the red hair, the sleeping guards, all of it."

"Wait. Sleeping guards?"

It was Dave who nodded. "Was gonna knock 'em out, but they was asleep already." He pouted. "Didn't get to hit nothin' except the wall."

Loth tucked that information away for later and held up the piece of paper. "Surely you were meant to get rid of this?" Because he couldn't see any plotter worth his salt not disposing of the evidence.

"Um, I'm not good with remembering things like town names, details," Scott admitted. "So I kept it. I was supposed to burn it."

"Right. When we light a fire later, in it goes," Loth declared.

"That's what I said," Ada muttered, "but it was all *think of the ballads, Ada.*"

"The Ballad of Scott and his dodgy ball sac!" Dave supplied, happy to have more fodder for his musical career.

Scott cringed visibly, and Loth bit his lip. He'd laugh about it later, when he didn't have more pressing concerns.

He rubbed his forehead. "So just to be clear, a man you don't know is paying you to bring the prince back to Callier to put him back on the throne, and you never thought to question his motives? Did it even occur to you that it might be a trap?"

Scott's vacant stare was all the answer he needed.

Loth chewed his lip thoughtfully. "Grub, was that your normal cell?"

"No. They moved me, something about needing me out of the way so they could clean. Like they ever cared before," he muttered bitterly, and really, Loth couldn't blame him.

Loth groaned internally as it all began to make sense. Prince Tarquin was dead and had been dead for years, except rumours of him persisted. So what did Lord Doom need to quash the rumours? A body. And that meant he needed a handy redhead to murder. He would probably explain it away as an attack by bandits or by rebels or something, but as long as he had a red-headed corpse to bury for the public, what was then to stop him from finally claiming the throne outright? Gods, he'd probably been intending to use poor Grub all along—maybe that was even the reason for his hostage status. But which poor sap had wandered unaware through the streets of Delacourt one night and accidentally come to the attention of the guards? Loth, with his henna-dyed hair.

Loth sighed and exchanged a wary glance with Grub. This just got worse and worse.

He knew he should have gone blond.

CHAPTER SEVEN

L oth attempted to bury his head under the pillow he was half-sharing with Grub, hoping to block out the disturbing noises coming from Benji's room. He was only partially successful, since Grub insisted on tugging the pillow back to cover *his* ears. They were huddled together as they tried to keep warm since there was no chance of a fire, and the night winds cut cruelly through the swamp. At least Benji had found an old shirt for Loth to wear. It was black of course and slightly too long, but Loth tied a strip of blue doublet around the waist and called it good. At least it kept him warm.

Dave and Ada were sharing a blanket, and one of them was snoring loudly. Scott was curled up on his own since he still stank of swamp water. And Calarian?

Calarian was the reason they were covering their ears.

Well, Calarian and Benji. Loth groaned as the night was once more disturbed by the creaking of bedsprings and the muffled shout of *"Yes! There!"* followed by the dull thud of the headboard against the wall.

"They're cousins!" Scott whined. "That's—"

"Yes, well," Loth snapped. "Elf families are incredibly close, apparently! Who knew?"

Loth was fairly sure the only reason Grub pulled his head out from under the pillow was to give him a judgemental look before observing, "That's rich, coming from someone whose own grandparents were second cousins."

Loth stared blankly for a second.

"Queen Frida and King Algernon?" Grub prompted. He obviously knew Loth had no idea what he was talking about, the little shit, and now Ada had lifted her head, listening.

Loth's tired brain kicked into gear. Right. The old king and queen had been distantly related. He remembered now. "Excuse me for not having memorised Warp's Peerage," he huffed. "Besides, the rules for nobility are different. We'll screw anything that takes our fancy, everyone knows that." Loth ignored Grub's hard stare in favour of tilting his head in the direction of the bedroom where the thud of the headboard had stopped. "Do you think they're done?"

His question was answered by Calarian shouting *"Ride me!"*, followed by what sounded like the crack of a whip, and then the steady thunk-thunk-thunk of charcoal on charcoal picking up pace.

Grub blushed bright red at the noises, and Loth regarded him more closely. "Tell me, Grub, are you blushing because you're embarrassed, or jealous?"

Grub's lips thinned, and he harrumphed and turned his back on Loth, taking most of the blanket with him.

Loth nudged at the prickly little beast. "Oh, come on, don't be such a prude. Honestly, listening to those two? *I'm* jealous. It must be *weeks* since I've had a good dicking."

Grub mumbled something into the blankets.

"What was that?" Loth curled up close to preserve the heat, leaning in to hear. "Did you say something?"

Loth could feel his bedmate practically vibrating with the

need to say something, and he didn't have to wait long before Grub jerked out of his grip, turned to face him, and hissed, "At least you've had one!"

That brought Loth up short.

Of course. Grub was anywhere between twelve and twenty. It was honestly hard to tell. But if he'd been locked up at say, fifteen or sixteen, and was the son of a nobleman, odds were good that he'd never had the opportunity to do anything fun. His sexual experience so far probably consisted of his hand, a straw mattress, and an audience of rats.

Loth wasn't sure if it was guilt, pity, or something else that prompted him to make the offer. "Well, if you want me to show you the ropes, I can. I won't even charge you."

Grub went still at that. "No, thank you," he said stiffly.

Loth wasn't sure what to say. It wasn't often words failed him, but then again, it wasn't often he got turned down, either. As he pondered it, there was a loud cry from the bedroom, *"Harder, Benji!"*

The room went silent, and then Scott declared, "Do they really have to be so... *theatrical* about the whole thing?"

Benji's voice came through the wall. "Shut up, Scott! You're ruining it!" before the squeaking of bedsprings started up again, and yes, that was *definitely* the crack of a whip.

Grub snickered, the tense set of his shoulders easing, and Loth pulled him back against his chest, smiling to himself.

LOTH WOKE to warm puffs of air against the back of his neck. He opened one eye and noted the dim, pre-dawn light filtering in, ghosting everything in shades of grey. Early, then. He closed his eyes again and snuggled back automatically against the warmth of another body, and there was a tiny sigh in his ear. Grub, he thought blearily. They must have rolled in the night.

He tried to get comfortable, but something was prodding at him through the fabric of his trousers, something hard and thick and... Loth was still mostly asleep, which was why it took a second to register that yes, that was definitely a cock pressed up against his arse. His eyes snapped open, and he allowed himself a moment of satisfaction. Grub might claim he wasn't interested, but his body was telling a different story. Loth rolled his hips so he was pushing back against Grub in a sinuous motion and grinned to himself when Grub picked up the rhythm in his sleep.

If they'd been anywhere but on a floor in a room full of people, Loth might have woken Grub, whispered sweet nothings in his ear, then rolled them over and put his skills to use. Really though, he wasn't the type to take advantage of someone who was asleep—he much preferred his partners awake and begging.

Besides, he'd been on horseback for two days, nearly been poisoned by swamp gas, and was covered in charcoal dust. In all honesty, he wasn't confident he could perform at his best, not knowing two elves with ears like bats would be listening in, and likely judging him.

So he settled for reaching behind him and shaking Grub's bony shoulder while whispering, "I'm flattered, Grub, but maybe later."

Grub's hips rocked once, twice, and then his whole body stiffened as he woke. "*Fuck!*" he hissed.

"We definitely could," Loth murmured, "I'd be more than happy to, just say the word. But maybe now's not really the time or place."

Grub scrambled backwards, and when Loth rolled over, there was just enough light to see the colour high on Grub's cheeks. "I didn't—I wasn't—it was an accident!"

"Was it? Or is it that you do find me irresistible after all? It's nothing to be embarrassed about, Grub. Lots of people feel that way about me." Loth blew him a kiss.

Grub sat up and scowled, slightly hunched over as if he

thought Loth might leap forward and grab his dick without asking, which was highly insulting—Loth *always* asked first. Loth sighed. "You seem very stressed about this whole thing." He waggled his eyebrows. "You know what's good for stress? Orgasms."

"You're impossible, you know that?" Grub threw aside the blankets and stalked over to the other side of the room and after a moment's hesitation, lay down next to Dave. Loth thought about warning him that Dave probably wouldn't be as under-standing about unruly erections. Then he decided to flatter himself that the odds of Dave having that effect on Grub were slim, so he settled under the blanket and went back to sleep, grin-ning to himself.

At least this time Grub hadn't refused him outright. It was progress.

CALARIAN WANDERED out of Benji's bedroom later in the morning wearing nothing but a dozy smile and a whole lot of charcoal smears against his pale skin. Loth stared at him. Elves really were unfairly attractive, even if Calarian looked like he'd been dragged backwards through a bush several times. As he wandered out the front door, presumably to go and piss, Loth saw a set of very distinct charcoal handprints against the globes of his magnificent arse.

"Wh—what!" Scott exclaimed, flailing his blanket off. "Put some clothes on, Calarian! I can see your—your *thingy!*"

"It's a penis!" Calarian said, turning around and giving them all an eyeful. "Most of us have got one!"

"And I've had as many as I've wanted," Ada said.

"Scott's just jealous of your symmetrical balls," Loth said.

Calarian grinned. "They are nice, aren't they?"

"Top quality," Loth said. "Stunning."

Calarian turned around again, jiggled his handprinted arse, and continued on his way outside.

Loth turned to Grub. Grub was wide-eyed and red-faced. He was holding Pie in his cupped hand, and stroking the fingerdragon's back gently as he very, very pointedly didn't stare at Calarian's arse.

Unfortunately, when Grub turned to avoid the sight, he was greeted by Benji walking out the bedroom, just as naked and just as pretty. Grub froze on the spot, and Loth genuinely feared that he might spontaneously combust. That was the last thing he wanted in a house built of charcoal, so Loth wrapped an arm around his shoulders and steered him outdoors.

The air just outside the cottage was surprisingly clear, just like Benji had promised. Loth patted Grub on the back while Grub took several deep breaths, and Pie flew in tiny circles around them.

"So," Grub said at last, clearing his throat. He was still bright red. "If Benji can get us to the Torlere road, we can easily find our way to Callier from there."

"Hmm." Loth drew the toe of his boot through the mud. "If we're absolutely sure we want to go to Callier, that is."

"It's too convenient, isn't it?" Grub asked. "This rescue out of nowhere. You think Doom's behind it."

"I think it's possible," Loth said. "I think it would be in Doom's best interests to produce the corpse of his tragically murdered nephew, who had a run-in with some bandits on the way to the capital. The prince would be coming of age about now, so the timing fits."

Grub pressed his mouth into a thin line. For a moment he looked older somehow. His forehead creased in thought. "He could have as easily killed me, or you, in the dungeon back at Delacourt. I'm not saying this isn't Doom's doing, but it's possible that Scott's benefactor is actually working to secure the rescue of the prince."

"Well, he'd be a fucking idiot then, wouldn't he?"

Grub's mouth twitched. "Probably that too, yes. But it's not like there's any shortage of idiots in the world."

Loth liked Grub, he decided. He was cranky, cynical, and he had a quick mind. It also didn't hurt that after a decent night's sleep—once the elves finally ran out of energy, at least—he was passingly attractive in the right light. What a shame he'd declined Loth's offer to rid him of his virginity last night. Still, they had some more time together, and if this morning was any indicator, he wasn't entirely immune to Loth's charms, so Loth could always offer again at some point. Grub was definitely on the top of his list when it came to his newfound companions. Calarian might have been stupidly attractive, but after last night Loth was pretty sure he didn't have the stamina to keep up with him. Not that it wouldn't be fun to try, he supposed.

He turned and watched as Calarian and Benji made their way back towards the cottage.

"Wow," Grub said. "Just..."

"It's like watching a pair of swinging pendulums, isn't it?" Loth mused. "Oddly hypnotic."

Grub surprised him with a laugh. "I'm not sure what's more entertaining; those two, or Scott clutching his pearls about it."

"Definitely Scott," Loth said. He couldn't help but add, "Disloyal little git. Trying to sell me off to Benji like that."

"Lucky you're not the prince then," Grub said with a wry twist of his lips that Loth couldn't quite interpret. Before he could overthink it, Grub, with a mischievous smile on his face, asked, "You know what git rhymes with, don't you?"

"It does! You're right!" Loth brightened at the reminder and turned and made his way into the cottage to tease Scott some more.

~

IT TOOK four miserable muddy days to make their way through the Swamp of Death. At least Benji kept them supplied with food, and seemed to know which paths were the safest to take, both to avoid the stinking, sucking mud and the worst of the swamp gas. Benji supplied them with powdered charcoal to wrap in a cloth and keep close to their face, meaning they all had smudged faces that looked like shadowy charcoal beards when the cloths were removed. (In Scott's case, it was a vast improvement on his own facial hair, a fact Benji gleefully pointed out.) Although Loth found himself getting light-headed on a few occasions, it was nothing like when they'd first entered the swamp. The horses got stuck several times, sinking into the mud up to their knees, and only Dave was able to extract them.

Scott took the journey the worst. Not only was Dave still happily composing his Shit Ballad out loud, but Scott clearly objected to Benji having taken over his position as leader. Loth suspected it particularly rankled with Scott because Benji didn't even want to be their leader—he just wanted them out of his hair. Possibly the only reason he didn't let them all wander off into the swamp and die was because Calarian kept blowing him every chance they got. For all his snootiness, Calarian went weak at the knees for a bad boy—literally and figuratively. Not that Loth could begrudge him that. Elves really were stupidly attractive.

Scott was scandalised, naturally. Ada and Dave didn't seem to care. Loth was highly appreciative of the free show, and Grub... poor Grub was red as a beet for most of the trip. Loth wasn't sure if it was the way the elves were so open with their affections, the fact they were having such a good time, or their unfairly pretty cocks that were making Grub blush and stutter every time he glanced their way.

Possibly all three.

Whatever the case, Grub warmed to Loth a little during their journey through the Swamp of Death. Loth suspected a lot of that was because he knew he couldn't hide his embarrassment and was grateful for Loth not teasing him about it. Grub was sharp-minded and quick-witted, and it seemed almost incongruous that he was innocent as well. However, to laugh at him for it wouldn't be just teasing him over the fact he'd never slept with anyone, it would be teasing him over the fact that he'd spent around a quarter of his life in a cell. And some blows were too low even for Loth to consider.

Huh.

It turned out he had a conscience after all. Who knew? Certainly not Loth, or anybody who had ever known him. It had really never come up before, and Loth found it quite unsettling. His parents were going to laugh themselves silly if he ever made it back to Callier. Loth fully intended to make it back, but he couldn't help worrying that they were playing right into the hands of Scott's mysterious benefactor. Who was to say they could trust him? At first, ditching the party when they reached Callier had seemed like the smartest thing to do, but now Loth wasn't sure he wanted to go to Callier at all.

Callier was home, in so much as any place could be home to the sort of man who often had to leave his lodgings in the middle of the night to avoid complications with the law. Loth had been born and raised there. His father was a tailor and his mother was a brewer, hence Loth's inherited love for the best things in life: fashion and intoxication. He wondered idly what Grub's parents were like, and how different their upbringings had been. Grub might have been a bastard son, but his father obviously acknowledged his existence. He almost certainly loved him in some way, because otherwise what value would he have been as a hostage? But whenever Loth tried to ask Grub about his childhood, Grub shrugged it off and muttered that it didn't matter.

"Let's just say my family isn't nearly as close as theirs," he deflected, nodding at the elves, who were heading into the trees holding hands.

"I'm not sure anyone's family is as close as theirs," Loth said with a grin. He'd discovered Cal and Benji weren't actually cousins per se, although they were distantly related, but he didn't intend on telling anyone else that—it was far too much fun watching Scott have conniptions.

Benji had assured them that another day's walk should take them to the road, and as much as Loth was hesitant to head home, he was looking forward to getting away from the mud, the gas, and Scott's constant whining every time Dave broke into song and the rest of them joined in with the chorus. And Grub had said there were villages along the Torlere road, and villages meant amenities, possibly even a tavern or an inn with warm meals, comfortable beds, and hot bath water. And if those warm meals were less turnip-based and more chicken-or-beef-based, then Loth certainly wouldn't complain about it. Hell, he'd settle for rabbit.

He'd noticed that even with Benji's vegetarian meals, Grub was already looking less drawn, and his elbows jabbed less brutally at night. Of course, Loth conceded that could also be because he'd stopped asking Grub if he wanted to stop in at the closest stables when they got a chance. In return, Grub did his best not to steal all the blankets and squirm too much. Regardless, Grub was less bone and more skin, now, and it made Loth pleased in a way he tried not to think too hard about. He tried to concentrate on the journey out of the swamp instead.

The surrounding landscape barely changed for most of the trek through the Swamp of Death: twisted, ghostly trees, and miles and miles of stinking mud. Finally, just when Loth was beginning to think he'd never escape the stench of sulphur and the stinking mud that sucked at his boots with every step, he looked down to discover that he'd stepped on a clump of stringy green grass. The surprise of seeing something alive and verdant almost made him stumble.

From that moment it seemed that every step brought a new sign of life: fresh grass, a sapling with a green trunk, buzzing insects and, finally, as the haze of the swamp cleared, birdsong. Loth took his first breath of clean air in days.

"Well," Benji announced at last, "this is the edge of the swamp." He nodded toward a screen of trees. "If you go straight through there, you'll find the Torlere road. Turn east on it when you reach it, and Torlere is about an hour away."

"What's east?" Dave asked. "I only know left an' right."

"East is left," Scott stated confidently.

"East is *right*," Ada corrected with a sigh and a roll of her eyes. When Scott scowled at her, she pointed up. "You do know the sun rises in the east, right Scott?"

Calarian and Benji clapped each other on the back manfully, like they hadn't just spent the last few days perched on each other's dicks.

"Good luck on your quest. Come see me again if you're ever passing," Benji said, with a final slap of Calarian's pert arse.

"I just might." Calarian said with a grin. "Long live the revolution!"

"Fuck the state," Benji said fondly.

They all took a moment to remove the various cloths from around their faces and climbed back on their horses. Loth watched Grub slide into the saddle and just this once, resisted the horse joke that was begging to be made. Grub caught his eye and raised an eyebrow. "Are you getting on, Your Grace, or do I get to mount this beast all on my own?" he asked with a grin.

Loth burst out laughing. He swung up behind Grub and wrapped an arm around his waist, still smiling, because, despite the odds, they'd survived the Swamp of Death.

IN LOTH'S OPINION, there was no more glorious sound than hooves on a hard-packed road, a tangible sign that they'd really left the swamp behind. He breathed deep, tugging absently at his scarf so he could feel the fresh air on his face and accidentally waking Pie, who grumbled and hissed at him before going back to sleep.

Somehow the dragon's home was in his scarf now. Pie invariably crept into what Grub called his thievery pockets to nap and when he tried to shoo him back to Dave, Pie turned sad green eyes on him and chirruped pitifully until he gave in and let him stay. Loth could swear he was being played by the dragon, but he didn't mind much.

They'd passed a few cottages on the side of the road, and Loth knew Torlere must be close. Sure enough, another twenty minutes' ride had them passing the outskirts of the town. It wasn't much to look at, just a few streets of houses clustered around a bedraggled little green, but after spending the last few days in the Swamp of Death it rivalled the height of civilisation in Loth's opinion. And the best part was there was an *inn*.

"Scott," Loth called, "has your benefactor made provision for us to stay anywhere on *this* road?"

He knew damned well that he hadn't, and he wasn't overly concerned about it—he had ways to ensure they didn't starve. He just wanted to make Scott squirm. He may have still been nursing a small grudge over Scott offering him to the swamp monster so readily.

Scott scowled and opened his mouth, but it was Calarian who spoke. "I have money."

Loth and Grub both turned to look at him. "Since when?" Loth demanded.

Calarian grinned broadly—he was still in the sort of good mood that follows exceptional sex, and had been since he and Benji disappeared into the bushes one last time, forcing the rest of them to wait uncomfortably while they listened to Cal's cries of *"Fuck me, Daddy!"*

("I thought they were cousins?" Dave had asked. Loth hadn't bothered to explain.)

"I have money," Cal repeated. "Benji thought we might need cash. He has all the money he's taken off his victims, and he says there's only so much you can spend when you live in a swamp." He reached into his saddlebag and drew out a bulging purse with a smirk.

"Are you gonna throw it in a bog an' spit on it?" Dave asked, eyes wide.

"No, I'm going to hire us rooms at the Torlere Inn and buy us a hot meal that doesn't have turnips in it," Calarian said.

"And a hot bath?" Loth asked.

"And a hot bath. Just for tonight though, to get rid of the bog stench. And we might have to share rooms if we want the money to last for the trip to Callier."

"Bags not Scott," Grub said immediately, and Loth was torn between admiration for his quick thinking and annoyance that he hadn't thought of it first.

"Same," he promptly echoed, taking petty delight in the way Scott's face fell as everyone else followed suit, leaving only Dave for a bedmate.

"S'okay, I'll try not to roll on you," Dave assured him. "Maybe you can listen to the new verse of the ballad! Help me find a rhyme for wet fart."

Loth snorted quietly and felt Grub shake with silent laughter. He much preferred this version of Grub to the scowling beast he'd been at first. It really was amazing what fresh air, adequate food, and not being locked in a dungeon did for some people's constitutions. He propped his chin on Grub's shoulder and peered into the fading daylight, looking for the inevitable inn that every town had. Scott had stopped in the middle of the road, looking distinctly lost, but Grub twitched his reins and rode past him confidently. "This way. We don't want the inn on the main road, we want the other one, trust me."

Calarian exchanged a look with Loth, who shrugged. This was one part of the kingdom he'd never been kicked out of—that was to say, had never been to in the first place, because the two normally went hand in hand. Calarian made a clicking noise and his horse turned after them. Dave and Ada, riding abreast, followed him, and finally, muttering under his breath about how it wasn't right, came Scott.

Grub rode past the inn and along the road, then turned sharply right and followed an alleyway to a small, unobtrusive building. Loth could tell just by looking that Grub was right—the other inn was for passers-by, with inflated prices and watered-down ale. This one though, had the look of a place that wasn't out to impress anyone—if you didn't know it existed, you didn't deserve a room there.

"I'm not even going to ask how you know about this place."

"Good," Grub said. "Because I'm not going to tell you."

There was definitely a story there, and one day Loth was going to find out what it was, but for now, the aroma of roasted meat wafting out of the tavern had all his attention. He tipped his head back, sniffing. Grub did the same, letting out a low moan that wouldn't have been out of place in the bedroom.

"Oh my gods," he groaned. "Real food."

Calarian's face drew into a pinched frown. "There's nothing wrong with vegetarian meals!"

"Of course not," Loth agreed, eager to soothe the holder of the purse strings, "not normally. But Grub's still all ribs and bad temper. We should probably do something to put some meat on his bones."

"Fair," Calarian nodded, somewhat appeased, "I'll get the rooms. Scott can stable the horses."

Scott, in an effort to wrest back control of the party, waited until Calarian was inside before clearing his throat and declaring loudly, "I'll go and take care of the horses, while the elf gets the rooms."

He needn't have bothered. Nobody was listening.

CHAPTER EIGHT

L oth watched, fascinated, as Grub ploughed through his third plate of stew. He wasn't sure where the boy was putting it all, but he was definitely enjoying it, seemingly unaware of the filthy noises he was making as he ate. They'd secured a table in the back corner of the tavern where they'd be away from prying eyes. Calarian must have paid handsomely because every time Loth blinked there seemed to be a maid with more food and drink for them. Everyone ate and drank eagerly, differences put aside for now, and Loth guessed he wasn't the only one in the mood to celebrate their escape from the swamp.

He allowed himself to relax, just a little.

For now, at least, they were safe. He leaned back in his seat, tilted his head back and took a long swallow of ale, and when he lowered his tankard, Grub was watching him intently. Loth couldn't resist licking his lips suggestively, and the boy flushed and ducked his head to avoid Loth's gaze. Before he did though, Loth caught sight of something in his face. A hunger perhaps, that had Loth speculating that despite Grub's protests, spending his nights sleeping next to another man—an *attractive* man, though he did say so himself—had awakened more than Grub's curiosity.

He stretched, enjoying the fullness of his belly and the warmth of the fire, before prodding at Calarian. "You arranged the bath?"

Calarian nodded towards the maid. "Just let Jenny know and she'll have them bring the tub to your room."

"Jenny? On a first name basis already, are we?" he leered.

He didn't really expect Calarian to wink and say, "What can I tell you? The ladies love an elf."

Loth was seeing a whole new side to Calarian, confident and almost—dare he say it—agreeable. Perhaps, Loth reflected, what he'd mistaken for teenage sullenness was no more than a desperate need to get laid. *Apparently,* he thought, grinning, *he still likes at least one type of meat.*

Grub stifled a yawn, and Loth noted the way he was slumped in his chair. "Come on, Grub. You can have the water after me. It'll still be warm."

"How come you get to go first?" Grub grizzled as Loth beckoned the maid over and gave his instructions.

"Beauty before the beast," Loth replied airily, easing out of his chair.

He'd moved far enough up the staircase that he almost didn't hear Grub's muttered reply of, "Shit before the shovel, you mean."

Almost.

He might have been annoyed if it was anyone else, but coming from Grub, it was funny. He still stopped and turned, though. "Look at me, Grub. Now look at you. If you bathe first, I'll come out dirtier than I went in."

"Fair," Grub conceded, and they continued up the stairs.

THE BATH WAS BLISS. Absolute bliss. Loth didn't care that he'd had bigger baths before, or even hotter baths. He didn't care that he'd been to the bathhouses in Callier before, where underground ovens kept the rooms filled with steam and the water was so hot it almost simmered. No bath in Loth's life had ever been as glorious as this one, where he got to squat in a tub and remove four days' worth of swamp mud. He might have even moaned a little, and he didn't miss Grub's startled expression as he did so, before Grub scurried to the window and pretended to be very interested in the absolutely nothing that was happening outside. Loth smiled to himself. It hadn't escaped his notice that although Grub had turned his back when Loth stripped, he'd been sneaking glances at him once he was safely in the tub—had been stealing glances for days, now Loth thought about it.

Loth turned his attention back to getting clean. There had even been fresh water and a paste of sage and salt to clean his teeth with. He ran his tongue over them and revelled in the freshness before setting to work on the rest of himself. He scrubbed every inch of skin he could reach thoroughly and was attempting to get to his shoulders, grumbling under his breath, when Grub inched closer.

"I could—I can reach your back, if you want?" he offered shyly.

Loth raised his eyebrows. "You do mine and I'll do yours?"

"Something like that." Grub nodded, cheeks pink, whether from the heat of the tub or from embarrassment, Loth didn't know.

"Deal." He fished in the water for the washcloth and threw it at Grub, who caught it deftly and then stared at it like he had no idea what to do next. He probably didn't. Loth leaned forward in the tub and beckoned Grub over. "Don't be shy. Best get started before the water gets cold."

Grub looked suddenly unsure, but then he straightened his shoulders, gave a terse nod, and walked across the room. He positioned himself behind the tub, and then there was a warm, soapy cloth dragging over Loth's shoulders, followed by the whisper of fingertips against his skin, cool and delicate. Loth shivered at the contact. Had he called the bath glorious before? He took it back. *This* was the most glorious bath ever. A sigh escaped him, and Grub's hands stilled for just a moment, but when Loth rolled his shoulders the hands started moving again, the movements becoming stronger, surer.

Grub worked his way down Loth's back, and while his touch wasn't quite sensual, it wasn't entirely platonic either. Loth didn't comment on the way Grub's fingers pressed in when they curled around his ribs, or how they hovered just over the swell of his arse, lingering a beat too long, but he didn't pull away from those inquisitive hands either.

Once Loth's back was thoroughly scrubbed, Grub hauled a fresh bucket of water over, and, using a scoop, he tipped the water over Loth's head before working the sliver of soap they had through his wet locks, attempting to work up a lather. He wasn't very successful, and when he rinsed Loth's hair, he peered at it dubiously.

"It's... almost clean?"

Loth shrugged. In his book, 'almost clean' was acceptable, and still a lot better than 'thick with bog mud.' He stood up with no warning, just to hear Grub squawk at the sight of his naked backside, and he wasn't disappointed. He stepped out of the tub, and Grub thrust a towel awkwardly at him while staring at a particularly interesting spot on the floor.

"Your turn!" Loth said brightly and refused to turn his back at all.

Grub stared at him expectantly, but Loth ignored him and continued to dry himself. It didn't take long before Grub decided hot water was worth more than his modesty. He let out a sigh. He stripped without ceremony and then slid into the tub quickly, although not before Loth was able to observe that even a week of regular meals and fresh air had taken him from *practically skeletal* to merely *far too thin*. It was a hell of an improvement.

The noise that left Grub as he sprawled in the steaming water was positively filthy. Of course, so was Grub, so Loth did his best to ignore the sound. He tucked his towel around his waist, knelt behind the tub, and started scrubbing him down. But this was no gentle pass of the cloth over skin. Loth *scrubbed*. Grub let out a hiss between his teeth, and Loth muttered an apology, but he didn't stop. He started with the back of Grub's neck, tackling the ingrained dirt that he'd been staring at for days now, and he made a small sound of triumph when under the dirt he found clean skin with a light dusting of freckles.

"Angel kisses," he said, quietly delighted.

"What?"

"Angel kisses. That's what they call freckles."

Grub huffed out a laugh. "You'd think if angels spent all that time kissing me they could have rescued me from that damned dungeon sooner."

Loth ran both soaped-up hands over Grub's shoulder blades, pleased to find that the skin that had been covered by clothing was easier to clean, and it didn't take long before rivulets of grey water ran down Grub's back, leaving more heat-pinked skin and freckles that did, indeed look like a smattering of kisses. Loth rinsed the skin one last time, stopping just short of the top of Grub's arse. "Maybe I'm an angel, sent to rescue you."

Grub flat out snorted. "Right. And maybe I'm the lost prince." He reached back and plucked the washcloth from Grub's hands, soaping it up and washing his face and neck. "I'll do the rest, and then can you wash my hair?"

Loth nodded and watched while Grub cleaned himself efficiently. They were the movements of someone used to washing as quickly as possible and gaining no pleasure from it. There was something undeniably sad about the thought that Grub had spent five years cleaning himself with cat-licks and damp cloths.

Loth gave himself a shake. He wasn't the one who'd locked Grub up. He had no reason to feel guilty. Still, once Grub was done, Loth was gentle as he poured the barely hot water over Grub's tilted-back head, and set to work washing his hair. Grub let out another one of those filthy sounds as the water streamed over him, and once Loth had worked his fingers through his tangled mop and rinsed it again, he was surprised to find that the red was much brighter than he'd previously thought; a shining copper that gleamed in the firelight.

"Oh, that's good," Grub sighed, before running his hands through his hair and pushing it back from his face to reveal a genuine, proper smile. It was at that exact moment that Loth came to a startling realisation.

Grub was attractive.

Not just in that 'in the right light if a man was desperate' way that he'd previously thought, no. Now that Grub didn't smell of swamp and straw and despair, now that Loth could really *see* him, he was genuinely pretty. Washing his hair had yielded unexpected curls, and combined with his porcelain skin and delicate features, he was almost fae-like in his beauty. Loth could have stared at him all day, except Grub chose that moment to splash him with bathwater playfully, laughing when Loth jerked back to avoid the spray. Grub splashed at him once more, before standing without warning and giving Loth a perfect view of his backside, perhaps as revenge for Loth doing it to him earlier.

As far as revenge went, it failed. Loth drank in the sight of the pert globes eagerly, struck dumb by their pale perfection, and it was only when Grub stepped out of the tub that he thought to hold out a towel. Grub took it, and he didn't pull away when their fingertips brushed. His skin was warm where Loth was touching him, and Loth wrapped a hand around his slim wrist and caught his gaze. Grub bit his lip and his cheeks flushed, but he didn't move away.

One thing Loth was good at was reading people, and Grub

was no exception. Something in his shy glance told Loth that while the prickly, bad-tempered, underfed Grub from before would never have accepted an offer to bed him, there was at least a slim chance that *this* Grub—this clean, damp, bashful sprite, with tiny droplets of water dripping off his curls and beading against his pale skin—might not turn him down. Not tonight, not if he asked nicely. The words were out of his mouth before he thought twice. "Come to bed with me, Grub?"

Grub barely hesitated before answering, "Yes."

Well, that was unexpectedly easy. He'd thought he might have to cajole at least a little. "Yes?"

"Yes." Grub ducked his head and rubbed a hand over the back of his neck. "Unless—unless you're teasing." His cheeks burned and his gaze grew wary.

Loth took a step nearer, draped the towel around Grub's shoulders, and pulled him in close, close enough to look him in the eye. Grub's gaze was wide, and both hopeful and fearful.

"I'm not teasing," he assured him, and leaned in for a kiss. Nothing extreme, just a brush of lips, a hand running through Grub's curls, but it was enough to draw a quiet sigh and for Grub to relax against him.

Grub.

Loth didn't have many standards, barely any in fact, but he did have one hard and fast rule. "If I'm going to sleep with you, I need to know your name. I can't keep calling you Grub."

Grub stiffened. "Why do you need to know?"

Loth ran his fingertips in a line down Grub's spine and felt him shudder. "Well, I have to know what to whisper in your ear as I seduce you, don't I?" he said lightly.

Grub relaxed under his touch. After a moment, he said "Cue. You can call me Cue."

"That's... certainly a name," Loth said carefully.

Grub—no, Cue—grinned unexpectedly. "It should be easy enough for you to remember while you're seducing me," he pointed out and then, perhaps tired of waiting for the promised seduction, he leaned in and kissed Loth before he could say anything else.

As far as kisses went, it was terrible, all teeth and awkward angles. Loth didn't care. He tilted his head and pulled back just enough to guide their mouths a little, tasting the tang of salt and sage, revelling in it. Cue (*not Grub, not Grub* he reminded himself) let out a soft, breathy sound, and when they parted, he was wide-eyed. "Was that—was it all right?"

Loth gave him his most devastating smile. "It was wonderful," he lied, one arm wrapping around Cue's shoulders and guiding him across the room towards the bed. "Why don't we get comfortable, and you can tell me what you want to try?"

Loth gave the tiniest of shoves. The back of Cue's legs hit the bed, and he sat down suddenly, making the straw in the mattress crunch as he bounced a little.

Cue stared up at him, mouth opening and closing, before he admitted, "I don't know. I don't have any idea what I like." His brow creased, as though he was afraid this was a test and he was failing it.

Loth stepped forward into the vee of Cue's legs, resting his hands on his shoulders for a moment before gently shoving him backwards so he was lying flat, and crawling up onto the bed next to him. "I'll tell you what," he suggested, "why don't I show you some things I know you'll like?"

Cue swallowed and nodded dumbly, and what was Loth supposed to do with blind trust like that except lean in and kiss the boy? It was better this time—less urgent, more careful, and Loth felt the thrum of arousal run through him, getting stronger the longer they kissed. Loth had always loved sex in all its forms. He considered himself a considerate lover—partly professional pride and partly because he loved to watch people fall apart. So by rights, he should have been confident. For some reason though, there was the briefest moment where he found himself hesitant, worried he'd mess this up. *Don't be an idiot*, he told himself sternly and pushed determinedly through his sudden bout of nerves.

He ran a hand over Cue's ribs, letting his thumb slide over a nipple, and was rewarded with a sharp intake of breath. So he did it again, his self-assurance returning. He was *good* at this, he reminded himself. He ran his hands over as much of Cue's skin as he could reach as he kissed him, drinking in the small noises that the boy let out whenever he found a sensitive spot, taking note for later.

Cue was panting slightly when their mouths parted, and Loth saw with satisfaction that Cue's cock was fully hard. It was a very pretty cock too, jutting upward from a nest of copper hair. It was long and lean and pale like the rest of him, though the head was easily as rosy as Cue's flushed cheeks. Loth tugged his own towel off and threw it aside, and didn't miss the way Cue's eyes widened at the sight of him naked, nor the way they lingered on his erection.

He did not preen. He did *not*. He did prop himself on his elbow though, so the boy could get a better look. And perhaps he arched his back the slightest bit to show off the length of his body, splaying a hand over what he knew for a fact was an impressively muscled stomach. It was more habit than anything, but it was still gratifying when Cue breathed out, "Wow."

"I'm glad you like it, sweetheart." Loth grinned. "Now, how about I suck your dick til you can't remember your own name?"

Cue's breath hitched. "Um. Pl-please, yes. That," he stammered out, breathless.

Loth hummed to himself, wrapping one hand around Cue's hard dick. No freckles there, he noted idly. "Relax, sweetheart. You just lie there and let me make it good."

He got a strangled moan in reply and took it as permission to carry on. He settled his forearm across Cue's belly, brushing against his razor-sharp hipbone—gods, this boy really did need feeding—and proceeded to kiss and lick at the very head of his cock, gently at first, just enough to make Cue shiver, easing his mouth down slowly, taking his time, caressing the velvet-soft skin with the very tip of his tongue.

Cue let out a squeak, and Loth hummed around the hot length in his mouth, putting every ounce of experience he had to work. Bobbing his head up and down, laving his tongue over the entire length, he used his hand to cup and fondle Cue's balls in a gentle rhythm. Cue whined and squirmed beneath the hand on his belly, before his hips bucked up and he gasped out, "Oh! Oh!" and came in a flood down Loth's throat.

The whole thing barely took a minute, and when Loth finally took his mouth away, Cue was staring at the ceiling, jaw slack. Loth couldn't help the soft laugh that escaped him. "Told you you'd like it," he teased, feeling unaccountably proud.

"That was…" Cue let out a sigh and let his arm flop bonelessly to the side.

"It was, wasn't it?" Loth agreed easily.

Cue let out a breathless laugh. "Consider me seduced."

Loth slid up the bed and tilted Cue's chin so he was facing him. "Do you want to stop, or do you want more?"

Cue's eyes flicked down the bed to Loth's cock. "Um, more? I want you to… to fuck me." His voice shook the tiniest bit, but his tone was sure, and Loth did him the courtesy of assuming he knew his own mind.

"Sweetheart, it would be my absolute pleasure."

He pulled Cue close and lined their bodies up so they were pressed together, and then he spent some time nuzzling at Cue's neck just to get him to make those pretty noises again. Cue for his part let his hands roam, fingers gentle as they brushed against bare skin, careful and curious. Loth kissed along his collarbone and flexed the muscles in his back so they moved under Cue's hands because he had a very nice back and it would be a waste if the boy didn't get to appreciate it in all its glory.

Loth worked his way down Cue's ribs, pressing his lips against as much freckled skin as he could find. He slipped a hand between them and wrapped it around Cue's cock, which was already stirring against his thigh, plumping up beautifully as it came back to life.

Loth climbed out of bed to grab the tiny pot of grease that he always carried in his pants, and when Cue made a curious noise he held it up, head tilted in silent enquiry—*are you sure?* Cue regarded him silently, and for a split second Loth wondered if he'd changed his mind, but then he rolled onto his stomach, head cushioned on his arms, and with a confidence he probably didn't feel, said, "Go on, then. Let's see if you're as good as you say you are."

Loth never was one to back down from a challenge.

He took his time, sliding one grease slicked finger in and then adding another, gently easing the young body under him open one whimper at a time, all the while crooning out soft assurances as Cue writhed under his touch. He knew when he'd got the angle right when Cue arched into his touch, panting out, "Oh, gods! Do that again!"

Loth laughed and eased in a third finger, aiming for the same spot, teasing and massaging, not going any further until he heard what he'd been waiting for, a broken, "Pl—please!"

He took his hand away and rolled Cue onto his back. He told himself he wanted to see his face to make sure he didn't hurt him. If he also had an intense desire to look into those wide green eyes when he sank inside? Well, Loth freely admitted that he'd popped plenty of cherries in his time. There was something so very satisfying about the look of surprise on a boy's face when he took a cock for the first time, and Loth didn't want to miss it, that's all.

Loth was the first to admit that he had an average cock. There was nothing special about it at all. What he could do with it though, now *that* was extraordinary. He'd spent a long time cultivating those skills, and he eagerly put them to use now. He propped himself up on his elbows, greased his cock, and pressed the head against the soft little mouth of muscle, waiting until Cue gave a tiny nod.

"Deep breaths and bear down," he murmured, and then eased himself into the clenching heat in one long, smooth stroke.

Cue gasped, his eyes wide and his mouth open in that perfect O of surprise that Loth loved to see, and gods, he felt amazing. Hot and tight, and Loth had to still his hips, close his eyes, and take deep breaths just so he didn't embarrass himself right then and there. He gave Cue another few moments to adjust, waited till Loth felt like he wasn't quite so close to losing control, then pulled out slowly and pressed back in, angling his body in a way that he knew from experience would hit all the right places. Cue's eyes widened again when he repeated the motion and Loth wondered briefly if it was too much, but then Cue's arms wrapped around his back, pulling him closer, his legs tangling with Loth's as he arched his back, letting out a series of tiny, breathless moans.

Loth rolled his hips, slow and gentle and devastatingly effective, and the whimper he got in return wasn't one of pain.

"More," Cue whispered, breath dancing hot on the skin of Loth's neck, and Loth picked up the pace, hips pumping steadily as Cue rocked against him, the boy's cock twitching, his hands gripping his shoulders tightly. It was intoxicating, and Loth gave up all hope of making this last. He could already feel that tingling deep in his gut that meant he was close.

He wasn't prepared when Cue threw his head back and his hands slid down Loth's back to his arse. Cue squeezed hard, holding Loth deep inside, his cock pressed against Loth's abs, grinding desperately as he let out a needy whine, and it was that noise that did Loth in. His hips stuttered once, twice, and then he was groaning out his climax. He buried his face in Cue's shoulder, whole body trembling, as he wondered briefly how, exactly, he was the one who was falling apart here.

Cue was breathing rapidly, desperation on his face, and Loth pulled himself together enough to slip a hand between them and tug at Cue's poor, needy cock. It was slick with precum, pulsing under Loth's fingers. He only got to enjoy the weight and warmth against his hand for half a dozen strokes before Cue was coming with a whimper, heels drumming against the mattress.

Loth took a moment to catch his breath, and when he was able to move, he eased carefully out, rolling to one side. Cue lay there panting, a tiny, pleased smile on his face like he'd achieved something marvellous. Loth supposed he had. Loth gave himself a few minutes to recover, but when he caught his eyes closing, he knew he'd have to move soon or he'd fall asleep, and he'd always considered it the height of rudeness to leave his partner laying in the mess. It took some effort, but he dragged himself out of bed and retrieved the washcloth, dipping it in the tepid remains of the bucket of clean water. He cleaned himself up, then did the same for Cue, who seemed to have turned into a boneless heap.

He dropped the cloth on the floor and pulled the slight body closer, covering them both with a blanket. Cue remained silent, and a tiny seed of doubt wormed its way into Loth's brain. It had certainly seemed like they'd both enjoyed it, but maybe he was being presumptuous? It wouldn't be the first time.

Finally, he shook the boy gently. "Sweetheart? Was that all right?"

The only reply Loth got was a gentle snore, and he wasn't quite enough of a bastard to wake Cue up, so he was forced to go to sleep with his question unanswered. His only reassurance was the faint smile on Cue's face as he slept.

CHAPTER NINE

Loth woke to sunlight streaming through the window, and an empty space in the bed beside him. Normally the empty space wouldn't have bothered him—he liked it when the people he slept with had the good sense to creep out in the middle of the night—but Cue? Cue was different. Loth might have liked to wake up beside him, but Cue had deprived him of the chance to find out.

Grumbling, Loth pulled on his clothes and his mood soured even more. Last night's bath had been amazing and tugging his dirty clothes on after it felt disgusting. He stared at his boots for a moment, still damp from the swamp, and decided that he'd go barefoot until they left the village.

He headed downstairs, the steps creaking under his feet.

It was early still, and the taproom of the inn was empty except for the maid from last night, who was putting fresh straw on the floor.

Loth flashed her a smile and headed outside into the sunlight. He glanced around the street. He saw a man leading a goat, and a woman lugging a bucket, but no sign of his missing bedmate. Loth slipped down the side of the tavern into the stable yard.

He dodged around a pile of dung—perhaps leaving his boots off had been a mistake—and slipped into the stable. He was about to call out for Grub (*Cue*, he chided himself) when he heard the low murmur of voices. He slipped forward silently and craned his head to see around the corner into the stalls.

Cue was standing in front of one of the stalls, scratching their horse's nose as it chuffed happily. Calarian was there as well, leaning up against a post and looking unfairly gorgeous for someone with unbrushed hair and soiled clothing.

"So you'd never done that before?" Calarian asked. "Never?"

"No. It was the first time." Cue sounded a little... brittle, and Loth felt a rush of concern well up in him. Had he *hurt* Cue? The thought of it left a sour taste in his throat.

"Did you like it?" Calarian asked frankly.

Cue ducked his head briefly, and the horse chewed on his fringe. "Yes. It was... It was incredible."

"Loth does look like he knows how to fuck," Calarian agreed. "He's got that swagger, you know? Like his hips know just the right way to move. And really muscular thighs. I'll bet he's got a nice dick too."

"Um. I... I suppose so? You're right about the hips, anyway," Cue said.

"Benji has a great dick," Calarian continued blithely. "So do I."

"I... yes, I noticed. So did everyone else."

"So." Calarian folded his arms over his chest. "You and Loth. How mind-blowingly hot was it? Who topped? What positions did you use?"

"Positions?" The word squeaked out of Cue.

"You know," Calarian said. "Monastical, paladin, reverse paladin, reverse double paladin—no, wait, you'd need someone else for that—alewife, oarsman, spreading peacock, dirty alchemist... What'd you try first?"

"I don't know what any of those things are."

Loth blinked. He only knew about half of them himself.

"Wow, it really was your first time, wasn't it?" Calarian shrugged. "You're sure you liked it though, right?"

Cue hid his face in the horse's muzzle. "Yes," he mumbled. "Yes, I liked it a lot."

"Good," Calarian declared, and then turned his head and stared at where Loth was standing. He caught Loth's gaze and winked. "Because I think maybe Loth was worried you didn't."

Shit.

Loth straightened up at the same time Cue did.

"Ah," he said, stepping forward. "Here you are. In the stables, of course."

Cue's face was pink, his eyes wide. He didn't take the bait. "G-good morning."

Calarian walked outside, whistling to himself.

Cue chewed his bottom lip for a moment, spots of high colour in his cheeks. "Were you really worried?"

And Loth didn't have the heart to bullshit at that moment. "A little," he admitted. "I woke up, and you weren't there. I thought that perhaps I'd done something you didn't like."

"I liked it." Cue twisted his face up like the admission had been dragged out of him through torture.

"Don't sound so enthusiastic, sweetheart," Loth deadpanned. "It'll go to my head."

Cue snorted. "Sorry. I don't know why I'm so shy about it. I feel stupid, I think. I don't like not knowing things and did you hear Calarian just now? Clearly there are a whole lot of things I still don't know!"

"To be fair, I think Calarian is on a whole different level to the rest of us," Loth said. "I didn't know what half of those things were either."

"But you knew the other half?" Cue dragged the toe of his boot through the dirt.

"I did," Loth said. "And I'd be happy to show you them. Well, apart from the reverse double paladin."

"We'd need someone else for that," Cue said, his mouth twitching in a grin. "Think Calarian's interested?"

The tension between them resolved, and Loth reached out and tugged Cue forward by the hips. He liked the way his hands settled there naturally. He liked the way Cue's mouth quirked, and his gaze flicked to Loth's, somehow shy and challenging at the same time. He especially liked the way that Cue didn't protest when Loth kissed him. He liked the way Cue opened his mouth under the pressure of the kiss, and their tongues met. He liked the way the kiss left Cue smiling.

"Not Calarian. I don't need that kind of competition. Now come on," Loth said. "Breakfast. You need some more meat on your bones."

He took Cue's hand and let him back to the inn.

CUE WAS on his third bowl of porridge by the time the party was more or less assembled in the taproom.

"Nicer without eels, isn't it?" Loth teased.

"Much." Cue shovelled another spoonful in his mouth. "You fucking deserved that though."

Loth grinned. "Maybe."

He liked this new Cue, and he suspected that this new Cue liked him too. They could still tease one another, but they were doing so now in the sense that they were on the same side. And not just as potential redheaded corpses in whatever scheme unknown rich men were hatching around them, but also because last night they'd shared a closeness. And it wasn't just about sex. Loth was no stranger to sex, and certainly no stranger to one-night-stands. Frankly, anything longer than a half-night-stand made him jittery and anxious to flee. But not with Cue, for some reason.

And maybe Loth hadn't quite figured out yet why Cue was

different, but the realisation that he was hadn't spooked him yet. Cue might be the inexperienced one when it came to sex, but Loth was certainly a virgin when it came to feelings.

Loth glanced around the room. Dave was squatting in front of the fireplace, watching as Pie dug through the embers. Pie's wings were extended, and the glow from the embers shone through the thin membranes like sunlight through stained glass. Calarian was slouching against a wall, his eyes half-closed, probably daydreaming of impossibly athletic sex acts, and Ada was stomping out of the kitchens.

Ada stomped over to the table. "I've talked to the maid. She's said if we stay on this road, we'll be in Callier in four days."

Cue scraped his spoon through his porridge and glanced at Loth.

"Ah," Loth said. "Excellent news. And then I shall be handed over to this mysterious benefactor, yes? Who is no doubt planning on restoring me to the throne and not slitting my throat and tossing me in a shallow grave?"

"I see your point," Ada said, because of course she did, "but you don't know that."

"I don't," Loth agreed. "But you don't know otherwise."

Ada hummed and tugged her beard thoughtfully. "Well, we were only hired to deliver you safely to the benefactor. What he does with you after that is really none of our business."

"Comforting."

"Practical," Ada corrected him. She stomped away again.

"We are almost certainly going to die," Cue murmured into his porridge.

"Almost certainly," Loth agreed. "How would you feel about ditching these idiots and heading north?"

"Why north?"

Loth raised his eyebrows. "Why not?"

Cue leaned back in his chair, his gaze falling on Ada, where she now stood in front of the fireplace and stared back. "Ada's too smart to let us run off. She'd have Calarian and Dave after us in moments."

"Not Scott?"

Cue shrugged. "Scott would go the wrong way." He chewed his bottom lip for the moment. "These are good people, Loth. They don't intend us any harm, but they're also not taking Lord Doom into account. If he's behind this, then we are in absolute danger. The man is a viper."

"Is that personal experience talking?"

Cue jolted and then scowled. "Why would it be? Everyone knows it."

"*I* don't know it," Loth said. "Or, at least, I don't *care*. But I suppose we run in very different circles, don't we?"

Cue pressed his mouth into a thin line. "Do people really not care?"

"Most people, sweetheart, don't give a fuck about anything else as long as their bellies are full and their families are safe." Loth sighed. "If half the noble houses slaughter themselves in a fight for the crown, all the average person wants is to be left out of it until the cards have fallen where they will. Politics looks very different from the bottom of the heap."

Cue nodded slowly, his brows tugging together. He stared down at his porridge and dragged his spoon through it again. "I don't know if we should go to Callier, Loth," he said at last. "But at the same time, if there's even a chance to..." He shook his head.

"To see your family?" Loth asked quietly.

"Yes." Cue stared at the scarred tabletop. He didn't lift his gaze. "To see my family."

Loth reached out and put his hand on Cue's knee. He squeezed it under the table out of sight of the others and hoped that it offered Cue at least a tiny bit of comfort. While it was clear that he and Cue came from vastly different worlds and had vastly different priorities, Loth thought of the smiles on his parents' faces whenever he darkened their doorstep from time to time. He decided that yes, if there was a chance their mysterious benefactor really did think Cue was the prince and wanted to rescue him, then that would at least get him back into the embrace of his family. Loth wanted that for Cue, because he'd seen the longing in Cue's gaze when he'd mentioned his father, however briefly, and he knew that Cue wanted it more than he could bring himself to say.

At the same time though, Loth wasn't an idiot.

"We're not on the road we should be," he said, "and that's to our advantage. But we should perhaps only travel by night, and it wouldn't hurt to dye our hair to make ourselves a little less conspicuous. I've already decided on blond, so you can't have that. I think you'd look lovely as a brunet." He frowned. "Although it may be a moot point. We are travelling with a seven-foot green orc, a dwarf, an elf, a fingerdragon, and an idiot. We're going to draw at least a little attention."

Cue tilted his head to the side, considering. "No," he declared. "We leave our hair as it is. If it is a rescue, they're only interested in saving a redheaded prince. And if it's a trap, then having two redheads might buy us some time, if they don't know who the prince really is."

"Ooh! A decoy!" Loth was impressed. "There's a devious streak that runs right through you, isn't there?" He winked. "Don't give me that face, sweetheart. It's a compliment."

"Is it?" Cue looked dubious.

"Of course." Loth lowered his voice. "Consider Scott."

Cue raised his eyebrows. "Must I?"

"There it is again," Loth said. "Delightful. Although that was more nasty than devious. Don't worry, that still gets my blood rushing to all the right places, if you know what I mean." He rather worried that Cue's wrinkled nose meant that he didn't. Oh, well. "My point is, consider Scott. He's got all these ideas about heroism, and about *deeds*, but what has that ever gotten him? Absolutely nothing, because he's also an idiot. Whereas you,

Cue, look like your arms would snap if you even tried to lift a sword, but I'd stick by your side in a heartbeat, and do you know why?"

"Because you're fucking me?" Cue asked.

"Well, yes," Loth admitted. "But that's not the only reason. You're smart, Cue, and you're devious, and all of my sharply honed survival skills are telling me that you're the one worth listening to."

Cue licked his spoon. "I'm not sure that really is a compliment though, coming from someone like you. No offence."

"None taken."

Cue narrowed his eyes. "None taken?"

"Honestly none," Loth confirmed. "It's much smarter to be a live rat than a dead..." He frowned. "a..."

"Are you thinking of an animal that doesn't live long and also has a reputation for being pure and good?" Cue asked curiously.

"Yes," Loth said. "But I can't think of one."

"Hmm." Cue shrugged. "Me neither. It's a shame, because otherwise that might have been a half-decent analogy." He dropped his spoon back into his empty bowl. "Your point has been taken, Loth. Don't strain yourself."

Loth tilted his head. "I'm thinking *pelican?*"

"They tear their breasts to feed their young," Cue said. "But I think they probably live longer than rats." His mouth twitched. "Don't overthink it, Loth, or you'll be forced to entirely reject your worldview."

"You have a lot more sass in you this morning." Loth squeezed Cue's knee and then trailed his fingers up his thigh. "I quite like it."

Cue smirked. "I quite like it too."

What felt to Loth like the beginning of excellent foreplay was ruined when Scott came clattering down the stairs and into the taproom. He was unshaven and his hair was wild. Sharing a bed with Dave, Loth supposed, was probably not very restful.

"Scott." Loth beckoned him.

Scott bobbed and dipped his way over to the table, and it took Loth a moment to realise his contortions were because he was trying to walk and bow at the same time. "Good morning, my grace. *Your* grace. *Grace.*"

"Good morning," Loth said. "Now, Scott, what's the plan today? Are we leaving for Callier?"

"Yes," Scott said. "Absolutely. Unless no." He wavered. "What is your wish, My Prince?"

Loth exchanged a glance with Cue. "I think that we should be cautious, and travel by dark."

Scott blinked at him.

Ada stomped over. "That's not a bad idea, actually."

"Um, the roads are *very* dangerous at night," Scott said.

"Are they?" Loth asked.

"That's what my mum says," Scott replied, nodding earnestly.

"Does your mum travel with an orc for protection?" Loth asked.

Scott opened his mouth and then closed it again. He shook his head.

"Then we travel by night," Loth said. "Calarian, what's your night sight like?"

"Like a fucking hawk's," Calarian said with a grin. Then he looked pensive. "Can hawks see at night?"

"Nobody in this group knows anything about animals," Cue muttered, but he was smiling.

"Then that's our advantage," Loth said. "We have Dave's muscle, Calarian's sight, and it would take a bandit with balls bigger than a giant's to try to rob Ada. And if we travel at night, we are unseen. There will be nobody reporting our journey to Callier until we're knocking on this benefactor's door to announce it ourselves."

He looked around the group.

Calarian and Ada nodded. Dave just looked happy to be there.

"Excellent idea!" Scott exclaimed. He cleared his throat. "It is my decision that—"

"Shut the fuck up," Calarian said, and smacked Scott around the back of the head.

Loth couldn't have said it any better himself.

THE DECISION TO travel at night meant that they got to partake of a luxury even greater than a hot bath. Loth made enquiries of the maid in the inn, and a little while later a washerwoman turned up to collect their clothes and take them away for cleaning. Loth and Cue returned to their room, wrapped in blankets, and ate cheese and bread and pickled onions. Loth was ready to offer to teach Cue a few more of Calarian's mysterious sex positions, but Cue crashed out in the bed before he could suggest it, and Loth didn't have the heart to wake him.

The washerwoman returned their clothing at dusk, and it was a very different group indeed that gathered in the taproom for dinner that evening. Everyone was clean and pink-skinned—apart from Dave, who was clean and green-skinned—and their clothes, although worn and patched here and there, were no longer various shades of mud.

"Look at you," Loth said when Cue wandered into the taproom. He was wearing a faded mustard shirt that didn't clash too badly with his hair and was a massive improvement on the rags he'd been wearing in the dungeon cell at Delacourt. Loth suspected those hadn't survived the washerwoman's attentions. "You look like a new man, Cue."

That got everyone's attention.

"Who?" Scott asked.

"Cue," Loth said. "Well, look at him. I can hardly call him Grub now, can I? He's practically shiny!"

"Yes, someone's given him a very thorough spit and polish,"

Calarian said, raising his eyebrows.

Ada chuckled under her breath, and Cue turned an even pinker shade. But he sat down next to Loth in the space Loth had left him and kept his chin up.

The maid brought food, and they ate. Loth was aware of Calarian carefully counting out their money for the meal. He figured that today's laundry had sucked their funds dangerously dry, but he wasn't too worried. Loth had survived on a shoestring before, and there was no Swamp of Death between them and their destination this time. As soon as they were somewhere new, Loth would give his tingling fingers a workout, and bolster their funds enough to see them fed all the way to Callier.

Loth wasn't quite on his home turf now, but he was finding his feet again. And there was nothing like a hot, filling meal of rabbit stew and fresh bread to really build up his confidence.

He should have known it was too good to be true.

"Horses," Calarian said suddenly, tilting his head to listen. "Maybe five. Coming fast."

Loth leapt up from his seat, dragging Cue by the wrist. He trampled up the stairs. Had he left anything in his room? Was there even time to check?

Dave lumbered up the steps behind him, Ada pushing at him.

Loth hurried into his room and peered carefully out the window that overlooked the entrance to the stable yard. He only caught a glimpse of the men on horseback heading for the front entrance, but a glimpse was all he needed: soldiers.

"Shit." He motioned for Cue to shut and latch the door.

Someone banged on the door downstairs. "Crown Guard! Open up!"

Loth pushed the window open and peered down into the stable yard. "How hard does that ground look to you, Cue?"

Cue looked at the ground, and looked at Loth, and then looked at the ground again. "There's only one way to find out."

"Good boy," Loth said, and then they jumped.

CHAPTER TEN

L oth and Cue darted into the trees surrounding the inn's yard and then ducked down into the undergrowth and watched. Calarian slung a long, shapely leg over the windowsill, and slipped as smoothly and silently down the outside of the inn as a trickle of water. He barely made a sound when he landed in a crouch in the dirt. Then he stood and reached back for Ada, the first time Loth had seen her at any type of disadvantage through her lack of height. But she didn't hesitate, falling into Calarian's careful arms, and he lowered her gracefully to the ground.

Dave and Scott had been in an attic room. Dave dropped from the window like a rock but seemed none the worse for wear. Pie, sitting on Loth's shoulder, chirped happily to see Dave land safely.

Scott wobbled on the attic windowsill, tipped into space, changed his mind and veered backwards, scrabbled for a hold, and then, with a loud cry of "Catch me, Dave!" launched himself forward, arms spread wide. "AAARRGH!"

Dave stepped neatly sideways, and Scott's thin scream was cut off with a thump when he hit the ground. Dave stood next to him, arms firmly at his sides, and let out an unconvincing, "Sorry. Missed."

Loth would have laughed if he hadn't been so busy trying not to get caught.

Calarian nudged Scott with the toe of his boot curiously, his hands on his hips.

Ada jogged towards the tree line with Dave ambling along beside her. Calarian jogged after them.

"Hey," Calarian said, settling into the undergrowth beside Loth and Cue. "You guys made it."

He held out his hand for a fist bump, and both Loth and Cue obliged.

Over by the inn, Scott groaned.

"Oh, he's not dead then," Dave said.

"Nah." Calarian sounded disappointed.

Loth sighed. "You know we're going to have to rescue him. If the soldiers find him and he's not dead, he'll sell us out in a heartbeat."

Calarian raised a single brow. "We could give him a moment. See if he succumbs to his injuries?"

Over by the inn wall, Scott staggered to his feet. "You guys?" he yelled, peering around in the gathering darkness. "Where are you guys?"

"That fucking idiot," Ada muttered. "Dave, go and grab him before the soldiers hear him."

Dave lumbered out of the tree line like a bull. He charged at Scott, grabbed him, and tucked him under his arm before lumbering back into the trees. Dave had only stepped back into the trees when the first of the soldiers appeared in the yard.

Fuck.

So much for getting the horses from the stables then.

As silently as they could, thankful for nightfall, they slipped further into the trees.

"What now?" Ada asked in an undertone. "We can't stay on the road now, and we don't even have a map."

Cue lifted his chin. "I... I might know a place."

LOTH LOST TRACK OF TIME, but he thought they walked for about half an hour, following a twisting trail through the dark woods. Cue led the way, with Pie fluttering around his head like a manic firefly. He stopped a few times, his forehead creasing as though he was trying to remember the way.

"It looks different at night," he said once, before choosing a fork in the path.

Loth really hoped he actually knew what he was doing, but he wasn't very optimistic. And then, just when he was about to suggest that Cue was leading them in circles, the trees opened up and Loth saw it:

It was a manor house, built of dark stone that gleamed in the moonlight. It must have been magnificent at one point. The grounds were overgrown, one whole wall had been overtaken entirely by creeping ivy, and at least one of the chimney stacks had collapsed. It was clear that the house was abandoned; there was no light coming from inside.

Loth's boots crunched against broken roof tiles as the group approached the dark facade of the house.

"What is this place?" Dave asked wonderingly.

Cue didn't answer him. He seemed a shade paler in the moonlight that he should have been as he stepped up to the front doors of the house. He pushed them open.

"Not even locked." His voice was shaky, and Loth sent him a worried look.

They stepped inside the house.

It smelled of damp and decay, but it wasn't as dark as Loth had feared it would be. And then he realised that most of the window shutters were broken; moonlight streamed inside. There was an elegant chair sitting under the window closest the door, in the entry hall. It was speckled with mould and smelled terrible.

Loth glanced around the entry hall. The antlered heads of what must have been an entire herd of stags stared down at him from the wall opposite the main doors. Below them, wooden shields and crossed spears adorned the wall. Loth squinted at the crest on the shields.

"Holy shit," he said. "That's the *royal* crest!"

Cue shot him a look.

"Which I knew, of course," Loth said, recovering fast, "because I am the lost prince."

"Welp," Calarian said. "I'm gonna go loot some stuff, I guess."

Cue's face was pinched, and he threw Calarian a look of disgust before he strode further into the house.

Calarian and Ada descended on the place like a plague of locusts. Dave dropped Scott and followed them. Loth, although he was tempted to join them, followed Cue instead. He found him in a room at the top of a creaking staircase. It was a library, perhaps, although it stank so badly of decay that Loth was sure that the weather, and mice and insects, had destroyed all the books years ago.

Loth approached him. "Cue, we are absolutely going to be arrested and hanged if anyone finds us here."

"Does it look like anyone's been here in years?" Cue asked. He reached out and trailed his finger down the sagging spine of a book. Then he pushed, and his finger punctured the spine. Cue's mouth twisted bitterly.

"How did you even know it was here?" Loth asked.

Cue shrugged. "It's a hunting lodge. A holiday home. They came here sometimes. My—" He cleared his throat. "Sometimes, if you were important enough, the royal family would invite you to stay as well."

"And your father was important enough?"

"I came here sometimes," Cue agreed. "When I was a kid."

"That's how you knew the way from the inn."

"Sometimes we used to walk there," Cue said. "Me and the other kids who were staying. The cook at the inn used to make toffee apples when there were children staying at the hunting lodge. Our parents would let us go to get us out of their hair, I think."

Even in the moonlight, Loth could see Cue's eyes shining with unshed tears.

"Cue..." He reached out.

Cue shook his head and stepped back. "It was a long time ago."

A reminder of happier times, Loth thought, before Cue was made a prisoner to ensure his father's compliance.

"Anyway," Cue said, "it's at least somewhere to shelter for a little while, isn't it? There might even be preserved food in the kitchen cellar. There used to be jars of onions down there, and pickled herring, and salted beef. How many years does pickled herring keep?"

"Pickled herring should be destroyed the moment it's pickled," Loth said and warmed when he saw the twitch of Cue's smile. "But I'm sure if there's anything edible, Dave will sniff it out. Come on. Let's go and see what they've found."

He reached out again, and this time Cue took his hand and allowed himself to be led from the library.

At the top of the stairs was a portrait. It was covered in mould, like so much else in the house. It was a man and a woman. A girl stood beside them, and a younger boy sat on the woman's lap.

"Is that them?" Loth asked. He pulled his sleeve over the heel of his hand and swiped the fabric over the man's face. "Is that the old king?"

"No." Cue copied the sleeve thing. His touch was a lot more careful than Loth's when he wiped the girl's face clean. "This house used to belong to the queen's family, the Dumesnys. This is her when she was a child."

The girl was solemn-faced. Golden curls framed her face.

"Oh," said Loth. He squinted at the mould-speckled boy on the man's lap. "So that's..."

"Lord Doom," Cue said quietly.

Loth blinked at the boy. How strange that even men like Lord Doom had once been little boys. It seemed incongruous, somehow. It was easier to imagine ruthless men like him springing fully formed into the world, instead of once having been pudgy-fingered, apple-cheeked toddlers. The larval stage of evil was strangely underwhelming.

"Come on," he said. "Show me the way to the kitchen before our noble rescuers strip this place back to the bare bones."

Cue nodded once and led the way back down the stairs.

The kitchens were, as Loth suspected, mainly stripped bare (although there was a disturbing amount of pickled herring). At least they were able to arm themselves when Cue dragged out a drawer and found an old set of knives and a meat cleaver, which Loth tucked into his belt. He had no idea where everyone else had got to, but Calarian was rattling through a bunch of dusty jars.

Cue lingered in the back of the pantry, smiling to himself. "I used to hide in here sometimes." The sound of horses outside the back door interrupted Cue's musings, and Loth swore under his breath.

"Cal? What happened to a little bit of warning?"

Calarian pulled his hand out of a jar of pickled onions. "What? Oh, shit. Horses!"

Loth threw him a look as Ada came scurrying into the kitchen. "Horses!"

"Yes, we know. Where's Scott?" he asked as Dave lumbered through the door clutching a dusty lute.

"Did you know there are horses outside?" Scott called from

somewhere near the stairs, and then there was a rattling sound, a thump, and a groan.

Loth sighed. "Did he just...?"

"Fall down the stairs?" Ada asked. "Probably. Dave?"

Dave grumbled but headed towards the source of the moaning. He was back a moment later with Scott slung over his shoulder. "They're out front as well," he reported gloomily. "An' we're stuck in here."

Shit. They were trapped. Loth could see the outline of bodies through the dirt-streaked windows, and he steeled himself for a fight that could only end one way. He took out his meat cleaver and reflected that at least he'd die in battle and not hanged for petty theft like his mother had always predicted.

But then Cue was pulling on his arm, hissing, "Quiet!" and dragging him towards the pantry, beckoning the others to follow. Maybe Cue thought it would go better for them having their backs against a wall, but Loth had never in his life known 'backs against the wall' to mean anything good. Still, he followed, because what other choice did he have?

Cue pulled the doors of the pantry closed, and then made a tiny chirping noise, and Pie's head popped out of Loth's scarf.

"Light," Cue whispered, and Pie obliged with a flame just big enough to see by. Cue tilted his head, his eyes narrowing as he felt under a shelf. "No. No, no, no. Where...?"

"What are you doing, Cue?" Loth asked in a whisper.

"Shh." Cue squeezed his eyes shut for a moment, and then suddenly dropped to his knees and began to feel under the lower shelf. "Of course! I was smaller!"

From somewhere, Loth heard a sharp clicking sound, and then Cue was scrambling to his feet and pushing the shelf. For a moment nothing happened, and then suddenly the shelf creaked and swung backwards. Loth saw a set of narrow, twisting stone stairs that appeared to lead down into total blackness.

"Pie," Cue said. "Light."

Pie chittered, and fluttered down into the darkness.

"Go," Cue said, catching Ada by the arm and pushing her toward the stairs. "Go."

Calarian followed Ava, and then Dave squeezed down into the narrow space, tugging Scott behind him. Cue looked at Loth, eyebrows raised. "Coming?"

And suddenly, it all clicked into place.

The dead parents, the ducking and dodging around his identity, the knowledge of secret passages and royal breakfasts, the red hair, the strange tenderness as he'd brushed the mould and dust away from the queen's childhood portrait, all of it. Loth grabbed Cue's wrist. "What's Cue short for?" he asked quietly. "Is it... Tarquin? Or should I just call you... *Your Grace?*"

Cue met his gaze coolly. "Quinn is fine. But I don't really think now's the time, do you?"

And oh, didn't he sound every inch a prince? Loth couldn't believe he didn't see it before. "Unbelievable," he muttered.

Cue pulled his wrist from Loth's grasp. He scowled. "I told you the first night in the cell back in Delacourt, Loth. Don't act so fucking shocked now."

Well, the princely demeanour hadn't lasted long at all, had it? But Cue had a point. Grub had a point. *Tarquin* had a point. This little redheaded arsehole had a point. He *had* told Loth the truth. Loth just hadn't believed it until now. Because Loth was an inveterate liar who would say anything if it was to his advantage, and he'd assumed that Grub-Cue-whatever-he-was-called, was the same. Turned out he was wrong.

Cue was right about one thing, though. Now wasn't the time. There was the sound of boots tromping around in the kitchen, and Loth knew it was only a matter of time before it occurred to the soldiers to open the pantry. He followed Tarquin down the stairs, pulling the hidden door shut behind them, and hoped to the gods they didn't spot Calarian's half-eaten jar of onions and look any further.

The passageway was filled with cobwebs and dust. Loth pulled his scarf over his face to shield him from the worst of it as they surged forward. All the while his brain chanted 'the *prince* is alive, the prince is *alive,* the *prince is alive.*' No matter how he phrased it, the knowledge was overwhelming. It was followed with an increasingly hysterical answering refrain of *Oh shit, I* fucked *the prince.*

THE TRIP through the tunnel was mostly silent—in part because nobody wanted a mouth full of cobwebs, but mainly because they didn't have the breath to waste on talking. The tunnel twisted and turned until Loth had no idea which way they were heading, which he supposed was the point. After about half an hour he risked a mouthful of dirt to ask, "Where does this come out?"

"Near the tavern," the prince said. "If we're lucky, we'll be able to retrieve the horses."

Several twists and turns later, they came to a set of steep stairs with a trapdoor at the top. Ada clambered up the stairs and hissed, "It's stuck!"

Well. Fuck. Of course it was. Loth wasn't going to die in battle after all. He was going to suffocate in an underground tunnel while eye to eye with the *crown prince,* who he'd *fucked*—

"Got it," Dave called cheerfully. "Jus' needed a nudge."

Loth looked up to see that Dave had, indeed given the door a nudge—if ripping it off its hinges could be considered a nudge. Regardless, he could see the night sky and freedom. Before any of them moved though, he asked, "Cal?"

Calarian closed his eyes. "It's clear," he reported.

Dave pushed through the opening, dragging himself over the edge, then extended a hand down and helped Ada out. Calarian followed, and then Scott, who teetered on the edge for a moment before managing to haul himself up. Loth didn't think he imagined Calarian's look of disappointment when he didn't fall. He and Quinn looked at each other.

"After you?" Loth indicated the steps, suddenly uncertain about *everything*, because Quinn was *royalty*, and gods, the things Loth had said, the way he'd sneered... he wouldn't be surprised if Quinn handed him straight over to the hangman for treason once he was back on the throne

Quinn just nodded curtly and then he was gone, up the ladder and over the top. Loth followed fast on his heels, just in case Quinn decided to slam the top shut and trap him there as revenge for all the terrible things he'd said about the royal family.

THEY SNUCK through the woods quietly, with Calarian leading since he had both night vision *and* a sense of direction. When they arrived back at the tavern, Loth was relieved to see that their horses were still there. He'd been worried that the soldiers would have released them—it's what he would have done—but apparently catching the escaped prisoners had taken priority.

Calarian, Ada, Scott and Dave saddled up, and when Scott asked, "Are you coming, Your Grace?" it took Loth a second to realize that Scott was talking to him because of course, the others didn't know. They still thought he was someone worth rescuing.

He looked at Quinn and knew immediately that something was amiss by the way he was staring fixedly into space, drawing shallow breaths. "We're right behind you. We just need a moment alone," he said.

Ada snorted. Scott looked concerned, and Calarian made an obscene gesture involving his hand and cheek that said he had no doubt what they were doing. Dave was oblivious.

"Are you sure it's safe?" Scott asked, which was possibly the first time he'd asked an intelligent question since Loth had met him.

Calarian leaned over and whispered in Scott's ear, and Scott blushed bright red.

"Oh! We'll wait up the road a bit then, Your Grace. Um, take your time?"

And with that the rest of them rode out, leaving Loth alone with his prince. His prince, who was still staring at the floor, bent in half with his arms wrapped around himself like he was trying to keep himself from flying apart. Perhaps he was.

"Quinn," he said, unsure where to start.

"They're really dead," Quinn gritted out. His forehead creased. "I knew, of course I knew. But I hoped... When Doom first locked me up, I used to dream that maybe they'd made it to the lodge, that they'd hidden in the tunnels and escaped. That they were, I don't know, living on a farm somewhere." He made a derisive sound. "How stupid am I?"

Loth stepped forward and laid a hand on Quinn's shoulder. "Not stupid," he said. "Just a sixteen-year-old trying to hold on."

"I'm not sixteen now though, am I? I've known they were dead for years. I should be past this." He heaved a great, shuddery breath, and Loth's heart clenched.

"Perhaps," he ventured, "you only thought you knew."

Grub looked up at him, eyes wet. "Perhaps."

Loth was assaulted by the desire to hold Quinn close, stroke his hair, and assure him it would all be all fine. He didn't though. He could tell that Quinn was barely holding himself together right now, that he would fall apart at the slightest hint of kindness, and neither of them were equipped to deal with that. Besides, even he wasn't a good enough liar to make that sound convincing. Instead, he changed the subject.

"So, given what I now know about you, the question is, do we tell the others?"

Quinn swallowed and straightened up, throwing Loth a grateful look. "I think Ada's guessed. Dave and Cal won't care as long as they get paid. Scott though? We don't tell him. I wouldn't trust him as far as I could throw him."

"And you couldn't throw him that far, with your tiny arms," Loth observed.

"That's because I haven't been getting my royal porridge with added eel," Quinn said, the ghost of a smile on his face. "No, Scott can keep bowing and scraping to you, and we tell the others to keep it quiet."

"Agreed. And it's not like he'll figure it out, not if we don't tell him. He's dumber than…" he cast about for an example. "… than Dave."

Quinn's nose crinkled, and his smile turned into something more genuine. "I wonder, how far do you think *Dave* could throw Scott?"

"We should try and find out," Loth grinned. "If nothing else, it'd be entertaining to watch."

Quinn nodded. "And just think," he said. "It'll be marvellous in the ballads."

Loth laughed quietly. "It will, won't it? Now, come on, let's get the hell out of here."

Quinn nodded and checked their horse's tack.

Before they left the stables, Loth caught Quinn's wrist. "The things I said, about all royalty being bastards…"

Quinn shrugged. "You weren't to know."

"So… no hard feelings?" Loth didn't care about royalty or politics, but he was coming to realise that he *did* care about Quinn. It was most disconcerting.

"No hard feelings."

"And the whole sex thing? You're not angry that I took advantage? Because in my defence, I didn't know I was despoiling a prince."

Quinn stepped forward and pulled him close, pressing their lips together. "No," he said between kisses, "but I did. And I really rather liked being despoiled by you. Maybe we could do it again."

And then he slapped Loth's arse, patted the saddle, and gave Loth a distinctly lecherous look as he asked, "So, shall we ride?"

Loth was just about to answer when, from the vicinity of the dark stalls, someone cleared their throat. He turned, his heart racing, as a man stepped out of the shadows.

CHAPTER ELEVEN

The men who stepped out of the shadows and into the silvery moonlight didn't look terrifying, but Loth was immediately aware of how Quinn froze at his side like a rabbit under the gaze of a hungry wolf.

The man stepped closer, straw crunching under his boots. He had a sword in his belt, but his hands, when he held up his palms, were empty.

"Your Grace," he said, and his gaze fell unerringly on Quinn. He was a man of medium height and middle years. There were crow's feet around his eyes, and wrinkles at the corners of his mouth, as though he laughed a lot. He wasn't laughing now. He had hair that might have been blond once, but was greying now. His eyes were pale in the moonlight. "You're not supposed to be on the Torlere Road, Your Grace."

It struck Loth as an odd thing for their pursuer to say. He clenched his hand more tightly around the handle of the meat cleaver, wondering if he stood any chance at all against a sword, and very much doubting it.

Quinn lifted his chin. "Ser Greylord."

It took Loth a moment to recall that he'd heard the name

before. The Shire Reeve at Delacourt and, no doubt, a man very invested in tracking down any prisoners who escaped from his dungeon cells. Especially when one of those prisoners was the crown prince.

Loth felt anger burn low in his gut, simmering like a pot on a stove. This was the man who'd imprisoned Quinn. The man who'd been responsible for the wretched condition Quinn had been in when Loth had met him—pale and too thin, his bones jabbing at his skin as though they were searching for a way to escape.

"I'm afraid I heard everything you said," Ser Greylord said. "I too, have a son. Younger than you, Your Grace. Twelve, now. When I was rewarded by Lord Doom with a position in his guard, my boy was sent elsewhere to live. You understand what I'm saying, don't you, Your Grace?"

Quinn's mouth was a thin line, and then he answered. "I think so."

"And so you escape," Ser Greylord said, "through no fault of mine, and so you are supposed to be on an entirely different road, while I search *this* one."

Loth's brain ground to a halt, like a river freezing over.

"For all of that," Ser Greylord said, "I'm glad our paths crossed because I fear you should not go to Callier. I sent a bird to Lord Doom to tell him of your escape." He shook his head. "When I received his reply, he did not sound surprised."

"So it's a setup," Loth said. "Everything has been a setup, just as we thought."

"Not everything," Ser Greylord said. "You were supposed to be on the other road! Only a bunch of crazed fools would cut through the Swamp of Death! You're supposed to be miles and miles away from here!"

He sounded a little frustrated, and Loth couldn't blame him. The man had clearly done his best to *not* catch them, and, like a bunch of drunken, determined geese, they'd staggered into his path anyway.

"Well, if you're such a good guy," Loth said, "then why the hell was Quinn in such gods awful shape when he was broken out?"

Quinn put a hand on Loth's forearm but didn't take his eyes off Ser Greylord. "He'd only been there a few months, Loth. There was another reeve before him. My rations increased under Ser Greylord's... hospitality."

"I don't believe him," Loth said. "I don't believe he's our benefactor."

"I'm not," Ser Greylord said. "But I suspect we have the same one. Someone put coin into the hands of those who would rescue you. That same person put coin into my hands, to ensure that the chase would be slow, and down the wrong road. I was not given a name, except to say that the prince still had friends in Callier, men who would restore his rightful throne to him, and rid the kingdom of Doom." He inclined his head. "Except now I have reason to suspect, at least, that all is not as it appears, and that perhaps your life is in more danger now, out here on the open road, than it was in Delacourt."

"I still don't believe him," Loth said. He stared at Ser Greylord. "You said you have a son, yes? Being held as a hostage to ensure your compliance. He's twelve, you said?"

Ser Greylord held his gaze. "Yes, and I fear he is no longer safe."

Loth's chest squeezed.

"Doom is unhinged," Ser Greylord said. "More and more, he dangles my boy's fate in front of me, and I do not trust him when he is displeased." His voice cracked, and he cleared his throat. He looked at Quinn. "Thus, if there is anything good that can come out of all this, I wanted it to be *you*, Your Grace, because you do not seem like the sort who earns loyalty with a knife at the throat of a child. I do not hope to gain your trust here tonight, but please, travel cautiously, because you cannot know if it's a friend or a foe waiting for you in Callier."

Quinn stepped forward, and Loth caught him by the elbow.

"We need to leave," he said firmly.

Quinn held his gaze.

"We need to leave," Loth repeated. He looked at Ser Greylord. "If what you say is true, then now you know we're on this road, I expect you won't be bothering us too much anymore."

Ser Greylord inclined his head.

"But, you're right," Loth said. "We don't trust you. We don't trust anyone." He nudged Quinn sideways. "Get our horse."

Quinn didn't argue. He hurried to get the horse, tugging it forward gently by the bridle. He swung himself up into the saddle and held a hand down for Loth. Loth hauled himself up behind him, and Quinn turned the horse toward the stable door.

"Just one thing," Loth said.

Ser Greylord raised his eyebrows.

"Me," said Loth. "Where did I fit in with this plan? Was it a decoy you wanted, to muddy the waters in some way?"

"You?" Ser Greylord shook his head. "No, nothing like that. You weren't even supposed to be in the prince's cell."

"So why was I?" Loth asked curiously.

"It was Bring Your Child to Work day," Ser Greylord said. He looked slightly embarrassed. "And young Crispin, the head guard's son, put you in the wrong cell."

"Huh." Now that Loth thought about it, the guard had seemed quite young. "For a moment there I thought I was important."

Quinn twisted in the saddle, his mouth quirking up. "You are."

They rode out of the stable.

THEY CAUGHT up with the rest of the party a few minutes down the road. Quinn didn't say anything about their run-in with Ser

Greylord, and neither did Loth. They rode at the end of the party so that they could speak together without being overheard. Loth figured that Calarian could listen in if he chose. Despite his earlier failure to hear horses back at the manor, he'd proved time and time again to have acute hearing. Loth also figured that, being Calarian, he probably didn't give a fuck.

"Do you believe him?" Loth asked quietly, his hands on Quinn's hips.

Quinn sighed, and leaned back a little. His hair brushed Loth's jaw. "I have no reason not to believe him."

"You don't need a reason. Not believing people should be your default, because people are untrustworthy arseholes."

"Do you really believe that?"

Loth rolled his eyes. "Not always. But, come on, back to Greylord. What about that stuff with his kid? Because let me tell you, every single beggar I've met in every single town has either got a grandparent at death's door, or some other sob story about a sick puppy to make you feel sorry for them. It's the oldest trick in the book."

"And it works," Quinn said patiently, "because people can relate. Death is relatable because everyone knows someone who's died. And being threatened with the death of a loved one? Well, that's relatable to anyone who's ever been in a room with Lord Doom. Look, I don't know if Greylord has a son or not, but I *do* know that he was much kinder to me than the previous reeve. I was fed, and I was given more than one blanket, and some nights he'd even come and talk to me, and bring his chessboard."

"You were sleeping in rags in a pile of straw!"

Up ahead, Ada turned to look back, and Quinn shushed Loth.

"I was sleeping in rags in a pile of straw for two days before I was rescued," Quinn corrected. "I already told you that." And he had, Loth recalled dimly. "You really thought I lived like that for five years? Fuck that. The first winter would have killed me. They said it was because of the rats when they moved me to that cell, but it would make sense that I was being put in position for a rescue instead. After all, Ser Greylord wouldn't want Doom to find out the prince had been rescued from a *nice* cell."

"You believe him," Loth said. "You think he was playing both sides while he was getting ready to break you out of there."

"Loth, why didn't our rescuers have to knock out any guards?"

Well, shit. Quinn had an excellent point there. What was it Dave had said? That all the guards had been *sleeping*. Fuck's sake, this had been an inside job the whole time, and none of them had even realised it. Loth found himself replaying every moment of the rescue and every moment that had followed it, trying to see it all in a new light.

"Um... Loth?" Quinn's voice sounded strangled.

"Hmm?"

"Your *hands*."

"Oh." Without being aware of it, Loth's hands had slipped off Quinn's hips. One was settled on Quinn's thigh, but the other one was cupped over his dick, and absently massaging it into a very respectable erection. "Sorry."

"Don't you—" Quinn groaned and squirmed in the saddle. "Tell them we're stopping."

"What?"

"You're the prince, arsehole," Quinn said. "Tell them we're stopping!"

"Let's just take a five-minute break!" Loth announced.

"Ten," Quinn grumbled.

"A ten-minute break," Loth corrected, and then Quinn was dragging him off the horse and behind the cover of a large tree beside the road.

"Feel that!" Quinn grumbled, rubbing against Loth's thigh. "I can't ride like that!"

Loth leered at him. "Sweetheart, you could ride a number of things like that."

"This is your fault." Quinn fixed him with an imperious stare. "Fix it!"

"Yes, Your Grace, whatever you say, Your Grace," Loth mocked quietly, and dropped to his knees and tugged Quinn's trousers down.

"Why are you...?" Quinn blinked down at him.

"Why am I kneeling? Because I'm going to put your dick in my mouth, and my neck doesn't bend this far otherwise."

"Your *mouth*?" Quinn looked completely gobsmacked at the very idea. *"Here?"*

"Yes," Loth said, cocking a brow. "Problem?"

"I just thought..." Quinn blinked. "I thought *hands*. But, gods. No, no problem at all!"

Loth didn't reply, because his mother always said it was rude to talk with your mouth full. That was fine—Quinn babbled enough for both of them. *"Oh! What—yes... aaah... oh gods..."* and his hands tangled tightly in Loth's hair and tugged in a way that had Loth's own cock twitching. He hummed around Quinn's cock, just to hear him whimper.

Quinn's hips started to rock, and Loth barely had time to think that five minutes would be long enough after all, and then Quinn was coming with a low groan. Loth suckled him clean, licked his lips, and then looked up with a bright smile. "Now do me!"

Quinn's eyes widened.

Loth laughed. "I'm teasing." He climbed to his feet and brushed the dirt off his knees. Then he smacked Quinn on the arse. "That should take the edge off for you, hmm?"

Quinn blinked at him dumbly, as though he'd suddenly lost the ability to understand words, although Loth supposed that his confused expression could just be the result of the mind-blowing orgasm Loth had given him.

"Come on," he said. "We've got places to be."

Then he backed Quinn against the tree and kissed him until Calarian called out that they'd better hurry up.

Quinn was still a little dazed when they got back on the horse, and he leaned back against Loth uncomplainingly as they continued on.

Ada pulled her horse to a halt and waited until Loth and Quinn caught up. "You know something."

"Nope," Loth lied. "Nothing at all."

"Bullshit. We're being pursued by soldiers, and you take the time to go and suck Cue off in the woods?"

"Listen, what would even be the point of life if you didn't stop and make time for blowjobs?" Loth asked. "Besides, how d'you know I sucked him off?"

"Ears like a bat!" Calarian called.

"If I *do* know something," Loth said, lowering his voice, "I'd rather not discuss it in front of Scott."

Ada narrowed her eyes as she considered that, and then nodded. "That's fair. I wouldn't tell him the day of the week because he'd still find some way to fuck it up."

"Listen," Loth said, lowering his voice even further, "have you considered trying to find out who his contact is in Callier, and, you know." He drew his finger across his throat.

"Considered?" Ada asked. She tugged at her beard. "I've dug his fucking grave in my dreams, but Calarian keeps reminding me that we might need a meat shield at some point."

Loth hummed. "That is a good point."

"Can you guys maybe not plot murder in front of me?" Quinn whined. "I'm trying to enjoy the afterglow here."

"Murder gives a good afterglow," Ada said.

Quinn groaned. "Stop, please."

"Yes, let the boy get used to sex before we introduce him to anything else," Loth said. Quinn elbowed him in the ribs.

"What do you need to know, Cue?" Calarian called back. "Because I'm an expert!"

Quinn covered his face. "Make it stop!"

Loth ignored him and called out, "Tell us about the dirty alchemist!" At Quinn's outraged expression, he said, "What? Enquiring minds want to know!"

Calarian slowed his horse and waited until they drew level. Then he spent the next half hour explaining, in great detail, exactly what went where, and what made the alchemist so dirty.

When he rode on ahead, Quinn stared after him for a moment, mouth hanging open. "Wow," he said, and then grinned mischievously. "I think we might need to try it."

THEY RODE UNTIL DAWN, and then, just as the light was beginning to gently snuff out the starlight, they turned the horses off the road and followed a path into the trees. The trees were sparse here, which worried Loth a little, but on the other side of them they found some fields fenced in with hedgerows. Dave barrelled right through one, leaving a space big enough to draw the horses in after him, and so they set up a camp of sorts behind the tall hedgerow, and out of sight of the road.

They were sharing the field with an unhappy looking cow and a couple of hairy goats. Whatever the field was usually used for—and the furrows in the ground suggested it had been ploughed at some point—it appeared it was fallow for now.

"Who wants some milk?" Dave asked, setting out after the cow with a cup in his hand and a determined gleam in his eye.

It was... *nice*. Loth lay on the grass with Quinn and watched him sleep. Sunlight dappled his pale face and illuminated the faintest hint of freckles across the bridge of his nose. Loth hadn't noticed them before now. Angel kisses. Loth plucked a dandelion from the grass and tucked it into Quinn's hair. Quinn's nose wrinkled, but he didn't wake.

Loth's stomach rumbled, and he thought regretfully of all

those pickled onions and herring back at the manor house. Not his first choice for a hearty breakfast, but better than literally nothing.

Calarian wandered along and suddenly stooped to pluck the dandelion from Quinn's hair.

"Hey!" Loth complained.

"I'm making dandelion soup, but if you'd rather go hungry because you're decorating your boy here, that's your choice."

"We could eat a goat," Ada suggested.

"Oh, yes, a goat!" Calarian exclaimed. "Let's not only impoverish some poor peasant farmer already oppressed by the state, but let's also kill and slaughter a breathing, feeling animal, Ada! Let's do that!"

He stalked away.

"I don't think we're having goat," Loth murmured.

Ada grumbled into her beard.

"We could eat these potatoes," Dave said, walking over and dragging the remains of a long, straggly plant behind him.

"That's not a potato, Dave," Loth sighed.

Dave held the plant up, displaying the whitish round objects hanging from its roots. "Yes, it is. Potatoes hide inna dirt, they do. My mum showed me how to find 'em. Fallow fields always have leavings."

"As a prince I could hardly be expected to know that, but well done, Dave!" Loth cheered up at the thought of freshly cooked potatoes. They weren't very exciting, but what they were, was filling, and for now, in the absence of goat, he'd take it.

Quinn squirmed in his sleep and Loth glanced down fondly. He *was* fond of Quinn, as strange as that was for him. He looked up to find Ada watching him with narrowed eyes.

"What?"

Ada shrugged. "You don't see many noblemen take such tender care of their servants, is all, Your Grace."

"Well, being in a cell for the last four years has changed my perspective, somewhat. I've learned to think more about the little people."

Ada grinned. "Five."

"Excuse me?"

"You've been in a cell for *five* years."

"Of course," Loth said, refusing to flinch under her knowing look. "Five years."

"We'll talk later, you said." Ada reached out and punched him on the shoulder and then climbed to her feet. "I'm going to look for more potatoes."

"Great idea," Loth said. He figured he should help or something, but he couldn't quite bring himself to get up. It was just too nice lying in the sun with Quinn. So he closed his eyes and fell asleep instead.

CHAPTER TWELVE

L oth was woken by Scott prodding at him. Having slept exactly long enough to feel like shit, he blinked blearily and scowled before hauling himself into a sitting position.

"What?" he snapped.

Scott had woken him at the very best part of a dream, one involving dirty alchemists and Quinn and a feather mattress. Now he'd never know how it ended.

Not until they got somewhere with a mattress, anyway.

"Breakfast, Your Grace," Scott held out a plate, and the aroma of baked potato soothed Loth's ire. Quinn was already awake, his own plate in front of him and a face full of potato, and if Scott hadn't woken him, Loth suspected the obscene noises Quinn was making as he ate would have.

Loth leaned over, gave Quinn a gentle shove, and nodded at his plate. "Should I be jealous?"

Quinn stopped eating just long enough to poke his tongue out and then went back to his meagre feast.

"That's no way to act around a prince!" Scott hissed, looking outraged. "You can't just poke things at him!"

Loth bit back a laugh before saying, "Actually Cue, you can poke whatever you want at me. Or in me. It's a two-way street, you know."

Quinn's eyes widened and he choked on his potato, blushing beet red—and that, Loth decided, was worth waking for after all. Quinn kept shooting him sideways glances as if he was trying to figure out if Loth was serious, so once Scott had made himself scarce, Loth said quietly, "I mean it, you know. If you ever want to try." He didn't need to elaborate.

Quinn ducked his head, cheeks burning, then swallowed convulsively and nodded, as if he was afraid to speak. Or maybe, Loth decided, it was just that he still had a mouth full of potato.

Once they'd eaten they spread their bedroll, tugging it into the shade to avoid the glare of the sunlight, and prepared to sleep the day away. The rest of the group did the same, all bar Calarian. "I'll take first watch," he said, "and then Scott can take over."

"Why me?" Scott whined, rubbing the heel of his hand over his eyes like a cranky toddler. "I'm tired!"

"Because you're our glorious leader, remember?" Calarian told him drily, and Scott had no reply to that.

Loth settled in beside Quinn and pulled him close. Quinn wiggled his arse with a hum, and Loth stiffened at the unexpected contact before murmuring in his ear, "Careful, sweetheart. I wouldn't start anything unless you want an audience."

"So? Who's watching?" Quinn countered. Loth wondered when his cranky little grub had gotten so bold, before he remembered—oh, right. It was since he started fucking him.

"Well, a cow and two goats, for a start. Plus, ears like a bat," he said with a soft laugh.

As if on cue, Calarian called, "Don't mind me!"

Quinn wasn't serious though, Loth knew—they both needed sleep more than anything else. With that in mind he threw an arm around his waist, and muttered, "Go to sleep."

They did.

Loth wasn't sure how long they slept for, except that he was tired and aching when he finally crawled to his feet. He really was too old to be sleeping on the ground. Quinn, stretching like a cat, didn't appear to have the same problem.

It was dusk. Dave was guarding the gap in the hedgerow, and Pie was sitting on his head. When Pie saw that Quinn was awake though, he chirped and buzzed over toward him like an oversized bumblebee. Dave lumbered after him.

"He likes you." He beamed at Quinn, his tooth-tusks gleaming in the late, golden light of day.

"I like him too." Quinn held Pie in one hand and stroked his finger down his spine. Pie arched and fluttered his wings appreciatively. "I've never seen a dragon before Pie."

"They're very rare," Dave said. "S'why the eggs cost so much."

"You know, they say that dragons are powerful and wise and good," Quinn said. "They say that dragons detest tyranny and evil, and destroy them wherever they find them."

Pie shuddered happily under his touch, and Loth knew how he felt.

"I think Pie is definitely powerful and wise and good," Quinn said, smiling down at the fingerdragon. "But I can't imagine him razing cities with fire, can you?"

"He singed a wasp once," Dave said proudly.

"Good job, Pie!" Quinn scratched the dragon under the chin.

"It might have been an accident," Dave admitted.

"I'm sure it wasn't." Quinn's smile grew as Pie puffed, and a couple of sparks tumbled out of his mouth and fizzled into nothing on Quinn's palm. "You're a big, scary dragon, aren't you, Pie?"

Alright, so there was no way hearing Quinn give a pep talk to a baby dragon should have given Loth an erection, and yet here he was, his dick straining in his breeches just because Quinn was so fucking adorable. Loth turned away and pretended to stretch while he readjusted himself. When he turned back again, Pie was trying to climb headfirst down Quinn's shirt, and Loth could respect that. He might have tried it himself if he'd thought he'd fit.

Ada stomped over towards them. "So, we should be in Callier in what, about three days?"

Loth glanced at Quinn, and Quinn nodded.

"Three days is about right, yes," Loth said.

"Good." Ada frowned. "Because as soon as I get paid, I want nothing more to do with any of you, to be honest. Something stinks about this whole thing."

"Is it Scott?" Dave asked. "Because I did throw him in the swamp after he was covered in shit that time."

"I meant metaphorically," Ada said, her expression softening.

"I didn't throw him in that," Dave said. "If he stinks like that, he must have fallen in a pool of it on his own."

Loth left Ada to attempt to try to explain that one and walked over to where Calarian was standing with the horses. Quinn followed him.

"Did anything happen today on your watch?" Loth asked.

"Nope." Calarian hoisted his saddle onto his horse. "I saw two farmers with carts, and one dog with three legs. And none of them saw me. This might be the main road once we get closer to Callier, but this far out? There's nobody."

"Have you been to Callier before?" Quinn asked suddenly. "Any of you?"

Calarian shook his head. "I haven't. Scott's never left Delacourt until now, and Ada hates dealing with humans, so I can't imagine she's been this far south before. Dave didn't even know what a paved road was—he wanted to know how the stones knew to line up like that—so I'm thinking he's never seen an actual city either." He levelled a stare at Quinn. "Why are you asking?"

"Just curious," Quinn said. "The benefactor must have offered you a lot of money, right? Ada wouldn't agree to it unless it was a lot, and Dave's dragon eggs aren't cheap. I guess I'm just wondering why someone with so much money would throw it on a crazy plan to rescue the prince instead of, you know, raising an army against Doom. Or at least hiring an assassin."

"You can't just kill a king," Calarian said.

Quinn scowled. "He's *not* a king."

"Whatever. My point is, you can't just kill the guy in charge without someone to replace him," Calarian said. "Because humans are stupid and like to be subjugated. They get confused when there's no figurehead to bow to." He nodded at Loth. "That's where you come in. Bring you back to the city, knock Doom off his perch, put you back on the throne, and they're happy. Idiots," he added under his breath.

"Or he might kill me with an audience, or have me killed at least, and claim the throne," Loth pointed out.

Calarian thought for a moment. "Oh, yeah. That'd work too. Sneaky! You would make an excellent House Master." And then, at Loth's blank look: "The person who runs the game in Houses and Humans. Talk about a plot twist!"

"My life is not a plot twist!"

"How would he kill you though?" Calarian mused, before he froze. "Wait—bandits!"

"Yes, that would be one way, but you're taking far too much leisure in planning my death," Loth grumbled, right before Calarian shoved him into the hedge.

"No—shhh—listen. Bandits! *I can hear bandits.*"

"How can you even tell that?" Loth hissed.

"I can hear the weaponry clanking. Nobody wearing that much metal is up to any good," Calarian whispered. "And they're leaving the road and coming this way!"

There was a dull thud and a rustle of leaves as Quinn threw his body into the hedge next to him. Loth pulled him close instinctively as Calarian peered out of their hiding spot. Dave and Ada must have sensed something was up because they were craning their necks this way and that, trying to see what was going on. Scott was, of course, oblivious, right until Ada kicked him in the shins, and by then it was too late.

The bandits had spilled through the gap in the hedgerow and spotted them. There were seven of them, all huge and leather-clad and yes, adorned with a variety of swords and knives and other things Loth couldn't name, but definitely didn't like the look of. They did, as Calarian had said, clank slightly with every step. Their leader strode up to Scott and hauled him up with one giant hand in his collar so his feet were several inches off the ground.

"Where's the prince?" he demanded.

"In the hedge!" Scott squeaked, pointing.

Weaselly little shit.

Footsteps behind him alerted Loth to the fact that Calarian was heading towards the danger, his long stride covering the ground between him and the bandits startlingly fast, and then he paused and an arrow flew through the air, striking one of the bandits in the thigh. He howled and dropped to one knee.

"Fucking missed," Calarian muttered, and stopped just long enough to nock another arrow and take a second shot. This one didn't miss, and the man collapsed to the ground, gurgling and clutching at the shaft protruding from his throat.

"The prince!" the leader shouted and shook Scott violently. "We want the prince!"

"It's the redhead!" Scott sobbed out, and oh, Loth was going to kick him right in his lopsided balls if they managed to survive this.

The bandit leader dropped Scott in a heap, apparently satis-fied, and then kicked him for good measure. He turned to his men. "Well? Capture the redhead!" he yelled. "Kill the rest!"

"There are two of them!" one bandit, who had an eyepatch, called out. "Two redheads!"

"Then take them both!"

The one-eyed man darted forward and grabbed Quinn, twisting an arm up his back and dragging him away, away from Loth, and much to his surprise, Loth found himself off and running. Except, instead of heading away from the danger, which had been his lifelong default, Loth was running *towards* the bandits, and the overriding thought in his head was *save Quinn.* Was this what bravery felt like, he wondered, or stupidity? He hadn't had much experience with either.

The rest of the bandits, who'd been shuffling their feet and staring at the body of their comrade, seemed to pull themselves together and ran forward in a roaring, thundering wall of leather armour and weaponry, swords drawn and at the ready. There were six of them, not counting the man Calarian had already killed, and they were all armed to the teeth. Loth wished *he* had a sword.

Wait. He did—sort of. He clasped at the handle tucked into his belt.

Dave opened his mouth and bellowed, and Loth saw the two men heading for him falter. He didn't have time to see how it played out over there though—he was too busy grabbing his meat cleaver and diving into the fray.

Nobody had ever told him that battles were so... *messy.* They weren't choreographed from afar, like sweeping dances. There was no single battle occurring at all where bandits met rescuers: just a series of scrappy individual fights. Loth caught a knee in the stomach and swallowed a mouthful of grass and dirt, before catching his assailant in the side of the neck with the meat cleaver. It wasn't the death blow he'd intended—the blade glanced off the guy's collarbone instead of splitting flesh—but it must have stung like fuck because the guy screamed and flailed back. Loth swung the cleaver again, and this time there was a wet sound and the blade was dripping and bloody when he yanked it back. His stomach lurched, but he ignored it, intent on finding Quinn. He'd done enough damage for his attacker to let go of him, and he had the faint reassurance that at least they wanted him alive.

That gave him an edge, he realised. It meant he could try and rescue Quinn at least, because someone was trying to hurt him, and the very thought of it made Loth burn with rage.

Loth had always thought the expression *seeing red* was just a metaphor, but his ears were filled with the sound of his blood pumping, and he was unaware of anything except that *they were threatening Quinn*. It was enough to make him scramble to his feet, cleaver held over his head as he surged forward, screaming at the top of his lungs. He couldn't have told you what he was aiming for, he just slashed wildly, hitting nothing. "Quinn!" he shouted, "Save him—"

He was cut off when an arm grabbed him around the waist, lifted him, and slammed him into the ground, driving all the breath from his body.

It was Ada. She held him in place, then sat on him for good measure. "Sit down, you bloody idiot, before you hurt yourself."

"But—Quinn—bandits—"

"Dealt with."

Loth blinked and lifted his head and tried to make sense of the scene in front of him. The bandits were gone, all bar one, their leader, and Dave was holding him aloft while Calarian kept an arrow trained on him.

The rest of them were scattered around the ground, dead or unconscious. "What happened?"

Ada rolled her eyes. "I took one out because I'm a dirty fighter, Calarian shot one of them while you were waving your little knife and screaming like an idiot, and then..." The look she gave him was pure evil. "One of them threatened Pie. And well, Dave." She grinned and shrugged.

"Dave?" Loth croaked out.

A hand stroked Loth's arm and he heard a voice he wasn't expecting. "He didn't take his dragon being threatened well.

Remember we wanted to find out how far Dave could throw Scott?"

Loth turned his head to find Quinn sitting in the dirt next to him, dust and blood smearing his face. He was grinning madly, chest heaving.

"Turns out it's about fifteen feet," Quinn said, "when you clean up a couple of bandits on the way. Once he'd knocked them over, he hit them on the head to make sure they stayed down."

"You're okay," Loth breathed, and he'd never been so relieved in his life.

"I'm okay," Quinn confirmed. He held up the kitchen knife he'd armed himself with. It was smeared with blood, too. "Turns out I have a vicious streak and surprisingly good aim."

"But..." Loth's head was still spinning. "But I was going to be a hero."

"We already have one of them." Quinn said. "Nobody likes him, and Dave used him as a shot put."

And then Quinn flopped down on top of Loth, still grinning like a loon, and smeared their mouths together in possibly the worst kiss Loth had ever experienced. He didn't even care when their teeth clashed though, because Quinn was safe and alive, and smiling at him. A laugh bubbled up inside him, and Loth let it out, and then they were both laughing and kissing and kissing and laughing, and Loth had never felt so alive.

"When you guys are done doing the horizontal galley rower, can I shoot this bandit, or what?" Calarian asked.

Quinn wrinkled his nose. "The *what?*"

"I'm starting to think he's making these things up on the spot," Loth murmured, but he gently pushed Quinn off him, and sat up. "Don't kill him yet. I want to know who sent him."

"We all want to know," said Ada. "But more than that," she lowered her voice and glanced over to the heap that was Scott, checking he was still unconscious, "I want to know when you—"

She prodded Quinn. "—had another name change? Who's Quinn? What aren't you telling us, *Prince?*" She glared at Loth.

Loth craned his head. "Scott's still unconscious, right? Or dead?"

"Be nice," Quinn said. Loth looked at him, surprised, and Quinn added, "He was actually useful for once."

"As a projectile." Loth gestured around them. "We could have used the cow for that!"

Dave, still dangling the bandit leader from his grip, looked horrified. "I would *never!*"

"Fine," Loth said. He climbed to his feet and held his hand down to help Quinn up. "But this is for your ears only. Not Scott's, and..." He waved at the bandit. "Not his either."

Dave clocked the bandit on the head and dumped him on the ground. "He's sleeping!"

Well, that was one way of putting it.

Loth cleared his throat. "Yes, Cue is now Quinn. Which is short for Tarquin."

"That's your name too," Dave said.

"No, it's just his name," Loth said. He gestured to Quinn. "He's the prince. I am not the prince."

His exciting revelation didn't get the reaction he'd anticipated. In fact, both Ada and Calarian looked slightly bored.

Ada grunted. "Figures."

Calarian shrugged. "Yeah, I heard you talking about it the other night."

"So there... *aren't* two of you," Dave said, his forehead creased in thought as the wheels in his brain turned very slowly. "If he's the prince, and you're not the prince, then who am I?"

"You're still Dave, Dave," Quinn said gently.

Dave gave a relieved smile. "Oh, that's good."

"And the thing is," Quinn said, stepping forward, "we know someone hired Scott to get me out of that dungeon, but we don't know who it was. Maybe there are still noblemen in Callier who are loyal to the crown, and who want me to take the throne now I'm of age, but—"

"Death to all kings!" Calarian exclaimed.

"No," Quinn said firmly. He pinched the bridge of his nose. "Can we just leave the revolution aside for now—you're not even *from* this kingdom anyway, Calarian—and worry about the fact that this whole thing could be a trap set by Lord Doom? Because even Ser Greylord, the Shire Reeve in Delacourt, said that he suspected Doom could be responsible. This escape could be nothing more than a chance to get me killed in an apparently random manner, leaving Doom to take the throne in my place."

"Well, I don't care about any of that," Ada said. "My job ends when we get to Callier and I get paid."

Calarian shrugged. "All kings are tyrants. I'm just here for the quest."

Dave puffed his chest out. "You're my friend, Grub-Cue-Quinn. I'll smash Lord Doom for you."

A gentle smile tugged at Quinn's mouth. "Thanks, Dave. I appreciate that."

On the ground at Dave's feet, the bandit leader groaned and stirred.

Loth strode forward. "Well then, let's see if we can get some answers."

CHAPTER THIRTEEN

The bandit leader was a man of middle years. He had stubble that was almost a beard, a scar that bisected his cheek, and a very angry scowl as he finally woke up and discovered he was tied to a tree. He struggled, tugging at the ropes and kicking his legs out, but Calarian, who had admitted quietly that he'd once been a Junior Wood Scout, had tied the ropes securely.

"Aw," Ada had said. "Did you wear a little hat with a feather in it and everything?"

Calarian hadn't answered, but he'd blushed bright pink.

Not that there was any hint of the little apple-cheeked Junior Wood Scout in him now. Now, Calarian stood over the bandit, pointing his bow at the centre of the man's chest. There was an arrow nocked and ready to loose. Calarian's stare was icy.

Quinn's was just as cold and proud, and how had Loth ever doubted he was a prince? He had no doubt at all that Quinn could order the death of a man with just the nod of his head, and watch impassively while it happened, and was it wrong that Loth was insanely turned on by that?

No, of course it wasn't wrong. It felt too good to be wrong.

Loth struggled to drag his mind out of the gutter—well, bedroom—and Quinn asked the man, "Who sent you?"

The bandit scowled, and for a moment Loth wondered if the man would keep his silence, but then he eyed Dave, the arrow, and Ada's clenched fists, and said, "I don't know."

"You must know," Ada insisted. She thumped him, Loth suspected, just on principle.

The man groaned and shook his head. "I don't, I swear. We got given a bag of coin and told there was a party on the road with an orc, a dwarf, a pointy-eared bastard, and a human, and that they had the prince. We were meant to grab him, take him the next town over, then kill him where they'd be sure to find his body. Nobody mentioned two princes." He glared at Loth and Quinn like they'd personally offended him.

"Pointy-eared bastard?" Calarian hissed. "I'm an *elf!"*

The man gave a sort of shrug in his ropes. "It's all the same to me. We were just meant to kill you all and grab the prince. They said it would be money for jam, that the leader was an idiot and the rest of you were hopeless."

"I like jam," Dave said. "And mustard."

"Yes, well. Obviously we're not hopeless," Loth said, "although Scott *is* an idiot." He thought for a moment. "Who delivered the coin?"

The man shrugged again. "Dunno. Some guy dressed in black." Calarian nudged him with the tip of the arrow and the man stiffened. "I really don't!" he insisted. "Please, you've got to let me go! I've got a little girl, she's sick! I'm only doing this for the money!"

Loth and Quinn exchanged a look, and Loth knew Quinn was thinking the same thing he was. *Every single beggar I've met in every single town has either got a grandparent at death's door, or some other sob story about a sick puppy to make you feel sorry for them. It's the oldest trick in the book.*

Calarian made an impatient noise. "He doesn't know

anything. Can I shoot him?"

Loth opened his mouth to answer but was interrupted by the clatter of hooves. A man on horseback swept into the field.

"I'll take care of him," said Ser Greylord.

Loth groaned. "You again?" He glared at Calarian. "And no warning from you?"

The elf shrugged.

"The speed you're going, I was bound to catch up," Ser Greylord said. "What are you doing, *walking*? Picking the flowers along the way?" He swung a leg over his saddle and dismounted, walking over and prodding the tied bandit with his foot. "I'll take him and his friends to the nearest town, lock them up for highway robbery."

Well. That would certainly be handy.

"What will you tell Doom about your search, though?" Loth asked. "Aren't you meant to be pursuing the escaped prince?"

"Didn't see another soul," Greylord said, expressionless. "The escapees must have gone back into the Swamp of Death. There's a monster, I hear."

"Benji!" Dave said happily, before looking more closely at Ser Greylord and turning to Loth with a frown. "Do we know him? Or should I hit him?"

"No, Dave," Quinn said gently. "He's on our side."

Greylord gave them a smile—a small, brittle thing—and Loth realised that Greylord wore an expression he'd seen before, although it normally graced the faces of peasants and whores in the jails he'd stayed in. It was the look of someone who had absolutely nothing left to lose.

"Yes," Loth said. "I believe he is."

Ada narrowed her eyes and squinted suspiciously. "He's in crown livery. How come he's alone?"

"I left the rest of my men searching a town five miles up the road. I actually had to go *backwards* to catch you," he said, and tipped his hat to Ada. "Pleased to meet you, ma'am."

Loth wondered how he knew, or if it was a lucky guess, but either way, Ada's expression softened slightly, and she gave him a nod in return.

"This bandit gentleman was just telling us how he was paid to assassinate a redheaded prince travelling to Callier," Loth said.

Pie was buzzing excitedly around the bandit leader's head, chirping happily when the man swore at him and tried to shake him off every time he landed in his beard. "Get it away from me, it's probably poisonous!"

"Pie's not poisonous," Dave insisted with a frown and knocked the man out—perhaps for calling Pie an *it*, but possibly because he just liked hitting people.

Ser Greylord stared down at the unconscious bandit leader and then moved away from the tree. He beckoned Loth and Quinn to follow him.

"So, it's the truth then," Ser Greylord said with a sigh. "It wasn't men loyal to the previous king who paid for the escape. Not if the bandits were paid too."

"It seems that way," Quinn said, and lifted his chin.

"Hmm." Ser Greylord squinted in the fading light. He stepped closer to Loth and Quinn and lowered his voice, checking that the bandit leader was still unconscious before he spoke. "Do you remember how we'd play chess together, Your Grace?"

Quinn nodded.

"Terrible players, both of us," Ser Greylord said. "Which is a shame, really, because a little bit of strategic thinking would be useful right now. I think you should come back to Delacourt with me. If you go to Callier, you're clearly walking into a trap. As for me, it's only a matter of time until Doom deals with my treachery, even if he set it up to begin with. But we could buy you passage on a ship, and you could travel to another kingdom. There's no need to meet your death in Callier."

Quinn stared past him, nodding slightly to himself.

Ada marched up to them.

"Excuse you, but we're taking the prince to Callier," she said firmly.

"Ah, dwarves don't renege on contracts, of course," Ser Greylord said. "An admirable trait. Admirable. Unfortunately, I may have to kill you for it."

Quinn held up his hand. "There will be no killing," he said, and then looked around at the dead bandits lying on the bloody field. "Well, no more killing. Well, no more killing *yet*." He sighed. "There will be no killing of anyone I *like*, clear?"

Ser Greylord nodded, but he didn't look convinced.

"I'm going to Callier," Quinn said, and stared at them all in turn. His gaze fell on Loth last, and it was steely. "I'm going to Callier, and I'm going to take my throne back, or at least end it one way or another."

THE ROAD at night was pleasant, Loth decided, if one ignored the dark trees swaying in the breeze and the ominous hooting of owls from somewhere in the distance. Also, foxes screamed. That was a thing. A very inconsiderate thing in Loth's opinion, that really added to the atmosphere of this entire venture.

Loth turned his thoughts inward to avoid thinking about every ghost story he had ever heard as a child. He found himself thinking about riding to his inevitable death instead, which wasn't really any more comforting, but Quinn was a warm weight at his back, and that seemed to help.

Somewhere, a few horses away, Scott groaned as he slowly regained consciousness.

"So, this whole revenge and birthright thing," Loth said as they rode at a leisurely pace down the road, Quinn's arms firmly around him from behind. "It's hot, don't get me wrong, but have you considered that it's also stupid?"

Quinn hummed in his ear.

"I don't trust Ser Greylord," Loth murmured. "He turned coat too quickly."

He felt Quinn's breath on his next. "He was constrained because his son is being held hostage. Which means he is being held hostage too, in a way."

"I don't trust *anyone*," Loth said. "It saves being caught by surprise at their moment of inevitable betrayal. Fine, I trust that he has a son. I trust that his hopelessness about his son's fate is what finally moved him to throw caution to the wind and try to help you. I even trust that he was going to take you back to Delacourt and put you on a ship to somewhere safe. But suddenly he's part of this? He's willing to ride into Callier and *die* for this? Now *that*, I don't trust."

"Have you never had nothing left to lose?" Quinn asked softly, and Loth figured that he wasn't talking about Ser Greylord anymore. "Sometimes, when there's been a sword dangling over your head for so long, you just reach a point where you're so sick of it that you just want to cut the string yourself, you know?"

"Is that what you think is happening here?"

"I think..." Quinn hummed again. "I think I've spent the last five years of my life locked up in Delacourt. I think that I'd very much like to look my uncle in the eye and remind him whose son I am. I want to hear him admit he killed my father and my mother. His own *sister*, Loth."

"And what good will it do you to hear him admit it?"

Quinn tensed. "I want him to know how much I hate him. And then I want him to *die*."

Quinn's dreams of revenge didn't feel so hot now, not that Loth knew exactly how they'd play out.

"You don't have an army," Loth pointed out. "You have Ser Greylord, who has nicely agreed to accompany us on what he absolutely believes is a suicide mission. You have Ada, who fully intends to hand you over to the benefactor, who we're fairly certain is Lord Doom, who wants you dead. You have Calarian, who seems to like you enough personally, but, politically, would slit your throat and use your blood to paint banners for the revolution. You have Scott, who doesn't know what's going on even when he's not concussed, and you have Dave. And Dave is about the only one here who would actually have your back in a fight."

"And you," Quinn said softly. "I think you proved that already."

"That was an aberration," Loth said, pushing down the warmth that rose up in him at Quinn's praise. He sat up a little straighter in the saddle nonetheless. "Please don't ever count on that. I'm sure my natural cowardice will come back in full force any moment now. And Quinn, even if it didn't, I'm a pickpocket with a meat cleaver. Lord Doom has actual trained soldiers."

"Technically, you're a scribe. And he has *my* actual trained soldiers," Quinn said. "They swore an oath to the crown. That's me."

Loth turned that over in his brain for a moment. "You'd risk your life on the fact that they'd do the right thing when it counts? That's a hell of a gamble."

He took his hand from the reins and pressed it to his abdomen, where Quinn's cold fingers were now resting. He squeezed Quinn's fingers, the small gesture saying more, he hoped, than his words. Because at the heart of this whole thing wasn't a figurehead, or a prince, or a crown. At heart there was a young man made of flesh and blood, who Loth hoped to know for longer than a few more days. It made him restless, and uneasy, and angry, and a hundred other different emotions he couldn't prise apart, let alone name.

Loth didn't give a fuck about the kingdom, but he thought he might just give one about Quinn.

Quinn pressed a kiss to the nape of Loth's neck. "I know," he said quietly.

And then he sank into silence, and nothing Loth said could draw him out of it again.

They clopped down the dark road, with the haunting calls of the owls echoing behind them.

An hour or so after their fight with the bandits, they stopped in the town where Ser Greylord had left his men hunting rumours of redheaded princes. They handed the bandit leader and his survivors over to the local constabulary, which in this small town seemed to consist of a man with one leg and a woman with a pitchfork. Then they waited anxiously while Ser Greylord rounded up his soldiers and spoke to them. Well, Loth was anxious. Quinn seemed strangely unaffected, though he did grip his kitchen knife tightly until Ser Greylord announced that his soldiers were now coming with them. It meant they were safe from bandit attacks, Loth supposed, but not that they were safe from, well, soldiers. Loth didn't trust them as far as Dave could throw them, and Ser Greylord must have felt the same, because he was careful to address Loth as the prince, and not Quinn.

It was a very uneasy fellowship indeed that headed to Callier. The four soldiers took up the lead, with Ser Greylord riding behind them. He wouldn't slow them down too much if they had a moment of independent thought and decided to turn on "Prince" Loth, but Loth appreciated the sentiment. He was thankful that none of the soldiers appeared to be interested enough to betray them. Then again, he supposed that in their line of work, a total lack of curiosity when it came to questioning their orders was a good thing. Soldiers weren't supposed to be creative thinkers, and Loth didn't see any signs that these four were eager to break the stereotype. These four, in various degrees, seemed to be mostly entertained by Pie, intimidated by Dave and Ada, and quietly fascinated by Calarian, who really had no business being that attractive.

Scott had to stop and vomit every few miles because he was

convinced he was going to be arrested every time Ser Greylord glanced at him. Calarian kept calling the soldiers bootlickers just to see if any of them would fight him. Only Ada and Dave didn't really seem to care about their new companions.

Loth was worried. He was worried that he was going to die, but, oddly; he was more concerned that Quinn was going to die. Mostly, he thought, because if he died it would be tragic and unavoidable, but if Quinn died, it would just be stupid. Ser Greylord had offered him an escape on a ship to an entirely new kingdom, so why the hell was he so keen to go and get himself killed in Callier? Was revenge that important? Did he not want to live? Had nothing that had occurred between them convinced him that there were better options than certain death?

Ah. There it was. The fact that Quinn was lining up to be a martyr hurt Loth's pride. He'd foolishly thought that maybe he'd showed Quinn a couple of things worth living for—mind-blowing sex being the most obvious—and somehow Quinn hadn't yet turned around and embraced him and said, dewy-eyed, *"Oh, Loth, let's just forget all this prince nonsense and run away together, you and I, and get married and spend the rest of our lives fucking like rabbits, because your dick is magnificent, and I want to sit on it forever."* Quinn was choosing certain death over Loth's dick. Clearly, he was irrational. Maybe he was even unwell. He'd probably eaten the wrong sort of mushrooms or something because anyone in their right mind would choose Loth and his dick. Mushroom poisoning and the subsequent hallucinations were the only explanation.

Of course, that didn't explain why *Loth* was still on the road to Callier. By rights, he should have handed Quinn's care over to Ser Greylord and made himself scarce, but somehow he couldn't bring himself to do it.

He told himself that it was because Scott still thought he was the prince, and it would be just his luck that the untrustworthy little bastard would track him down and ruin his plans of a quiet life as a gigolo. Yes. It was Scott's fault—which reminded him.

"Scott!" he called out. "A word?"

He stopped his horse, dismounted, and walked to the side of the road, and Scott scurried over to meet him there, still doing that weird bob-walk-wobble thing that made him look like a drunken seagull on stilts. Loth beckoned Scott closer and leaned in like he was about to impart great wisdom.

"What is it, Your Grace?" Scott asked, eyes wide with excitement.

Loth punched him right in the balls, holding nothing back. Scott dropped to the ground like a sack of shit, a strangled noise coming from him as he clutched at his squashed nuts.

Loth shook his fist out and flashed a grin at a slack-jawed Quinn. Yes. That had felt just as good as he'd imagined.

At Quinn's stunned expression, Loth said, "I told myself I'd do that if we survived the bandits, and I'm trying to be a better person and keep my promises."

"He certainly had it coming," Quinn said, and for the first time in what felt like days he gave a smile.

"He seems to have missed the basic premise of being a hero—the part where you protect others instead of ratting them out," Calarian observed. "Can I punch him as well?"

"He didn't try to throw *you* to the wolves," Loth said.

"No, but he's a pain in the arse and I didn't get to shoot the bandit leader, so I should at least be allowed to give him a boot to the meat and two veg."

Loth shrugged. "I mean, I see your point."

He hopped back on his horse behind Quinn and rode off leaving Scott laying in the dirt groaning, and he didn't need ears like a bat to hear the sound of a good, solid kick followed by a yelp, a groan, and a kind of crunching noise as Scott tumbled face-forward into a carpet of leaves.

It was an incredibly satisfying sound.

CHAPTER FOURTEEN

I t took three days to reach Callier.

They still travelled at night, the road growing busier and the villages more tightly packed together as they drew nearer the city. And then, one night, and one bend in the road, and there it was: the city wall rising up in the distance, with the scattering of towers and spires rising up behind it. It shone even in the darkness. Tiny points of light from thousands of different windows, different fires and different lanterns, different candles, all coming together in a glittering, glowing patchwork that mimicked the field of stars blazing above it.

They stopped and took it in for a moment, and Loth felt Quinn's hand sliding into his.

Ser Greylord cleared his throat. "I need to go to the castle. I'm expecting news, and I have to report to Lord Doom. If I don't go straight away when I've been seen entering the city, it'll look suspicious. So my men will go to the barracks, and I'll be inside the castle. There's a door around the back, near the laundry. I'll leave it unlocked, and it's generally unguarded."

Loth nodded—every castle had a door like it, in practically the same place—a door where a pickpocket or a noble's bedwarmer could easily slip in and out unnoticed, their purse a little heavier than before.

"And where are *we* going?" Scott asked. "What's happening?" It was the first time he'd spoken in hours, cowed into submission by the presence of the royal guard.

"I know somewhere," Loth said. He was fairly certain they'd be welcome—after all, what was that saying? *Home is where the stomach is.* Or was it the heart? Something along those lines, anyway. It didn't matter. The point was, they'd be able to get a good meal there, at least. The others looked at him expectantly, so he flicked his reins and led them forward, through the gates of Callier. As they rode he murmured to Quinn, "Listen, when we get there you have to pretend to be me, okay?"

"Pretend to be you how, exactly? Be an arsehole and accuse people of horse buggery? Or steal everything in sight and shag anything not nailed down?" Quinn asked, and Loth was fairly sure he was joking to hide his nerves.

He played along. "I'll have you know you just listed my best qualities!"

"What, lechery and theft?"

"I prefer to think of it as mergers and acquisitions." That earned him a stifled laugh against his shoulder. "Just follow my lead, okay?" he said, trusting Quinn to do just that. He'd proven over and over on the trip that there was more to him than just the prickly little urchin that Loth had first met in a pile of straw. Really, there always had been—it had just taken Loth a while to see it.

They turned through city streets familiar to Loth. He knew his way around Callier with his eyes closed. A familiar sense of *home* stole over him as the horses' hooves clopped against the worn-down cobbles and echoed in the night. Loth had grown up in these streets and taken his first wobbly steps in them. Later, he'd used his knowledge of the narrow, twisting back alleys to evade pursuit by creditors and angry spouses on more than one occasion, people who were bigger than him that he'd shot his mouth off to all the same, because he'd always been a slow learner in that regard. The city even smelled exactly as Loth remembered: a little grimy, a little bit like seawater and, in this neighbourhood at least, overwhelmingly like hops and yeast.

"Lead the way, Your Grace," Ada prompted, and Loth realised he'd stopped his horse at the turn into the cobbled street where his parents lived.

He turned and surveyed his rescuers and prayed to whichever god would have him that his parents would take this in their stride like he hoped. Looking forward he rode down the hill towards the house at the bottom, the place he'd grown up: the house right beside his mother's brewery.

They rode into the courtyard in front of the house and dismounted, and Loth pulled Quinn close and murmured, "Follow my lead," before knocking on the door in the distinctive two-three-two rhythm that he always used.

There was the sound of voices and then the door flew open, and his mum was standing there, beaming. "Son!" she said, surging forward, arms wide.

Loth sidestepped neatly and gave a shove, sending Quinn flying into her arms. By the time either of them realised what was happening, they were already locked in a hug. Loth's father looked over his wife's shoulder, eyebrows raised. Loth gave a tiny shrug, and at that, his dad stepped forward and slapped a meaty palm on Quinn's shoulder. "So good to see you my boy!" he said loudly, and Loth breathed a tiny sigh of relief.

Quinn twisted his head to stare back at Loth, and the gaze he sent was half confusion, half utter panic, with a dash of something much more fragile underneath it all.

Loth cleared his throat. "May we come in? We're in dire need of somewhere to stay, and Quinn said his family would be willing to help."

His mother had by now registered that the body she was

embracing wasn't the one she was expecting. But that didn't stop her holding on tight, only raising her chin to ask, "And you are?" with a gleam in her eye that Loth knew meant she'd play along.

"Mum," Quinn said, his voice shaking only the slightest bit on the word, "we've rescued the prince. Can we come inside, and we'll explain?" He glanced around. "It's not exactly safe out here."

Mum's jaw dropped, but she rallied quickly. "Rescued the prince, hmm?" she asked. She pressed a kiss to the top of Quinn's head. "I had my money on minstrels, to be honest. Joined them, slighted them, stolen from them. It's always you and minstrels, isn't it, dear?"

"Um," Quinn said, the inflection in his voice making it sound like a question. "Not this time?"

"Well," Mum said. "I suppose that's what they call personal growth. Come inside then, all of you, and let me get a good look at you."

She dragged Quinn inside and Dad held the door open as everyone trooped in after them. Loth was last inside and got the full effect of Dad's raised eyebrow stare. He met Dad's gaze with a tilt of his chin that he hoped conveyed *trust me,* and it must have come close because Dad let out a sigh and closed the door before asking "So, which one of you is the prince, then?"

Loth cleared his throat, but before he could say anything Scott stepped forward. "I'm the one who bravely rescued him and led the party to freedom and victory. May I present your Graceness, Prince Tarquin of... um... anyway, the prince!" he said with a flourish and bowed down so deeply in front of Loth that his nose almost scraped the ground.

"Tarquin of *um,*" Dad said, his one cocked eyebrow almost vanishing into his thinning, grey hair.

Loth lifted his chin and attempted to look regal. He wasn't sure he pulled it off.

"Well, what an honour." Dad sounded about as honoured as if

he'd stepped in dog shit. "Did you hear that, love? It's Prince Tarquin of Um. Under *our* humble roof."

Mum was bustling Quinn toward the kitchen. "Well, make sure he wipes his feet, same as everyone else." She tutted at Quinn. "You've gotten so thin, son! And you're a mess." She reached into her apron pocket and pulled out a large handkerchief and Loth knew, just knew what was coming. He wasn't sure whether to laugh or cry when his mum spit on the hanky and rubbed at the dirt on the cheek of Tarquin, Crown Prince of Aguillon, rightful heir to the throne.

Quinn screwed up his face as she scrubbed.

"That's better, love," Mum cooed, and Loth recognised that look. His mum had decided to take Quinn under her wing. She'd always been weak for a lost cause—Loth supposed it was second nature, with him as a son.

He caught a glimpse of the look on Quinn's face as Mum tugged him further into the house—that same one where confusion battled with heartbreak. When was the last time Quinn had a mum to fuss over him? Loth might have been a grown man, but he'd still put up with all the spitty hankies in the world if they came with a hug from Mum. He didn't think he'd ever be old enough or grown enough *not* to need his mum. And Quinn... well, Quinn had been even younger than he was now when his mother had been stolen from him.

By the time Scott straightened up from his spectacular flourish, Mum had already decamped with Quinn, and Ada and Dave had followed. Loth stepped around Scott and headed after them. He found them in the kitchen.

The kitchen was actually Dad's domain. Mum spent most of her time at the brewery next door, but Dad worked mostly from home. The big table in the kitchen was covered in swathes of fabric, spools of thread, and pincushions that bristled like hedgehogs. The fire was still burning in the fireplace, despite the late hour. Mum had already got Quinn sitting on the stool closest to its warmth and was attempting to tug his tousled hair into place. Quinn stared up at her, his cheeks flushed and his eyes wide. Loth didn't blame him. Mum was a force of nature when there was mother henning to be done.

"Stay here and get warm, *son,* and I'll find you something to eat," she said with a kiss to the clean spot on his cheek, and Loth pushed down an irrational surge of jealousy. He wasn't sure if it was because Quinn was getting his mum's attention, or because Mum was kissing Quinn and Loth wanted to be the only person whose mouth was on him. Which was... yeah, that was weird, and exactly the reason that Loth didn't do feelings. They were way too messy and confusing.

Except apparently, he had one now, didn't he? A lone feeling, errant and unexpected and unasked for.

Fuck.

He pushed the thought away for later. For now, he had to sell himself as the prince, if only to stop Scott asking awkward questions. Or any questions. Or opening his mouth at all, really. It would probably be easier to just get Dave to knock him out again. However, Loth wasn't sure that even Scott's thick skull could take much more of that treatment, and his parents, as easy-going and understanding as they were, might not forgive him if they had to bury a body.

He cleared his throat. "It's very good of you to take us in like this," he said, as if he didn't know his parents were dyed in the wool anti-Doomers who hated the ruler with a passion, if only because of the exorbitant taxes on hops and silk. "I'll be sure to remember this once I retake the throne."

His father couldn't hold back a snort, but he covered it with a cough.

Mum put her hands on her hips and said, "Nobody will be retaking anything tonight. We'll get you fed, find somewhere for you all to sleep, and talk about it in the morning."

Loth knew that supposed prince or no, there'd be no arguing with her.

Dad cleared the swatches and sewing equipment from the table and shuffled the chairs around to make room for them all, making sure to seat Loth at the head with an exaggerated bow.

"My Liege," he said, and Loth could hear the smirk in his voice. His father was *so* going to milk this, he realised, and wondered why he was surprised. After all, he'd gotten all his worst traits from his parents. At least Loth didn't have to fake his royally pissed off expression.

Mum dragged Quinn off the stool and sat him at the table, as though he was a little lost lamb who needed shepherding even across the big, scary kitchen.

"Now then," she said as she rattled around in the pantry, "we've got bread and cheese and cold meat. Who's hungry?"

"Excuse me, Mrs Mum," Dave said. "Calarian is a vegetablarian."

Mum wasn't the least put off. She'd always liked a challenge.

It didn't take long at all until everyone was digging into the best spread Loth had seen since leaving Callier weeks ago. Pie, curled around a jug of beer, trilled happily as Loth fed him a spoonful of honey.

"So, then," Dad said. "You've got yourself a prince and a dragon and a ragtag group of adventurers. No offence, Scott, but I'll bet that looked a lot better on paper."

"Pie burned our paper in the Swamp of Death," Dave said. "But it was an accident."

"You were in the Swamp of *Death?*" Mum's eyes blazed on Loth for a moment, and then she remembered herself and turned to Quinn. "The Swamp of *Death?*"

"I'm sorry?" Quinn mumbled.

"Swamp of *Death,*" she repeated under her breath.

"To be fair," Loth said, "It's less Death and more Swamp of

One Slightly Murderous Anarchist Elf, but that wouldn't sound as impressive."

Calarian gave a dreamy sigh. "You mean one very handsome and virile anarchist elf."

"Oh, here we go," Ada muttered, "And while I'm eating, too."

"Anyway!" Loth said far too brightly. "We escaped the swamp. And other than one or two hiccups along the way…"

"Bandits, soldiers, assassins, getting lost in the woods, deadly gas, jumping out of second story windows," Ada listed before Loth glared her into submission.

"*One or two hiccups,*" Loth continued, "we made it safely, and that's the main thing."

"Give me strength," his mum sighed. She turned to Quinn, her whole demeanour softening. "Are you sure you've had enough to eat, sweetheart? I'm sure I have some cake somewhere."

"I'd like cake," Loth said eagerly. His dad made the best cakes.

"Not for you, *Your Grace.* I would be way too embarrassed to serve it to a man of your noble blood. Why, the flour was hardly milled at all! This is only fit for commoners, and of course my precious baby boy." Mum scruffed a hand through Quinn's hair, and the little shit had the cheek to poke his tongue out at Loth when nobody was looking. Still, he'd lost that startled deer look he'd been wearing since they arrived, so Loth supposed that was almost worth missing out on his dad's cake for.

After everyone had finished their cake (except for Loth, because his mother really was the *worst),* Mum clapped her hands together. "Right. We need to find somewhere for you all to sleep."

"As the leader," Scott started.

"You'll be watching the horses and guarding the gate, excellent," Mum said, silently daring him to disagree. "There's a blanket out in the stables. It's almost clean."

She nodded at Dave, Ada and Calarian. "There are two spare rooms upstairs. You can work out who shares with whom."

"Can Pie stay near the fire?" Dave asked. "He likes it."

Pie chirruped his agreement and licked Dave's ear.

"Of course he can. Quinn will be in his old bedroom." Mum's eyes narrowed as she looked at Loth. "I'm not sure where we should put you, Your Grace. You might have to sleep in a chair, but with your royal breeding you'd probably like that. It'll be good for your posture."

Loth was about to object because giving his bed away was taking it a step too far, but Quinn beat him to it.

"He can share with me, Mum," he said quietly. "We've shared for most of the trip. We're... friends."

Calarian let out a snort, and Loth kicked him under the table.

Surprise flashed across Mum's face for a split second. "Friends," she said finally, giving Loth a raised eyebrow. "Is that what you're calling it, Your Grace? Because I'd hate to think my son was taking advantage of you—or the other way around."

Loth wasn't even sure which one of them she was talking to, truth be told, but he knew she'd tell him what she thought soon enough. In great detail. Whether he wanted to hear it or not.

"Nobody's taking advantage of anyone, I assure you," he said, and he almost believed it for a second, right before he remembered that they were only here because he'd put his hand up and claimed to be the prince, without giving a damn about Quinn's protests. To be fair, he'd thought they were *both* lying.

Still, it had worked out for the best, right, having two of them? Loth had saved Quinn's life in the Swamp of Death. And fine, if he hadn't been there, one of the others probably would have, but that had to count for something, right? And Quinn had saved all of their lives in the hunting lodge, and they'd fought the bandits side by side, so surely Loth wasn't quite the opportunistic bastard he had been at the start. Was he?

Mum watched his face carefully for a moment and then sighed. "Off to bed with the lot of you, and I'll come and tuck you all in in ten minutes," she said to a sea of disbelieving faces.

Dave grinned happily. "That'll be nice, Mrs. Mum. Nobody's tucked me in since I was an orcling."

"Well then, tonight's your lucky night." Mum gave Dave's arm an absent pat, and everyone stood and followed Dad as he showed them where the wash basin was and where their rooms were. Scott was jostled out the back door with a blanket.

Loth made to stand, but Mum put a hand on his leg.

"Not you, Your Grace." Her tone was polite, but her gaze was steely. "We need to talk. Wait here."

Loth pulled his chair closer to the fire, knowing his parents would be back soon enough, and for a moment he closed his eyes and allowed himself to soak up the smells and comfort of home. It was nice, being here. Loth supposed that if they were all going to die in a failed rebellion tomorrow, at least he'd have this.

His dad joined him minutes later, sliding into the chair next to him. "Mum'll be a minute. She's still tucking them all in," he said. He turned his gaze on Loth, and the corners of his mouth twitched up in a smile. "I have to say, impersonating a crown prince? You've pulled some spectacular nonsense over the years, son, but I'm fairly sure this tops them all." He shook his head.

"Oh, I don't know," Mum said quietly, coming in to join them. "I'd say that where he's really outdone himself is actually falling for the prince."

Loth opened his mouth to deny it but, for just about the first time in his life, he was unable to push out a lie, when usually they fell from his lips unthinkingly. That errant feeling from earlier reappeared, and Loth swallowed thickly because he had, hadn't he? He'd fallen for Quinn.

Mum stared at him for a moment, and then patted him on the cheek just a smidge too hard. "Go to bed, dear," she said. "You look like you haven't slept in a month."

Loth hugged her and nodded, and then hugged Dad. Then, with both of them watching him thoughtfully, he climbed the stairs to bed.

CHAPTER FIFTEEN

Loth was unsurprised to wake and find an empty space where Quinn should have been sleeping. He rose quietly and wrapped a blanket around his shoulders before sneaking down the stairs. He avoided the squeaky ones through years of practice.

The fire in the kitchen fireplace had burned low, but the embers were glowing in the grate and the room was still filled with warmth. Quinn was sitting on the little stool, a poker in his hand. He leaned forward to stir the embers. Pie, curled up on his shoulder, purred loudly as the embers blazed brighter for a moment.

The stiffening of Quinn's shoulders told Loth he knew he was being observed. Loth moved forward into the kitchen. He took the blanket from his shoulders and draped it around Quinn's. Pie vanished under it.

Loth stared into the embers. "So, tomorrow we—"

"Don't," Quinn said. He looked up at Loth. The firelight made his skin glow. "Tomorrow I'm almost certainly going to die, I know. So for tonight, I'd just like to sit here in your parents' kitchen and pretend that I live here, and I've always lived here, and I always will."

Loth crouched down. "You don't have to die tomorrow, Quinn. We could run. We could go back to Delacourt and get on a ship like Ser Greylord said."

"I'm not going to spend the rest of my life being hunted like a dog." Quinn narrowed his gaze, but then he reached out and took Loth's hand, and his expression softened. "I don't want you to come with me tomorrow. I don't want any of you to, not even Scott."

"Ada will be coming for her money," Loth said. "And Dave is really hanging out for those dragon eggs. Scott will be there for the ballads, and Calarian wants to see this through to the end so he can brag to all his House and Human friends that he's been on a *real* quest."

"Stop." Quinn squeezed his hand tightly. "Stop, please. Just for tonight, I live here, remember?"

"Are you sure?" Loth asked. "It gets draughty in winter, and it always smells like hops."

Quinn's smile was sweet and faint.

"Ugh," Loth said. "This is really uncomfortable."

He released Quinn's hand and then sat his arse down on the warm stones in front of the fireplace. He stretched his legs out and then opened them and tilted his head at Quinn.

Quinn grumbled, but slid from the stool to the floor. He crawled into the space between Loth's knees. A few jostling motions and chirrups of a disgruntled fingerdragon later, he was leaning back against Loth's chest, and Loth's arms were around his waist. Loth put his chin on Quinn's shoulder and they watched the embers together.

"Tell me more about living in this house," Quinn said at last.

"It's stifling," Loth said, and then sighed and reconsidered. "Well, it felt that way when I was a teenager, just bursting to get outside and into trouble, but even when I managed it, my parents knew exactly what I'd been up to. I swear my mother has a network of spies in the city that would rival anything Lord Doom could come up with."

Quinn huffed out an amused breath.

"But my parents?" Loth felt his chest ache, aware that he was driving a knife into Quinn's heart, even if Quinn wanted him to. "I love them, and they love me. I don't think there's anything I could ever do that would mean they'd ever shut the front door in my face. And I have done some spectacularly stupid things, believe me."

"Oh, I do." Quinn's quick grin was sharp. "You don't need to convince me at all. Minstrels, wasn't it?"

"Excuse you, I have undiscovered musical talent just waiting to burst out of me." Loth pressed his mouth to the shell of Quinn's ear. "I mean, I'm no Dave, but I can hold a tune."

"That actually puts you ahead of Dave," Quinn said. "But don't tell him I said that. I'm sure he's very musical, for an orc."

"And his lyrics are certainly memorable," Loth mused. "I don't think I'll ever be able to forget *Scott got trapped when he was taking a crap*."

Quinn laughed softly before trailing off. Pie flitted over to the fireplace and scrabbled in the embers. Quinn watched him intently, his mouth opening and closing several times.

"I'm scared," he finally said, and he sounded so *young* when he said it that Loth felt his heart clench.

"Me too," Loth admitted, "but just this once, I thought I'd do the decent thing. The right thing. You know, see what all the fuss is about."

Quinn hummed in reply, leaning back further into his touch, and Loth's arms tightened imperceptibly around his waist as if that could somehow protect them from the coming day.

∾

"So," Dad asked, "What's the plan?"

The sunlight glinted in the window as the band of rescuers sat around the table, squinting in the light. None of them were morning people. Only Calarian looked alert and perfectly put-together, but that had more to do with genetics than the time of day, Loth figured. He hoped it wasn't just Calarian's vegetarian diet, because, if it was, Loth was vain enough to consider it, and he knew his tastebuds would hate him for it.

Dad was dishing out breakfast; thick bread topped with fresh honey, scrambled eggs and slabs of fried ham, and mushrooms for Calarian. They might be riding to their doom—ha!—but they were riding with full stomachs if Dad had anything to do with it.

"We have a way in," Loth said, and then he stopped, because really, that was as far as their planning had gone. Once they were inside, then what?

Dad raised his eyebrows. "Apologies, Your Grace, but it sounds like you're expecting to walk in, demand the crown and hope for the best. And if that's the case, I may as well just stab you now and save everyone the trouble."

"Lord Doom would probably reward us," Mum said from her seat by the fire, where she'd been polishing Pie's scales till they gleamed. "He might even appoint us the royal brewers for our service."

Scott leapt to his feet. "You can't kill the prince!" he shouted, except he tripped as he stood, and he had a mouthful of bread and honey, so it came more like "*ooo an't ill thprince*," which spoiled the dramatic effect somewhat.

Calarian swatted at him. "Shut up. They're not killing anyone. They're making a point, that's all. And they're right. We do need a plan." He got a distant look in his eye. "How would this play out if it was Houses and Humans? Does anyone have any dice?"

Ada rolled her eyes.

"There's two of them," Dave said unexpectedly. "Princes. But I'm still Dave."

At his mum's questioning look, Loth explained. "Scott was hired to rescue the prince, but the only description he got was that the prince had red hair. Quinn was sharing my cell and claimed to be the prince to escape. They decided to take us both since it's been so long that nobody knows what the prince looks like, even though it's obviously me." He wilted a little under Mum's stare. "Obviously."

"So, Lord Doom doesn't know what you look like either?" his father asked, drumming his fingers on the tabletop in a gesture Loth recognised from his childhood. It meant his dad was Having an Idea, something that might be either brilliant or terrifying. Loth took after his dad like that. "Isn't he your *uncle?*"

They were getting into dangerous territory, mostly because Loth didn't know enough about Quinn's background to actually answer a question like that with any depth. He floundered for a moment, opening and closing his mouth.

"Dad," Quinn said, the word a little faint and wavering on his lips. "The prince and I talked about this. Apparently, Lord Doom hasn't seen the prince since he was quite small, and, you know, then there were years in captivity on top of that. It's very likely that Lord Doom will think that the prince is h—uh, is *me*. At least for long enough to press an advantage."

They hadn't actually talked about it, but Loth appreciated the save. "Yes, that's what h-we said."

"I'm confused," Dave said, and he wasn't the only one.

"It's not much of an advantage though, is it?" Dad asked. "Won't he just kill you both?"

Loth blinked.

"Um, y-yes," Quinn said. He swallowed. "That is very much the downside to the plan."

"Except," Loth said, remembering what Quinn had said. He held up his finger. "Except I am the crown prince, here to claim the throne, and the soldiers will side with *me*."

"Will they?" Dad asked. "How sure are you of that?"

"I'm almost certain it's a possibility," Loth said, and that had definitely sounded more reassuring in his head.

"At least you have an orc and a dwarf and an elf to back you up," Mum said, but she sounded hesitant.

"And a professional hero!" Scott exclaimed.

Everyone ignored him.

"Well, the thing about that," Loth said, "is that they're just here to get paid. Once they deliver me to Lord Doom, their contract is up and they're done."

Ha! At least he had the satisfaction of seeing Ada, Dave, and Calarian wilt a little under the intense combined judgement of his parents' stares.

"Is that so?" Mum asked. "Hmmm."

Why were her eyes twinkling? Loth had never before known her eyes to twinkle when she was winding up into a furious rage. And yet... the furious rage didn't come as sharply and suddenly as a summer storm, like that time Loth had been dragged home by the royal guard after... well, no need to relive the specifics. The point was, nobody could prove that had been Loth's arse hammering up and down between that young man's thighs, in his house, while his father, who was lord mayor, was having tea with the Callier Ladies Guild for the Prevention of Immorality downstairs, even if Loth *had* been found a block away with his pants still around his ankles a few minutes after being disturbed. It was totally circumstantial. No, this time Mum's anger must have been less a summer storm and more of a tempest, building to something truly spectacular, simmering away as she turned up the heat. Loth couldn't wait to see it explode.

"Well," Dad said at last. "I suppose you're both going to have to look like princes then?" He clapped one hand on Loth's shoulder, and one on Quinn's. "Boys, follow me."

He drew them out of the kitchen.

Damn.

Loth was going to miss the fireworks.

DAD MOSTLY WORKED in the kitchen, but he did keep a small shop front attached to the brewery where he saw customers and measured them up. Loth had learned everything he knew about fashion here, and also everything he knew about measuring dick sizes. He was a gifted amateur on both counts. He could estimate an inside leg measurement at ten paces and tell what size trousers a man wore as well.

Dad hummed tunelessly as he flicked through the rack of doublets and cloaks he kept there. An assortment of clothing that while all beautifully tailored, had for one reason or another ended up in the reject corner, on the rack. These were the clothes that had been ordered and not paid for. Items where the customer had tried them on and been disappointed in how they looked, and even clothing where the wedding had been cancelled and the customers hadn't needed matching navy doublets after all. That particular cancellation *may* have had something to do with Loth helping out in the shop the day the grooms came in for their final fitting, but Loth refused to admit it. After long moments of consideration, Dad pulled out the two matching navy doublets, along with two pairs of black pants.

"These look like what we need," he said, handing them over.

They changed in the curtained-off corner of the shop, and when Quinn stepped out in the new outfit, Loth was struck dumb, unable to do anything but stare at the absolutely mouth-watering vision in front of him.

Quinn, in general, was attractive. Quinn dressed in clothing befitting his station was devastating, and every inch the prince. He'd unconsciously straightened his spine and tilted his head back, eyes cool and assessing. Loth had a sudden overwhelming urge to go down on one knee. Or, well, both of them.

Quinn must have mistaken his silence for disapproval. He

rubbed a hand over his chin and crossing his arms over his chest defensively, his confident demeanour leaving him all in a rush.

"I look like a scarecrow, don't I?" He tugged at the waist of his trousers and yes, now he'd pointed it out they were a little loose, but only in a way that made Loth wonder if he could fit a hand down there.

"Overall, I'd say you look completely convincing," his dad said. "We'll add a belt, and a cloak will cover a multitude of sins." He turned to Loth. "Wouldn't you agree?"

"You look marvellous, Quinn," he said, fighting the urge to crowd Quinn back into the curtained corner, drop to his knees, and either pledge fealty or suck royal cock.

Something of what he was thinking must have shown on his face because Quinn gave him a smirk. "Your turn."

Loth ducked into the changing area and dressed. Then he took a minute to admire his father's skilled handiwork: the intricate rows of stitching along the seams, and the gold embroidery thread winding down the front of the doublet in a pattern of swirls and points that added to the richness of the garment. Maybe he should have gone into the family business after all.

Maybe, if he survived all this, he still could.

He was admiring the way the pants fit him, accentuating the curve of his backside nicely, when his dad called out, "Hurry up. Or can't you fit that fat royal arse into those trousers?"

Loth had never had a fat arse in his life, and they both knew it, but that never stopped his father teasing him about it. It was almost a tradition between them, and it was comforting in its familiarity.

Loth tugged the curtain aside and stalked out, pretending to be offended. "The royal rear is spectacular, thank you very much. I should have you beheaded for suggesting otherwise."

His dad snorted. "You'd have to go through your mother first. Good luck with that." He looked Loth over, and his expression softened. "It suits you, son."

"Thanks, Dad." Loth spread his hands and turned to Quinn. "Well? Do I look like I'm you?"

Quinn's mouth was hanging slightly open. "Um, you look…" he stammered, and his throat bobbed as he swallowed, "… wow." Quinn licked his lips, and Loth wasn't sure he even knew he was doing it.

Loth allowed himself a moment to preen. He knew he looked good, but it was still nice to have it confirmed. Then he stepped forward and took Quinn's hand. "It'll be fine," he lied. "We have to win—we're the good guys."

Quinn squeezed his hand gratefully. "We have to win," he repeated, and then he said it again with more conviction. "We're going to win this."

Maybe he was a better liar than Loth first thought, or maybe he honestly thought they had a chance. Loth so badly wanted that to be true that he allowed himself a moment to imagine it. Maybe Doom would see the error of his ways. Perhaps the palace guard would turn. Maybe Doom would choke on a fishbone at lunch and there'd be no fighting at all. It was a nice thought.

But Loth still tucked his meat cleaver into his belt.

WHEN THEY WENT BACK INSIDE, everyone else was huddled around the table with Mum, eating cake and drinking mugs of tea. Dad had found two deep blue cloaks that did, indeed, hide the fact that their clothes weren't tailored to them, and the rest of the party looked up and made impressed sounds at the sight of Loth and Quinn in their matching outfits.

"There's two of them," Dave said with something like reverence. "They's both a prince."

Loth caught sight of his scarf draped over a chair. His dad had made it for him years ago, added what he called the 'sneaky bastard pockets' as a joke. More than once Loth had gotten out of difficult situations using what he'd stashed in them. He picked it up and wound it around his neck. The warmth and familiarity of the thing had him feeling instantly more like himself and less like the absolute imposter that he was. At Quinn's questioning look, he said, "For luck."

Pie grumbled from where he was burrowed in one of the pockets, poking his head out sleepily before nestling back in. Loth let him stay. Dragons were lucky too, right?

"So, Your Grace." Mum tilted her head in thought. "If Lord Doom's expecting Scott and his merry band to deliver you anyway, why are you bothering to sneak into the castle? Why not ride in all flags and trumpets, claim the throne publicly? Wouldn't that actually be safer?"

It was Ada who spoke up. "Because we were never really expected to pull this off. If we go in like that, then Doom knows we're coming, and he'll have an entire division of his guard surrounding him. He knows the prince will want to claim his throne, and he'll slit his throat as soon as he steps through the door. If we sneak in, we can catch him unguarded. And we can get paid before anyone gets their throat cut," she added, which Loth privately thought was just callous of her, but his Mum nodded in understanding.

"Of course," Mum said. "Dwarves always complete their agreements. So you'll go in, pretend you have no idea Doom wants to slaughter his nephew." She looked at Loth knowingly as he flinched at her words. "And once your 'hero' arranges payment, it'll be onto your next job."

Ada shrugged. "I'm loyal for as long as I'm paid to be."

"It is handy that we're going to the palace, we can meet Ser Factor while we're there," Scott said.

Loth sighed. "This would all be much simpler if you actually knew your benefactor's name. Scott."

Scott screwed up his face in thought, before shaking his head. "I've told you all before! Ser Bene Factor!" He dug in one of his pockets and pulled out a grubby slip of parchment, different from the one they'd taken off him and burned earlier. He flattened it against the table and hunched over it, one finger tracing over the letters, lips moving silently, before he straightened and announced, not-quite confidently, "Bean. E. Factor. Beany Factor."

"That's not a name, Scott," Quinn said, and rolled his eyes. "We've been over this before."

"Shut up," Scott said, full of self-importance and smarm. "You're just a grubby little peasant, so what would you know?"

It was immensely satisfying for Loth, watching his mum wallop Scott around the ears. "Don't you dare talk about my Quinn that way! That's my *son!*"

Scott whimpered under the assault. Years of hauling barrels of beer around had given Loth's mother plenty of muscle. Loth almost sympathised with Scott—almost—right until he remembered that he was very probably an accidental traitor and absolutely an idiot. He leaned over and gave him a swat of his own, and when Scott pulled his brows together and opened his mouth to object, Loth shrugged and said, "Royal privilege."

Quinn grinned for just a moment, before sobering. "I guess we'd better get moving, before Doom has time to prepare."

"One last thing," Dad said. He disappeared upstairs and came back with a pair of swords that Loth had never seen before. "You two can't go and defend your right to the crown with just a meat cleaver and a kitchen knife, Your Graces."

"That doesn't make sense. Only one of them is the prince," Scott interrupted, still cupping his sore ear and scowling.

Mum glared at him. "Maybe. But they're both my boys." She stepped forward and pulled a flustered-looking Quinn into a tight hug, and Loth heard her whisper, "At least try and stay safe, son."

Quinn's eyes were suspiciously bright as he nodded.

Mum let go and turned her attention to Loth, dragging him in for a hug as well and whispering the same thing. She'd been saying it for years, and Loth was hit with a wave of regret that he'd never bothered to listen.

He pressed a kiss to her cheek. "We'll do our best, I promise. We've got an orc, an elf, a dwarf, an idiot, and a dragon—what could possibly go wrong?" he said, with an assurance he didn't feel.

"We don't have an idiot," Scott said to the room at large. "Do we?"

Everyone ignored him.

Dad clapped them all on the back and wished them luck, and then they went outside, mounted their horses, and rode to meet their fate.

CHAPTER SIXTEEN

The castle was both intimidating and disappointing, somehow. It showed hints of having once been a truly beautiful building, but if he looked closer, Loth could see that whoever lived there now didn't really care—the gardens were scruffy and verging on overgrown, the windows dirty, the paintwork on the doors peeling. Quinn gazed about sadly while Calarian secured their horses, and Loth guessed it was just another reminder of what he'd lost. It hadn't even been a formidable sight to begin with either—just a slightly larger-than-normal manor house with a couple of towers and new wings added on at either end. Loth was pretty sure, from memory, that the lord mayor's house was grander. It was a few generations newer, for starters—but to be fair he'd only really seen inside the son's bedroom that time.

The laundry door that Ser Greylord promised was unguarded was around the back—and Quinn knew the way. He led the way through the back street, and then through several gates and down a couple of paths to get to it. Loth guessed they'd got to the right spot when they reached a scrubby yard with a bunch of freshly laundered sheets flapping and cracking like wet sailcloths as the wind caught them. They stood outside the laundry door for a moment, all waiting for someone else to make the first move, until Ada rolled her eyes, and muttered, "Let's get this over with."

She squared her shoulders, took a deep breath, and then shoved the door open.

The laundry room was dim after the brightness of the day outside, and the stone floor was wet and slippery.

Ada turned back to face them. "Careful how you—"

"I'm the leader! I should go first!" Scott darted forward, skidded, and then his arms windmilled as he smacked face-first into the wall. He reeled back again, blood pouring from his face. "*By mose!*"

"Well," Loth whispered in Quinn's ear. "At least if we die, we got to see that first."

"It is weirdly comforting," Quinn whispered back.

They made their way carefully across the wet floor. Ada and Calarian took the front, and Dave lumbered along behind Quinn and Loth. Scott staggered along after him, still whining about his nose.

They edged out into a deserted corridor and inched forward cautiously. They'd turned three corners when Calarian held up a hand. "Shh!" He tilted his head and then whispered, "It's Greylord."

"How can he know that?" Quinn asked quietly.

"Ears like a bat," Calarian answered, "I can tell his footfall."

Right on cue, Ser Greylord turned the corner. Upon seeing them, he gave a terse nod. "Come on. Doom's alone right now. He's unwell." A tight smile flitted across his face.

"Unwell how?" Ada asked.

"Something he ate disagreed with him." There was a gleam in Greylord's eye that hinted it might not have been a coincidence.

"Nice," Ada said, nodding her approval.

They made their way slowly forward, watching and listening

for any sign of the guard, but as Greylord pointed out, "Even if we see anyone, I'm already escorting you to Doom. What are they going to do, escort you more?"

It seemed to take forever to get to where they needed to go, and it still didn't take nearly long enough as far as Loth was concerned. Quinn's hand crept into his, and he wasn't sure who was more comforted by the press of skin on skin. This was possibly the bravest thing Loth had ever done, and he wondered if heroics were for him, after all. He cast a longing glance at a side door, but Calarian caught him looking and scowled at him.

"You don't leave a campaign at the last roll of the dice," he said in an undertone.

Loth desperately wanted to disagree, to tell him that yes, you did if it meant you were alive at the end of it, and bolt anyway. But he couldn't quite bring himself to do it, because that would mean tugging his hand out of Quinn's, and there was no power in the world that could compel him to do that.

Also, of course, he wouldn't make it as far as the laundry door if Ada had anything to do with it.

"He's in the solarium," Ser Greylord murmured.

Quinn nodded, his grip tightening on Loth's hand.

"Oooh, are there *fish*?" Dave asked.

"No," Quinn whispered. "A solarium is a room at the top of a tower, with a bunch of windows, so it's always warm and sunny."

Dave's big shoulders sagged. "So, no fish?"

"No fish," Quinn said.

Dave gave a small, sad sigh.

They reached a set of winding stairs and began to climb them. They were in the tower, Loth realised. His stomach swooped as they reached a landing, and Ser Greylord paused in front of a large, closed door. And then he raised his fist and knocked.

"What?" came a churlish voice from inside, muffled a little by the wood. "Is it the boy with the vomit bucket?"

Sir Greylord grimaced and opened his mouth to respond.

At that moment Scott pushed forward, his face shining with both blood and enthusiasm. "No!" he exclaimed, pushing the door open. "Ib is I, Ser Factor! I hab combleted the glorious task that you set be!"

It probably would have sounded more impressive if Scott hadn't been snuffling through a broken nose.

The petulance dropped out of the man's tone immediately, replaced by a cold, dead tone. "You've done *what?*"

Scott bounced into the room. "Id me, Ser Factor! Remebber? From Delacourt! We meb in the tabern! I'b rescued de pridce!"

Loth had no idea what came over him at that moment. He tugged his hand free of Quinn's and elbowed him back at the same moment. And then he stepped inside the solarium, pulling the door shut behind him.

Sunlight flooded through the immense windows that stretched to the ceiling of the circular room, and Loth got the impression of a space that was meant to be light and airy. Some of the effect was muted by the various dark draperies and tapestries that hung at intervals between the windows, working against the pale stone of the walls. It was a bigger space than Loth was expecting, scattered with couches and daybeds, no doubt for people to stretch out on and enjoy the sunlight. There was an imposing fireplace with a roaring fire. A man stretched out on a couch that had been placed by one of the windows.

The man stood and faced them. He was thin and sharp-featured, and not unattractive. He had piercing blue eyes and was wearing a purple silk robe and clutching a crystal goblet. He was still on the right side of middle age, and his golden hair was, if not lustrous, then at least not thinning yet. He looked enough like Quinn that Loth didn't need to make any guesses.

"Uncle," he said, stepping forward past Scott. "How lovely to see you again."

Lord Doom's gaze flicked down him, then up again, and then

down again, and then up. Loth stared back at him, chest puffed out in his glorious and expensive doublet, and curled his lip in a noble sneer.

Lord Doom narrowed his eyes. "Tarquin?"

"Yes," Loth said. He brushed an imaginary speck of dust from his doublet. "Here I am, of age, ready to take over my royal duties. Isn't that why you sent for me, Uncle?"

"Excude me! Excude me!" Scott bobbed and ducked. "Excude me, Ser Factor, bub wob is dat?" He pointed to a large tapestry emblazoned with a crest, hanging on the wall between two windows. "Why dub it say Dumbass Knee?"

"It says Dumesny, Scott," Loth said. "This is Lord Doom."

"No! This ib Ser Factor!" Scott's eyes widened. "Lord Doob? Lord Doob ib ebil! *Ebil*!" He took a step back. "Hab I been helbing the *billain*?"

Lord Doom huffed impatiently. "Are you an imbecile?"

Scott's brow furrowed. "I think I'b a Sabbitarius." He seemed to remember himself then, saying, "Dob't try and distrabt be. You're Ebil Lord Doob!"

"Evil's a matter of perspective. Didn't I keep my nephew alive all these years?" Doom looked Loth up and down again, frowning. "You look older than I thought you would."

"I look more *alive* than you thought I would, you mean."

"That too." Lord Doom set his goblet down on the small table beside the couch. He narrowed his eyes as he studied Loth critically. "But no, you're definitely older than you should be. You have crow's feet."

"I do *not* have crow's feet!" Even as he yelled it, Loth was aware that it wasn't really the thing to be focussing on right now, so he tacked on, "Uncle."

"Prove it's you," Doom demanded. "Tell me something only you'd know."

Loth blinked and then did what he did best. He thought fast

and lied through his teeth. "There's a lodge about an hour's walk outside of Torlere. We used to go there on holidays. There's a portrait there of you and my mother as children. You always were a chubby child."

"Anyone who's seen the portraits knows that." Doom sniffed, but there was a hint of uncertainty in his tone.

Loth closed his eyes as if he was reliving a fond memory. "My parents loved it there. I remember that sometimes they'd let the children go into the village, to the kitchen at the tavern. Not the one on the main road, the other one. They'd give us toffee apples." When he squinted through nearly closed eyelids, Doom was tapping a finger thoughtfully against his chin. So just for good measure, Loth added, "And of course, there's the secret passage in the pantry."

Doom froze, and Loth might even have pulled it off, if Scott hadn't chosen that moment to say, "You bean the bassage that Grub showed ub?"

"Who's Grub?" Lord Doom demanded, advancing on Loth.

"He'd a pedant who wad in the sabe cell. He'd got red hair ad well, so we redcued hib too," Scott explained, before frowning. "But hid nabe id Cue now, I thidk?"

Doom's face creased and his lips moved as he worked through what Scott had said. When he'd finally deciphered it, he asked, "So where is he, this other redhead?"

"A peasant, as the idiot said," Loth interjected quickly. "A nobody, a grubby little urchin with a bad attitude and a taste for horseflesh, which was what landed him in my cell."

"He... was arrested for eating horses?"

"Not eating, no." Loth watched a faint expression of disgust flicker across Doom's face and congratulated himself on a successful diversion.

Of course, it turned out to be a waste of time, because just then the door opened and Quinn pushed inside, declaring loudly,

"For the last damned time, I've *never* fucked a horse!" And then he stood next to Loth, tilted his chin defiantly, and said, "Hello, Uncle."

For a moment, nobody moved. Then Doom surveyed them both, eyes narrowing. His hand moved to his belt, and for the first time Loth noticed the knife there and his heart sank.

"One of you is lying."

"Quite possibly," Loth said. "Perhaps I'm the prince and the time I spent starving and freezing has dimmed my natural beauty, and this is an interloper that we've brought along to confuse you. Or maybe I'm the liar, and this is the prince." Doom started to approach, and Loth held up a finger. "But—think carefully—have you considered that maybe we're *both* lying?"

Lord Doom paused. "How can you both be lying?"

Loth smirked, warming to his subject. "Think about it. Maybe we're *both* a diversion. Imagine if the real prince is tucked up safely, somewhere far away, waiting til you least expect it to emerge and claim the throne."

"*There'd adother pridce?*"

"Shut up, Scott," Loth said, as Doom scowled at the pair of them.

"I could just kill you both," he said finally. "Make sure."

"Ah, but then you'd never know where the real prince is. You wouldn't be sure at all."

Somehow though, from the murderous gleam in Lord Doom's eyes, Loth didn't think that he was the sort of guy who was going to lose any sleep over it. He reached out and grabbed Quinn's sleeve, ready to pull him back.

At that moment Ada strode into the room with the rest of them in tow, stomping up to Lord Doom. "Pardon me, but we'd like to get paid. We've delivered the redhead as agreed—we've delivered two, so we should really charge extra, but I'll waive it in exchange for cash. Pay up."

Doom's jaw dropped. "I am a little busy right now! First with the vomiting, and now all of *this*!"

Ada put her hands on her hips. "Pay up, M'lord. Unless you want us to leave and take them both with us?"

She glared at Lord Doom, who did his best to stare her down, but Loth could have told him that getting between a dwarf and their promised payment was always going to be a losing battle—it was a matter of honour, after all.

"I'd pay her if I were you, M'lord," Ser Greylord, who'd slipped into the room behind the rest of them, muttered. "She has an axe."

Doom threw his hands in the air. "Fine!" He nodded at Ser Greylord. "I don't suppose you have any gold on you?"

"Actually, I do." Greylord detached a bulging purse from his belt and presented it to Ada with a slight bow. "Consider your contract complete, ma'am."

Ada beamed at him. Then she turned on her heel and barked out, "Right. The old contract is settled, and the new job's started! You all know what to do. Except you." She pointed at Scott. "You can stay out of the way."

And then the dwarf, the orc, and the elf stepped forward and stood shoulder to shoulder in front of Quinn and Loth, forming a human—no, an other-than-human—shield.

Lord Doom's expression tightened. "What the fuck is this? What are you doing?"

Ada grinned at him through her beard. "Our business is completed, Doom. We've got a new contract now." She tugged her axe out of her belt. "If you want the prince, whichever one he is, you're going to need to get through *us* first."

Loth's chest swelled with hope, and he glanced quickly at Quinn. Quinn looked as befuddled as Loth felt, his forehead creased and his mouth hanging open slightly, but the same unlikely hope shone in his eyes. Loth had no idea what the hell was going on here, but was it possible they were *winning*?

Holy crap, it was.

They had Doom outnumbered, and they were going to *win*!

Which, of course, was right when Scott, attempting to make himself scarce and stumbling around in the periphery, tripped and fell forward. To save himself, he reached out and grabbed desperately at the tapestry displaying the Dumesny crest, pulling it from the wall. An end of it landed in the fireplace. Flames licked at it for a moment, and then the thick fabric caught on fire. Scott screeched and tugged it free. Then, panicking, he tossed the flaming drapery right into the middle of their not-human shield. They scattered, and in the seconds that it took them to regroup, Lord Doom was rushing forward, raising his gleaming knife into the air and heading straight for Quinn.

Thump.

The sound of the knife punching into flesh was the loudest thing Loth had ever heard.

"Quinn?" Loth asked, his heart clenching. Why was he finding it hard to breathe, and why was he on the floor? "Quinn?"

"Loth!" Quinn was staring down at him, eyes wide. "What did you *do*?"

"Oh," Loth said, and looked down at where Lord Doom's knife was protruding from his stomach. "Holy shit. Did I stand in front of you?"

Quinn nodded, his eyes filling with tears.

"Wow," said Loth, because who the hell ever would have seen that coming?

From the door of the solarium, Loth heard banging and yelling. Soldiers, no doubt. Quinn might have hoped they'd defend the crown, but Loth more than had his doubts. So did Ada and Ser Greylord and Calarian, fortunately—they lined up to meet the soldiers just as the door crashed open again. Dave bellowed happily and dived into the melee at the door. Scott, meanwhile, was still crashing around over by Doom's couch, half dragging the smouldering tapestry with him.

Which left nobody between Quinn and Lord Doom at all.

Quinn roared, pulling his sword out of its sheath and advancing on his uncle. Loth saw the sneer on Lord Doom's face and watched as the man reached behind him. He had no doubt that Lord Doom had more blades secreted about his person, and no doubt that Quinn, who had spent the last five years in a cell, was totally and utterly mismatched in this fight.

His stomach hurt, and his eyes stung, and his throat... *wriggled*? Shit, no, that was Pie, still tucked up in the pocket of his scarf.

"Help him!" Loth tried to yell at the others. "Help Quinn!" But his voice was weak.

Quinn raised his sword just as Lord Doom produced another knife.

"Come on then, nephew," Doom said. "You're the only thing standing between me and the throne. I should have killed you years ago, but your mother begged me not to. With her last breath, even."

Quinn's expression twisted, but his sword-arm didn't shake. Tears shone in his eyes.

Lord Doom shook his head reproachfully. "Why couldn't you just have been killed by bandits like a good boy?" He tilted his head. "It's not an easy thing, Tarquin, to kill your last remaining relative. Still, I'm sure I'll get over it in time. I'll bet the weight of the crown will be quite comforting. And I promise I'll play quite the heartbroken uncle in public."

He darted forward with his knife just as Quinn swung the sword. Quinn missed as Doom sidestepped, and Loth heard the tear of fabric as a blade cut through it. He didn't even know which one of them had been struck. It became obvious when Doom dropped his knife and snatched the sword from Quinn's hands with a dry laugh. "You really thought you could take me on, you sad little boy?"

"Help Quinn!" Loth wheezed at the others desperately, but

they were knee-deep in soldiers at the door. All he could think was that he should have run after all, taken Quinn and left this whole mess behind, because there was nobody to help them, nobody at all.

Except.

A voice rang out. "No!"

Long legs strode past and Loth saw the silhouette of Ser Greylord, sword extended towards Lord Doom. Loth stole a desperate glance at Quinn, who thankfully seemed unharmed except for a slash in his sleeve, and silently willed him to move. By some miracle Quinn did the sensible thing and backed quietly away, and Loth allowed himself to breathe.

Doom still had the sword in his hand, but he dropped it to his side as he looked Ser Greylord up and down like he was some sort of interesting bug. "What on earth are you doing, Greylord?"

"My duty," Ser Greylord said, "I'm defending my prince."

Doom snorted. "Oh, isn't that noble of you. Tell me though, Ser Greylord, haven't you forgotten something?"

Greylord smiled, sharp and dangerous. "Have I?"

"There's the small matter of your son. I have him, and I won't hesitate to kill him for your treachery." Doom advanced, sword extended, but his movements were more cautious, less assured, and it was the work of seconds for Ser Greylord to knock the sword out of his grip. Doom's hand darted to his boot but Greylord was quicker, smacking at his hand with the broadside of his blade and earning a yelp as yet another knife clattered to the ground.

Greylord's voice was cold. "Except you don't. I knew you could only be trusted to keep my son alive as long as it suited you —after all, you killed your own sister. Luckily, I've been able to foster a lot of goodwill among the ranks over the past few years. It wasn't hard to find men willing to rescue him—they're loyal to me, not you."

"Rescues go wrong all the time. He could be dead," Doom sneered, but he suddenly sounded a lot less sure of himself.

Ser Greylord stepped forward, the tip of his sword grazing Doom's throat, and a shadow of a smile passed over his face. "You left me in charge of training an army and didn't think I'd send my best for my own flesh and blood? I received word last night that my son is safe. So there's nothing to stop me killing you here and now."

"You wouldn't dare! You can't seize power singlehanded!"

"I don't plan to, *M'lord*," Greylord chuckled, and Loth reflected that if he was going to die on the floor, at least he could do it knowing that his side had the last laugh. "I plan to seize it with an orc, an elf, a dwarf, two princes, and a dragon."

At that, Doom paled. "A *dragon?*" He ducked out from under the tip of Greylord's blade and ran to the window, repeating *"You have a dragon?"* frantically scanning the outside sky, trying to spot where the creature might be.

Loth made a soft clicking noise and prodded the wriggling lump in his scarf, and said dragon's head popped out. Tiny claws dug into Loth's skin as Pie squirmed free. He perched on Loth's nose, his tail dragging against his chin, and chirped, before blowing a tiny puff of smoke.

Lord Doom's head whipped around and when he saw Pie he froze for a moment, then pointed and made a dismissive sound. "That? That's not a dragon! It's barely a—a *newt!* I was actually worried for a moment there!" He laughed and wiped at the tears in his eyes. "Sorry, sorry, this is serious. Ooooh, you've got a *dragon!*"

Pie beat his tiny wings frantically and alighted from Loth's nose. He buzzed through the air like a dragonfly; the sunlight catching his stained-glass wings, and dove straight at Lord Doom, biting him soundly on the finger.

"Ow! What the fuck was that?" Lord Doom shook Pie off and stared where he landed on the ground. He looked incredulous for a second and then began to smile. "Is that—gods, is that the best it can do? A *nip?* Pathetic! That has to be the tiniest, most useless, absolutely fu—"

And then, without uttering a single word further, he suddenly jerked, his expression freezing, and then pitched face-down onto the floor, utterly stone-cold dead.

Pie puffed out his chest and trilled.

CHAPTER SEVENTEEN

The dull thumps echoing in Loth's skull weren't the last drawn-out beats of his faltering heart playing a solemn, fading tattoo to escort his soul into the afterlife. Loth craned his neck to see: it was Dave, in the doorway, knocking a pair of soldiers together like wooden blocks. He was beaming like a delighted child, his tooth-tusks gleaming in the light.

Loth turned his head. Yup. Lord Doom was definitely lying dead on the floor. Quinn stood over him, gaping. And Loth had been... stabbed? It was weird, but he didn't actually feel any pain. Possibly that was because he was already drifting between life and death, and his senses were no longer working. Oh gods. What a waste. He was so young and so pretty.

Ada stomped over to him and peered down at him. She tugged the knife free and inspected the tip of the blade for blood.

Loth's eyesight must have been going too because he couldn't see any.

"Get up, you idiot," Ada said, which Loth felt was very rude of her considering he was dying. He blinked at her silhouette, craning his head in case she was blocking the light he'd heard so much about, the one he was supposed to head into, but all he saw was ordinary sunlight, dust motes floating gently through the air, and a cobweb dangling from the ceiling. Huh.

Loth carefully felt around the torn fabric of his doublet. That was when he discovered that thanks to Dad's habit of always double-backing and triple-stitching everything he ever made, plus in this case adding a layer of padding to smooth out the lines, the stab wound in Loth's gut turned out to be less of a gaping hole and more of a...

"It's a scratch," Ada said with a derisive snort. "It's barely even bleeding. Get up, you wuss."

"Are you sure I'm not dying?" Loth asked and peered down at his stomach. "Because for a little while there I couldn't even speak."

"That's because you were winded from where you hit the floor." Ada nudged him with the toe of her boot. "Get up."

Loth ran his hands carefully over his stomach. "Are you sure?"

Ada raised her eyebrows and held up her axe. Her eyes gleamed. "If you want to be dead so badly, I can help you out."

Loth got up. "What about your contract to protect me?" he asked. "Or was that all nonsense, and secretly you and the others stepped in because shared adversity has made us all friends? Are we friends, Ada? Do you secretly love me? Because I'm amazing, I know! You can admit it. Say that you love me, Ada."

"No," she said shortly.

"Say it!"

"No."

"You love me!" Loth exclaimed, "My roguish charm and boyish good looks have melted your pragmatic, ice-cold heart!"

"I don't love you," Ada said frankly. "I think you're a dickhead."

"But you protected me!" Loth beamed at her. "You protected me because you love me! There's no contract. I don't have any money and—"

The blade of Ada's axe hit the floor right in front of the toe of his boot. Loth took a step back.

"There is a contract," Ada said, grinning at him through her beard. "But we're not contracted to protect you. We're contracted for *Quinn*." She put her hands on her hips. "Your parents could only afford one contract, and they probably figured you were slippery enough to get out of any trouble on your own."

"My *parents* are the ones paying you?"

"Your mum arranged it, offered us the job while you were off getting prettied up. Nice arse in those trousers, by the way."

"But—my own parents, and they paid you to protect Quinn and not *me*?"

Ada shrugged. "Well, to be fair, Quinn is a much nicer person." She patted his leg. "Besides, nobody was really expecting you to go through with your whole 'I'm the prince' routine and actually put yourself in danger."

Yeah, that had taken Loth by surprise too. He grunted at Ada and then stepped over to where Quinn was standing over Lord Doom's body. Pie was perched on Quinn's shoulder with his wings stretched wide, arching his neck and trilling as Quinn scratched under his jaw absently.

From over by the door, Dave cracked two soldiers' heads together, then came lumbering over to join them. "Pie!" he exclaimed.

Pie chirped and fluttered over to him.

"Dave," Quinn said quietly. "I thought you said Pie wasn't poisonous."

"He's not!" Dave's green brow creased in thought. "He's not poisonous, he's *venomenomous*."

"Venomous," Quinn murmured.

"S'wat I said!" Dave said with a proud grin. "There's a diff'rence!"

Quinn threw Loth a wide-eyed look, and Loth reached out and pulled him into a hug. Quinn clung like a rabid possum for a moment, and Loth could feel his shuddering breath on his neck.

Then Quinn straightened, blinking, and shook his head. "What just happened? I mean, I'm not going to lie, but I honestly thought we'd be dead right now, and my brain is having some trouble coming to terms with the fact that we're not."

"How about I convince you?" Loth asked, before pressing a very messy, very dirty kiss to Quinn's mouth. Quinn was unresponsive, and Loth drew back. "What?"

Quinn wrinkled his nose. "I mean, we're standing right over the corpse of my uncle. I don't think I'm a squeamish kind of person, but that's a little weird."

Loth looked down at Doom's corpse and hummed thoughtfully. "I suppose it is."

"Like, he's *right* there," Quinn said, gesturing.

"We could throw the tapestry over him," Loth suggested.

"Hmm." Quinn patted Loth on the arm. "Or you could keep your tongue out of my mouth for a little while until we're not sharing our personal space with my dead uncle."

"I mean, I'm not a fan of that plan so much," Loth said magnanimously, "but if it's what you'd prefer, then I unhappily concede."

"Unhappily?" Quinn's mouth twitched in a smile.

"My tongue loves being in your mouth," Loth said. "So do many of my other parts."

Quinn flushed, his cheeks taking on a bright pink tinge that clashed terribly with his hair. "I'm sure I don't know what you mean."

"Do you want me to explain it to you?" Loth asked with a wink. "Or perhaps offer a practical demonstration?"

"Please don't." But Quinn was fighting a smile again, so Loth figured he was going to count that as a win.

He pulled Quinn into another hug and pressed a kiss to the top of his head. It was perfectly chaste and perfectly respectable, and it earned him a perfectly pleased smile in return.

"I guess the ballads are right about one thing," Loth said, loosening his grip on Quinn at last. "It turns out that dragons *do* defeat evil. Even tiny ones."

Pie trilled proudly, puffed out a little spark, and fluttered over to Doom's corpse. Loth laughed aloud when Pie shit on the dead body from a great height, and it landed with a splat on the back of Doom's purple robe.

The sound caught the attention of Scott, who was sitting in a corner, watching the goings-on. He took it as a cue to get to his feet and scurry over, giving a sweeping bow to Loth. "You're alibe, my pridce! By band of berry ben sabed you!"

Loth personally thought that Scott's use of *my* was something of a stretch since they'd stopped listening to him somewhere around Torlere. Since he was feeling vaguely charitable by virtue of not being dead, he said, "They certainly did."

Scott straightened and shuffled closer, lowering his voice. "I'b sorry I wad working for the billain. I didn't know Lord Doob wab by benefabtor," he admitted, shamefaced. "Maybe I'b not a hero. I bight not be cud out for adbenturing abter all."

"Maybe not," Loth agreed. "Perhaps you'd do better going back to farming."

"Probably," Scott sighed. "Ad now I hab a broken node and I'm not eben handsob adybore."

Before Loth could offer his opinion that Scott hadn't ever been handsome, Quinn chimed in. "If you go and get your nose looked at, someone can probably straighten it. Why don't you clean up and go find one of the maids to see to it for you?" He handed a grateful Scott a handkerchief to clean himself with because Quinn was a far better person than Loth would ever be. Maybe Loth would have to reconsider his *'all royals are bastards'* stance after all, he reflected. But he'd think about that later. Right now, he had more pressing things to take care of.

Like holding Quinn tight and not letting go.

∼

Loth and Quinn sat together on one of the daybeds, hands entwined and shoulders pressed together. They watched Dave drag the unconscious soldiers over to Calarian, who was tying them up with the efficiency befitting a Junior Wood Scout before they came to. The odd soldier would open his eyes and try to speak, but Dave soon took care of them with a thump of his fist. He was clearly enjoying himself, hovering and looking for signs of movement, almost like it was a game. Whack-a-guard, maybe.

Another soldier was standing in the doorway, looking quite faint as Dave bopped a bunch of skulls, but Ser Greylord was talking to him in a low voice, and the man was listening and nodding. Greylord seemed to be doing a lot of talking to people generally. He'd already had a long, animated discussion with Ada, who'd seemed thrilled with whatever he was saying. Well, she almost smiled at one stage, which was practically the same thing.

At one point the soldier he was talking to now looked over at Quinn and Loth and caught Loth's gaze. Then he blanched and ducked his head, and Loth really wasn't sure how to take the gesture at all. Was it deferential? Loth wasn't practised enough at receiving deferential gestures to be sure. Moments later, the soldier left.

Ser Greylord came and sat next to them. "Your Grace," he said quietly, and they both turned their heads.

"Sorry," Loth said after a second, because Greylord wasn't talking to him, was he? Loth had forgotten, just for a moment, that he wasn't royalty anymore. "Habit."

Loth couldn't deny that there was a part of him that would miss being the prince—it had been nice to sweep his arms in the air and make pronouncements, to pretend that anyone cared what he thought. Still, it was only fair that Quinn got to claim his crown. He'd certainly earned it, and Loth suspected he'd be a decent king. He was pulled out of his musings by Greylord saying, "Actually, it's perfect."

"What is?"

"You, still answering to *your grace* like that. The way you do it automatically will work well for us." Greylord lowered his voice. "We can't be certain how the castle guard will respond to the prince being alive. They may say they're loyal, but that might just be lip service. It might be prudent if we continue to have two princes while we see which way the wind's blowing, so to speak."

"So I'm assassin bait?" Loth asked, somehow unsurprised. At least if he got murdered in his bed, it would be a *nice* bed.

"It's more like an extra layer of protection for the pair of you," Greylord corrected. "And there'd be no risk per se, because of course you'd both have a personal guard."

"Oh?" Quinn leaned forward, elbows coming to rest on his knees, giving Lord Greylord all his attention. Loth did not sulk when Quinn pulled his hand away to move. He did *not.*

"I've talked to the lovely Ada, and she's agreed to continue to guard Quinn as per her contract," Greylord said, and Loth and Quinn exchanged a glance. *The lovely Ada?* Loth tucked that away for later consideration and focussed on the matter at hand.

"And me?"

"Oh, I'll keep an eye on you."

Loth found himself comforted by that. He'd worried, just for a second, that they'd give him some useless, wet-behind-the-ears kid. He hummed. "And this is your plan to keep the prince safe? Us both pretending we're the heir?"

"For the time being, yes. Nobody here will admit to knowing who the real prince is, after all."

Quinn screwed up his nose doubtfully, but Loth could see where Greylord was going with this. "They won't, will they? They're under contract."

"Exactly." To prove his point, Greylord made a show of standing, clearing his throat and declaring loudly, "Well, I certainly don't know which one of you the prince is, and there's no way to tell."

Quinn grinned, and said," I can assure you, it's definitely not me. I'm just a horse-buggering peasant, remember?"

Loth gasped dramatically. "Well it's not me, I'm just a scribe, so it must be you!" When he glanced up, Ada and Calarian were approaching, wearing identical mischievous expressions. Dave lumbered after them.

"Is not. Ask anyone." Quinn's lips twitched. "Ada? Which one of us is the heir?"

Ada grinned. "No idea. It's definitely one of you, but as long as I'm getting paid I don't care."

"Cal?"

Calarian shrugged. "Collectivist anarchists don't believe in royalty, so I never bothered to find out. If there's ever a revolution and I need to shoot the prince, I'll figure it out then."

Oh yes, this was going to work wonderfully, Loth could already tell—just as long as Dave didn't have an unexpected moment of brilliance, although the odds of that were slim. Loth asked though, just to be sure. "Dave? Who's the prince?"

"There's two of them!" Dave said happily, and it was perfect, because who was going to argue with a seven-foot orc, especially one with a deadly dragon by his side?

"That's right, Dave. There are two princes," Greylord said, a tiny, smug smile on his face. Loth had the suspicion that Greylord would be excellent at chess, despite his previous denials, if he put his mind to it. "For now, it appears that most of the soldiers remaining are happy enough to continue doing their duty, as long as there's a prince somewhere in the mix. The trick during any transition of power, of course, is to let everyone continue doing the things they were doing, and not make any waves."

Loth saw Calarian's anarchist brow crease at that. He cleared his throat. "Do as little as possible. That sounds like an excellent plan. So, ah, the prince and I—or the peasant and I, who knows? —should probably just retire to one of the royal bedrooms, hmm? And keep out of everyone's way? For the good of the kingdom."

Quinn raised a single eyebrow. "For the good of the kingdom?" The expression he wore was both regal and hot as fuck,
and only made Loth more eager to get Quinn away from the
body of his uncle and out of his doublet.

"Definitely. It's my—*our*—duty as the new monarchs to facilitate a smooth transition of power."

The eyebrow inched higher, but then Quinn flashed him a
broad smile. "Well, if we have to facilitate for the sake of the
people, I suppose we'd better go ahead and do it."

"I thought they were already facilitating each other," Dave
said, brow furrowed in thought. Loth and Quinn were already
heading down the stairs when they heard a loud, "Wait, no. *Fucking!* That's what they're doing!" Then Dave paused before asking,
"Won't the horses get jealous?"

Loth couldn't help it. He burst out laughing, and once he
started he couldn't stop. Relief and adrenaline rushed through
him as he doubled over, letting out a series of distinctly un-royal
cackles. "We're making the horses jealous, Quinn!"

"Well we're not, but we can be if you can stop laughing long
enough to get down the stairs and into a bedroom," Quinn said,
grinning and slapping his arse.

It just made Loth laugh harder, and he probably should have
paid more attention to where he was going. As it was, he took the
curve of the stairs without looking, put his foot on a step that
wasn't there, fell arse over teakettle, and was unable to stop
himself until he hit the landing with a thump, a groan, and a
popping sound from his ankle that couldn't possibly mean
anything good.

Later, Loth would reflect on the irony of escaping the battle
unscathed only to laugh so hard he tripped and fell down the
stairs. For now though, he just lay at the bottom of the staircase
in a heap of limbs, ankle throbbing horribly, and waited for his
handsome prince to come and rescue him.

CHAPTER EIGHTEEN

Loth jolted awake with a start when someone landed a stinging slap on his naked arse. He yelped and swore. Then he rolled over onto his back and turned his head to glare furiously at a grinning Quinn. "What the hell was that for?"

Quinn sprawled on the bed beside him. "That was for saying, halfway through, that I was an excellent rider."

"You just can't take a compliment, can you?"

"Not when it's also a horse-fucking joke, no!" Quinn reached out and flicked one of Loth's nipples. Hard.

"Ow!" Loth cupped his hands over his nipples. "Stop it! I'm your injured hero!"

Quinn, like an idiot, stopped, and Loth seized the advantage and rolled on top of him, pinning his wrists to the bed. Quinn didn't seem too bothered by that. He just grinned up at Loth, his hair a tousled copper mess against the fine sheets, and waited to see what Loth's next move was.

"Ugh, unfortunately my ankle is the only thing that's throbbing," Loth said. He pecked Quinn on the tip of the nose before rolling off him. Then he sat up, wincing as he set his feet on the floor and all the blood rushed back into his swollen ankle.

Quinn made a sympathetic noise behind him, and the mattress dipped as he shifted. A moment later he was kneeling behind Loth, pressing warm kisses to the nape of his neck, and across his shoulders.

The room they'd claimed a few hours ago wasn't the finest room in the palace—neither of them wanted to fuck on Lord Doom's bed—but it was still the nicest room Loth had ever slept in. The bed was large, the rugs on the floor were thick and soft, and the window offered a fine view of the city all the way to the harbour. The room also caught the afternoon sun, and from the deepening golden shade of it, Loth suspected they'd both slept longer than they'd intended. Loth tried not to feel guilty about all the important things Quinn had to do as Quinn pressed another kiss to his nape.

Loth would miss this. He'd miss Quinn's quick wit and his perfect arse and his red hair, but it was never going to last. He consoled himself with the thought that he had a few weeks, at least, and dipped his chin so Quinn could kiss more of his neck.

Quinn's hands slid over his stomach, lingering on the scratch from Doom's sword. "*Such* a hero," he muttered.

"I'm legitimately injured," Loth grumbled. "I was almost a martyr."

"And now you're a prince."

Loth perked up at that because he was, at least for the time being.

Quinn sighed against his neck. "Do you think we can get someone to bring us something to eat?"

"Let's find out." Loth stood and limped over to the door. He opened it and looked outside. Ada was standing guard. Her arms were folded over her chest and she was watching the length of the passageway suspiciously. Loth cleared his throat. "Excuse me, but the princes are—"

"The princes are *noisy*," Ada snapped. "You're worse than Calarian and Benji."

Loth grinned. "I'll take that as a compliment." The guard on the other side of the door made a choking sound. He would have been seventeen at most, Loth guessed, and he was a delightful shade of purple under his helmet. Loth supposed they had been rather loud, but he couldn't bring himself to feel sorry about it. He nodded at the boy. "It turns out that a Dirty Alchemist works up quite the appetite. Be a good lad and bring us up something to eat, will you?"

The young guard took off running.

"He must have been intimidated by my regal presence," Loth said.

"Either that, or the fact you're waving your regal dick around everywhere," Ada suggested. "Which you really shouldn't, since it's pretty obvious you're not a natural redhead."

"Excellently pragmatic as always, Ada," Loth said. He closed the door and turned to see Quinn's judgemental face. A second later it was obscured by the pair of pants that Quinn threw at his head. Loth climbed into them with some difficulty and then opened the door again. "Come in, Ada."

She stomped inside and stared at Quinn, who was pulling his clothes on. "Now that one's a natural redhead."

Quinn spluttered and tried to hide behind a tapestry while he tugged his pants up.

"He's shy too," Loth said, for some reason deeply amused by that. "So, Ada, what's the news in the castle? And the city too, I suppose. Are the people delighted that Lord Doom is dead, or should Quinn and I expect mobs armed with torches and pitch-forks to turn up at any moment now?"

"Probably not. Doom upset a lot of people. It's not that they love the prince, it's just that they hated Doom more."

"The enemy of my enemy is my friend," Loth murmured, nodding. He made his way with difficulty over to one of the ornate chairs in the room and slumped down, extending his injured leg in front of him. "Ugh, I'm getting too old for this."

"How old are you, anyway?" Quinn asked, from the depths of the shirt that he was shrugging into.

Loth honestly had to think about it, he'd gotten so used to shaving off a year or two and then adding them back as it suited him. It took some serious calculation before he ventured, "Twenty... six?"

Quinn's head popped out the top of the shirt. "Is that all? Are you sure?"

Loth counted again and grimaced. "Fine. Twenty-seven."

"You mean twenty-one," Ada interrupted. Loth frowned. "Twenty-one," She repeated. "The prince is twenty-one, which is why he's come to take the crown, remember?"

Loth brightened immediately. He could live with twenty-one. And he'd blame the crow's feet on the time spent in jail. And then he remembered, with a sudden sinking feeling, that he wouldn't be playing a prince for much longer, and that very soon Quinn wouldn't need him at all. Quinn would go on to be a prince—or a king—without Loth by his side. He'd probably do an amazing job of whatever the hell it was monarchs actually did, and Loth would go back to doing...

His stomach sank even further.

Well. Loth would go back to doing what he'd always done, wouldn't he? Thieving, cheating and whoring, with the occasional scribing on the side.

He certainly didn't belong in a castle, with a prince.

"Loth?" Quinn asked. The way he said it made Loth think that he might have repeated it a few times before it caught Loth's attention. Quinn's eyes were wide, and his forehead was creased with concern. "Are you okay?"

Loth pasted on a fake smile and ratcheted it up a few gleaming degrees. "Of course I am. Why wouldn't I be? Sorry, Ada, what were you saying about the guards?"

He kept his smile in place and didn't risk looking at Quinn again while he listened to Ada give her opinion of the state of things in the castle and the city beyond.

THE NEXT TWO weeks were possibly the strangest of Loth's life so far, and that was saying something, given his adventures with the minstrels.

He limped around the castle, attending meetings with various palace officials as he tried to work out who was with them and who was a threat. Loth was surprised to find that what he'd once told Quinn about most people not giving a fuck as long as their bellies were full and their families were safe went far higher up than he'd ever imagined. As long as the kingdom was in safe hands, nobody seemed to care whose hands they were.

Sometimes he caught a glimpse of the pinched expression on Quinn's face and wondered exactly how much that stung. Everyone was full of praise for the previous King Tarquin, but they'd still bowed and scraped to the man who'd killed him, hadn't they? And they would have kept doing it if Quinn hadn't turned up.

"To be fair," Calarian had said one night when Loth had been ranting about it in private, "why the hell should any of them risk their lives for kings and princes and crowns?"

"Because it's *Quinn!*"

And Calarian had looked at him like he was an idiot. "But they don't *know* Quinn. To them, he's just another figurehead."

Frankly, Loth didn't know if that made him feel better or not.

Still, there were meetings to attend and committees, and more meetings. Despite telling himself that none of it mattered because he'd be gone soon enough, Loth got drawn into the discussions, if only because someone had to tell the idiots off for being, well, idiots. He found himself arguing against increased tariffs 'to cover the cost of our prince's glorious return', pointing out that the glorious return had, in the end, cost no more than a bag of gold coins and a lute for Dave. Quinn just watched quietly, eyebrows raised in something like amusement, when Loth went through the budgets for the army and slashed them ruthlessly, because no, the guard really didn't need new uniforms with an extra cape, thank you very much. Loth couldn't help but feel that the people who oversaw the spending of palace finances were pickpockets just like him, only on a far grander scale.

Loth had a suspicion the old hands were testing them, testing *Quinn*, to see if he would be an easy mark. Loth could have told them not to bother. Quinn was clever in his own right, and he kept Loth and Ser Greylord close. When he wasn't sure about something, he'd click his fingers and Pie would come fluttering over and perch on his shoulder, and Quinn would hum and say, "I need to think on it," then dismiss them all. At the sight of the dragon, the room would collectively remember what had happened to Lord Doom, everyone would scramble to leave, and when it was just them Quinn would shrug and ask, "Well?"

The Dumesny apple, Loth thought, hadn't fallen very far from the tree at all. And given the uncertain position they were both in, Loth approved.

And it wasn't all meetings.

A lot of time was spent in the royal bedrooms, the ones with the convenient connecting door. Loth discovered that if you prompted him just right, Quinn had a filthy mouth—in both senses of the word. They finally mastered the reverse paladin with only one pulled muscle, and Ser Greylord confided later that the poor young guard outside the door at the time had come to him, stammering and pleading not to be posted there again because he couldn't look his majesties in the eye.

Instead of turning bright red, Quinn only sighed. "Who are we going to ask to be the third member of our reverse double paladin attempt now?"

Loth was delighted.

Now that Quinn was finally getting enough to eat, he had all the stamina of youth, and all the adventurousness of the newly bedded, and although he'd never admit it, Loth was quietly glad that his sore ankle gave him an excuse to take a break occasionally.

Not that he was old. He was only twenty-one, after all.

All in all, life was good. Somehow they were ruling the kingdom, and if the lack of pitchforks and rioters was anything to go by, they were doing a reasonable job, and if it was up to Loth he'd have happily carried on that way, except it couldn't be that simple, could it?

It all came to a head one morning as Loth was dozing through yet another boring meeting.

"-oronation, Your Graces?"

Loth's eyes snapped open, and he found himself on the end of a disapproving stare from the lord high chancellor, a man who Loth secretly thought looked rather like a toad, with bulging eyes and rolls of flesh hanging off his neck. Loth pulled himself upright in his chair and regretfully removed his hand from Quinn's thigh under the table.

"What about it?" he asked and hoped it sounded like he'd been listening.

"We need to set a date. The kingdom needs clear leadership, and the people are eager to celebrate their new king." The man's gaze flicked between Loth and Quinn, narrowing, and Loth half expected his tongue to whip out and start catching flies. "Um, whoever that may be."

Loth caught Ser Greylord's expression and didn't like the way he looked worried.

"The problem is," Ser Greylord said later, as Loth and Quinn walked with him along one of the castle's galleries, "that in order to protect the rightful prince, we may have sown confusion at the same time."

"Well, that was the point, wasn't it?" Loth asked.

"It was," Ser Greylord said, inclining his head. "But now, of course, when Quinn takes the throne, what's to stop some troublemaker insisting a year from now, or ten, or twenty, that the *other* prince was the rightful one all along, and Quinn is a pretender."

"This was your idea!" Loth groaned. "You're right. You're a terrible chess player. You're probably also a terrible human being. And why are you carrying around a jar of beard oil?"

"Ah," said Ser Greylord. He slipped the small jar underneath his cloak. His face was pink. "That is a gift for someone. And yes, I know it was my idea, and it served its purpose at the time. But it does leave us with a difficult choice now."

"No," Loth said. He met Quinn's gaze. "It's not a difficult choice. I can make an announcement ceding any claim to the kingdom. And if I leave now, then you should have plenty of time before the coronation to sort it out."

Quinn's eyebrows drew together into a scowl the likes of which Loth hadn't seen since he was a grubby little pile of dirt, straw, and bad temper.

"You will *not*," he hissed, and grabbed the front of Loth's doublet, stomping down the corridor and dragging Loth behind, making him yelp as he was forced to put weight on his still-tender ankle. Quinn opened the first door they came to and pulled him roughly inside, slamming the door closed behind them.

Library, Loth noted dimly, but his attention was mainly taken by Quinn crowding him against the wall and jabbing at his chest with one bony finger.

"What do you mean, *leave*?" he demanded. His eyes blazed. "Who the fuck told you that you could *leave*?"

Quinn was hissing and spitting like a wet cat, and Loth was so surprised that he could barely push the words out. "You heard what Greylord said, and—"

Quinn twisted the front of Loth's doublet and pushed him harder against the wall. "I don't care what Greylord said. I don't care what *anyone* says!" His eyes shone, and not with anger this time, but with tears. And just like that, his anger seemed to vanish. He sagged against Loth, his breath hitching. "I can't—I can't do it on my own, Loth!"

Loth's mouth worked, opening and closing until he managed to speak at last. "You won't be on your own. You'll have Greylord to guide you, and help you rule —"

Quinn let out a frustrated noise. "I'm not talking about ruling. Greylord doesn't make me laugh. He doesn't make me feel alive, or take me to bed like you do."

"I'm sure if you asked nicely, he'd consider—"

"*I don't love Greylord!*" Quinn burst out.

Loth froze. "What?"

Quinn blinked back the tears, then drew himself up straight and jutted his chin out. "You heard me."

Blood roared in Loth's skull as he tried to make some sense of what Quinn was saying. "You love me," he repeated. Quinn nodded. "You love me." Loth said it again, just to make sure he wasn't hearing things, that he wasn't dreaming. "You *love* me?"

"Stop saying it like it's a joke!"

Loth blinked at him. "A joke? No, I didn't mean..." His chest ached. "Quinn, I'm saying it because I can't believe it. Because you could do a lot better than a penniless scribe with a limp and a penchant for scarves, you know? Ask anyone. Ask Greylord, or Ada, or Calarian or Dave. Hell, even ask my *parents*. But you... you're standing here telling me that you *love* me."

"That's what I said." Quinn held his gaze. "Is that a problem?"

Loth was still reeling from the news that Quinn loved him. Somehow he'd missed it, but that was okay. It was better than okay, because now he knew and he'd get to tell Quinn that he loved him back. He reached up and untangled Quinn's fingers from their death grip in his doublet, then laced their fingers together and took one tiny step forward.

"No," he said quietly, leaning their foreheads together. "As it happens I feel the same, so it's not a problem at all."

The smile Quinn showed him was dazzling.

Loth managed a shaky smile in return. "I'm not sure how it solves the whole two prince issue, though."

Quinn dropped to his knee.

Loth's blood heated. "I mean, it's a nice offer, but is this really the time? Wait what am I saying—it's always a good time. But did you lock the door? We don't want a repeat of that time in the—"

"Loth!" Quinn jabbed him in the thigh. "I'm trying to ask you to marry me."

Loth's mouth fell open. "Bullshit."

Quinn sighed and stood up. "You don't have a romantic bone in your body, do you?"

"You love me anyway," Loth said, just because he could, and saying it made him smile all over again. "Why did you get up? Are you checking the door's locked?"

Quinn rolled his eyes. "I'm not blowing you, idiot. I'm serious. I'm actually proposing. They want a legitimate heir on the throne? We'll give them one. They don't need to know which of us it is, do they? If we're married, we rule jointly."

A jar of buzzing wasps momentarily replaced Loth's brain. Because Quinn wasn't just offering marriage. He was offering Aguillon. He was offering the *kingdom*.

"I'd be stealing," he babbled, "and I've never stolen anything before that didn't fit in my pocket or my scarf."

Quinn poked him in the chest. "You're not stealing anything. I'm sharing it with you. Also, what are you talking about stealing?" His eyes widened. "The kingdom, or my heart?"

Loth spluttered with laughter. "Gods, you're right. I'm sorry, I really don't have a romantic bone in my body, because that was probably the nicest thing anyone has ever said to me, and I laughed. I should say yes now before you come to your senses and back out."

"Say it, then," Quinn said, his eyes shining. "Make your choice. You can either go back to being a penniless scribe, or you can say yes."

"Yes," Loth said, dizzy with emotion. "*Yes.*"

Quinn laughed, and leaned in and kissed him. Hard. And then he went and locked the door, and sauntered back to Loth with a wicked gleam in his eye.

This time when he dropped to his knees, there was no confusion.

CHAPTER NINETEEN

L oth tugged at the collar of his doublet. He wondered if he could undo the top clasp or if his mum would come over and fasten it again like she'd been doing all night, tutting and fussing and telling him to stop fidgeting. He didn't mind, really—not given how well she and Dad had taken the news. When Loth had told them that he and Quinn were getting married and that he'd be joint ruler of the kingdom, Mum had looked across at Dad and said, "Told you. And really, it's not a patch on that business with the Lord Mayor's son. Or his wife. Or the minstrels."

Loth had a sneaking suspicion his parents actually preferred Quinn over him, but then, he preferred Quinn over himself as well, so he couldn't fault their taste. He tugged at the collar again, and Quinn elbowed him. "Stop it, Mum will see." Because she was Mum to both of them now, of course.

"I am the ruler of Aguillon, and I'll undo my collar if I want," Loth said, pretending to pout. He mainly did it so Quinn would kiss him, and it worked wonderfully well.

The ceremony had passed in a haze, and, frankly, Loth was

still waiting for someone to come along and pinch him. But no, the weight of the crown he was wearing appeared to be very real. So did the weight of Quinn's hand in his, offering a comforting squeeze whenever Loth found himself starting to fidget.

The wedding ceremony had been quick, and so too had been the joint coronation. But the reception? Gods, Loth liked a party as much as the next dissolute troublemaker, but the reception was interminable! Loth didn't want people's congratulations—he wanted to take his new husband to bed and fuck his brains out. Was that *really* too much to ask? Loth didn't think so.

Loth gazed in the direction of Ser Greylord and Ada. *Lady* Ada, Loth reminded himself. It had seemed only fitting to elevate her, since she'd agreed to stay and train up the new recruits. Ser Greylord had a slight blush, and Loth couldn't quite hear what he was saying. He straightened in his chair and leaned forward to hear better, but he needn't have bothered. Calarian was sitting next to him, putting his bat-like ears to use.

"He said, *I find myself admiring your beard, M'lady. It shines so brightly.*"

"Oh?" The words caught Loth's interest, and he nudged Quinn. "Do you think he knows what it means, complimenting a lady dwarf's beard?" he asked quietly. "Will he know if she gives the right answer?"

"He'll know," Calarian said, grinning even harder. "He asked me before, to make sure he got it right." He tilted his head, watching Ada's lips move, and repeated, *"Thank you, good sir. Would you like to see the handle of my axe?"* as Greylord gave a bashful smile and ducked his head.

Maybe Loth did have a romantic bone in his body after all, because it barely crossed his mind to poke fun. Of course, that could also have been because he was more interested in other types of poking right now.

"Humans are so stupid," Benji announced loudly from beside

Calarian. "If he wants to do the slippery friar with Ada, why doesn't he just say that?"

Benji had been a late addition to the guest list, mostly because all of the palace messengers had been too frightened to go into the Swamp of Death. In the end, Calarian had volunteered. He'd come back two weeks later, dazed, bow-legged, and beaming like an idiot.

Calarian nodded. "Right?"

Quinn caught Loth's gaze, the question written plainly on his face.

"I have no idea," Loth said. "Honestly, I think they're just making them up."

"Imagine being kings and not even knowing what a slippery friar is," Calarian said and rolled his eyes. "Humans are so stupid. Kings are so stupid."

"Death to all kings!" Benji announced and finished his wine in one long gulp. "Is this silverware ours to keep?"

"Not technically," Quinn said. "But we figured you'd steal yours anyway, so we gift-wrapped you some to take back to the Swamp."

Benji pouted attractively and slid a wine glass into the neck of his tunic. It clinked against the rest of the things he'd steadily been stealing all night. "It doesn't count if you *give* it to me. I'm supposed to be redistributing wealth, not you!"

"Oh," Quinn said. "Sorry."

"It's fine," Benji said, and slid a spoon up his sleeve.

Loth sighed as yet another parade of servants brought in another course of dinner. Over in the far corner of the hall, the minstrels began another merry tune. Loth had been avoiding the minstrels all night, just in case any of them knew him. Both Dave and Scott had been drawn to them like moths to a flame though. Dave, because he wanted to play his purloined lute, and Scott, because... well, Loth didn't really know or care, but the important thing was it kept him out of the way.

Pie was nestled in Quinn's hair and had been since the coronation. Occasionally he poked his snout over the top of Quinn's crown just to see what was going on and let a puff of smoke or two tumble down Quinn's temple like errant curls, but Loth was fairly sure most people hadn't even noticed he was there. Watching the lights reflect off Quinn's curls, Loth was struck with a thought, and he tugged at Quinn's sleeve, eyes wide with horror.

"Quinn," he hissed urgently.

Quinn's brow furrowed.

"I don't get to be a blond now!" Loth whispered. "I'll have to stay a redhead!"

"And what's wrong with being a redhead?" Quinn said, lips curling up in a smile. "I like redheads. My *husband's* a redhead, and he assures me he's very handsome."

Well, when he put it like that.

"Blonds probably don't have more fun anyway," Loth murmured, and leaned in for a kiss.

"Not more fun than us, that's for sure," Quinn agreed with a bright grin. "So, what are we trying tonight? The innocent pageboy? The one-armed farrier? No, wait!" He waggled his eyebrows. "Maybe we could have a washerwoman's delight."

Benji suddenly stood up, a waterfall of silverware tumbling from his sleeves. He picked up a knife and banged it against a glass. The low roar of conversation in the hall slowly died down.

"Excuse me! Excuse me, humans!" Benji announced. "The king and the king are retiring now, before they start fucking at the table with stupid made-up sex positions that don't even really exist. But mine and Calarian's do. Thank you, and good night!"

"Well," Loth said in the sudden stunned silence from the entire great hall. "Yes. Goodnight."

He bolted from the great hall, dragging a red-faced Quinn behind him.

"At least we got out before Dave started singing," Loth said a little later, unfastening the laces on his doublet.

He liked to think that whatever Quinn said was in agreement, but it was hard to tell when his face was buried in his hands like that and his shoulders hadn't stopped shaking since they'd arrived in their bedroom and he'd sunk down onto the couch by the window.

"Please tell me you're laughing and not crying."

Quinn snorted and raised his face. "I'm laughing."

"Oh, thank the gods. I was worried you had buyer's remorse. Or marrier's remorse. Some sort of remorse, anyway. Of course, you'd have to be mad to regret marrying this." Loth tugged his shirt over his head to demonstrate just what a catch he was, but the effect was somewhat spoiled when the cloth got caught on his crown.

Quinn dragged himself to his feet, still letting out little huffs of laughter, and walked over, removing the shirt and then the crown, setting it to one side. Quinn then lifted his own crown off, and Pie climbed out of his mess of red curls, chirruping happily. Quinn carried him gently over to the window, cooing and making nonsense noises. It was adorable, and it made Loth wonder if he could get nonsense sounds out of Quinn later as well. It normally wasn't hard—ha!—to reduce him to a babbling wreck.

There was a faint glow coming from the southern tower: the solarium. The fireplace there was constantly tended ever since Dave had claimed it as a dragon hatchery, and there was currently a bunch of eggs nestled in the embers, waiting to hatch.

Quinn stroked Pie down his spine, causing him to let out an excited trill and a puff of smoke, and then Pie sailed out of the window, catching an updraft and gliding in the direction of the solarium.

Loth approached and stood behind Quinn, his arms laced around him. Together, they watched Pie dive and swoop toward the solarium, until he was too far away to see and was swallowed up in the darkness. They could still hear his happy trills and chirps though. Loth nuzzled the back of Quinn's neck and slid one hand up the front of his tunic. Quinn sighed softly, and Loth smiled to himself. Quinn was so easy for him.

Of course, it went both ways.

He was just in the process of laying kisses up Quinn's nape when Quinn pulled away with a frown. "I forgot. We need more oil—we used the last of it last night, remember? I'll go get more." And then he was gone, out the door before Loth could object.

Loth sighed. He'd had plans involving what he liked to call the Slow Roll, *urgent* plans, and now Quinn was making him wait, even if it was for a good reason.

Ah well. He'd undress, he decided, and then Quinn would walk in to find a naked vision waiting in his bed and it would be like a wedding present—after all, Loth's dick was a gift, even if he said so himself. Loth went to slip his trousers off, but in his slightly tipsy haste he forgot about his boots. The trousers got caught up, and he was left standing there trapped in a tangled mess of boot leather and cloth.

Well. There had been an *awful* lot of wine.

Loth sighed and plonked himself down on the floor, trying to get free of his boots, but unable to figure out quite how laces worked. So when Quinn dashed back in the door saying, "Right, I got the big bottle, so we can—"

He was greeted by the sight of Loth sitting there morosely, trapped by his pants and unable to get up.

Loth cleared his throat. "Well," he said, "I suppose you're wondering how I got into this mess."

Quinn snorted. "This? We're doing this again?"

"Shush, you." Loth held out a hand helplessly in a wordless plea. "I suppose you're wondering how I got into this mess."

"No!" Quinn laughed. "I didn't care then, and I don't care now!"

But he crouched and sorted out Loth's laces, then helped him tug his boots off while Loth grumbled, "You never let me soliloquise." Once his boots and trousers were off, Loth climbed unsteadily to his feet, finally free of the tangle.

Quinn, because he was slightly more sober and definitely more sensible, took his own boots off before attempting to strip, and then there was a swish of fabric and a pair of trousers hit Loth in the face. He batted them aside and took in the view that was his husband, the king.

Quinn was as far from the too-thin-too-angry boy Loth had met in a prison cell as he could get. In the weeks since they'd arrived in Callier he'd filled out, and his scowl was barely seen these days. His hair and his eyes shone with good health, days spent striding around the castle had developed the long lean muscles in his thighs, and there was almost a plumpness to his cheeks, a softening of the sharp angles that had been there before. He was beautiful, and there was no way that Loth deserved him, or any of this. He certainly wasn't dumb enough to try to give any of it back though. Hell, no. He wasn't stupid.

Also, Loth definitely wanted to fuck his new husband. Or be fucked—it could go either way, and hopefully it would. Loth stalked forward and wrapped his arms around Quinn, sliding his hands down his back and giving his arse a light slap. Quinn pulled away and began to walk backward to the bed, the light from the fireplace gleaming on his naked skin.

Quinn grinned. "No soliloquising, not tonight. Now get over here, *Your Majesty*, and fuck me until I can't see straight."

Loth sighed. Was a man never allowed to soliloquise? Then again, it *was* their wedding night.

"Fine," he grumbled, striding over to his husband. "Let's giddy-up!"

Quinn's jaw dropped. "Oh, you fucking didn't! A horse joke, Loth? Really?"

Loth laughed as Quinn tackled him onto the bed.

There would be plenty of time to soliloquise in the morning.

Early one morning
the day was dawning.
We was late because Scott's
map was broke
DAVE (that's me) punched a
wall

We found some princes
saved them all
There was ~~th~~ ~~~~ two of them

Scott said he was the leader
he set the map on fire
We got lost without it
Then a swamp monster came
Scott got trapped when he was
taking a crap
and left a trail of shit

The monster wasn't scary
like we thought
He was just an elf in a
bad mood
Him n' Cal are cousins but
they call each other daddy
and we saw them NUDE

Scott our LEADER is a useless
Little tit
got caught by an elf when
he WENT to take a shit
CAN't read a map (A)
ALMOST killed us all
got a crap beard an'
uneven BALLS

SCOTT

Lord doom tried to kill
Loth n Tarquequin, but
we helped coz we dint
want them to die
But the **HERO** who killed
doom was a ~~rat~~ ~~tiny~~
VENOMENOMUS
dragon called PIE!

Pie is the hero an' now
we got two kings
i got a place for all my
dragon eggs
the kings got married an
Ada cried when they weren't
looking
Benji says king Loth has nice legs
(he really said ARSE but that doesn't
RHYME)

AFTERWORD

Thank you so much for reading *Red Heir*. We hope that you enjoyed it. We would very much appreciate it if you could take a few moments to leave a review on Amazon or Goodreads, or on your social media platform of choice.

To connect with Lisa on social media, you can find her here:

Website
    Facebook
    Instagram
    Goodreads
    Bookbub
    Twitter

She also has a Facebook group where you'll be kept in the loop with updates on releases, have a chance to win prizes, and probably see lots and lots of pictures of her dog and cats. You can find it here: Lisa Henry's Hangout.

You can connect with Sarah on Facebook, or send her an email at
sarahhoneywriting@gmail.com.

ALSO BY LISA HENRY

Dauntless

Anhaga

Two Man Station (Emergency Services #1)

Lights and Sirens (Emergency Services #2)

The California Dashwoods

Adulting 101

Sweetwater

He Is Worthy

The Island

Tribute

One Perfect Night

Fallout, with M. Caspian

Dark Space (Dark Space #1)

Darker Space (Dark Space #2)

Starlight (Dark Space #3)

Playing the Fool series, with J.A. Rock

The Two Gentlemen of Altona

The Merchant of Death

Tempest

With J.A. Rock

The Preacher's Son

When All the World Sleeps

Another Man's Treasure

Fall on Your Knees

Mark Cooper versus America (Prescott College #1)

Brandon Mills versus the V-Card (Prescott College #2)

The Good Boy (The Boy #1)

The Boy Who Belonged (The Boy #2)

Writing as Cari Waites

Stealing Innocents

ABOUT LISA HENRY

Lisa likes to tell stories, mostly with hot guys and happily ever afters.

Lisa lives in tropical North Queensland, Australia. She doesn't know why, because she hates the heat, but she suspects she's too lazy to move. She spends half her time slaving away as a government minion, and the other half plotting her escape.

She attended university at sixteen, not because she was a child prodigy or anything, but because of a mix-up between international school systems early in life. She studied History and English, neither of them very thoroughly.

She shares her house with too many cats, a dog, a green tree frog that swims in the toilet, and as many possums as can break in every night. This is not how she imagined life as a grown-up.

Lisa has been published since 2012, and was a LAMBDA finalist for her quirky, awkward coming-of-age romance *Adulting 101*, and a Rainbow Awards finalist for 2019's *Anhaga*.

ABOUT SARAH HONEY

Sarah lives in Western Australia with her partner, two cats, two dogs and a TARDIS.

A teacher once told her life's not a joke.

She begs to differ.

Her proudest achievements include having kids who will still be seen with her in public, and knowing all the words to Bohemian Rhapsody.

Red Heir is her first published novel.

Printed in Great Britain
by Amazon